The Long Fingers

The Long Fingers

Gwyneth Graham

A catalogue record for this book is available from the National Library of Australia

For Olivia and Davida

Part One

Returning

Chapter One

Panic rose from her stomach, racing into her heart, flooding her throat, billowing into her brain.

A voice she had not heard for many years.

Usual Monday routine. In the office by 7.30 am, gym class done, eating spoonfuls of muesli as she cleared her inbox before the weekly executive meeting. Her favourite time of day before a queue formed at her door and the meetings started.

Then the phone call. Her father never rang her.

She swivelled away from the polished desk, taking her green tea to the window. Behind her, an office which shouted 'Emily' with its coordinated maroon leather chairs and clear surfaces, disturbed only by one in-tray and a single photo of a recent European trip; organised office, organised mind, one of her mantras. She regained even breath between sips of cooling tea, as she looked across the familiar picture of central London that surrounded her office tower.

She glanced down to the street thickening with the dark stream of workers trudging up Bishopsgate; black coats, coffee cups, laptops, briefcases. Some into the long nineteenth century government building opposite, a few through tall iron gates into St Helen's cobbled courtyard, protected from peak hour rumble of buses, taxis, cars.

Having spent years away from her birthplace, her history, she regarded Londoners' attachment to their past with some cynicism. A plaque on every church and theatre wall announcing their historic importance, events long gone. Even the wholesale meat market dripping with blood and intestines at 5.00 am had elegant plaques describing its history. Her eyes travelled across the competing tension of past and present; old church spires dwarfed by chrome and glass, the Gherkin's curves soaring above ancient stone buildings.

'She wants to see you ... mightn't last long', he'd said in that gravelly voice, instantly recognisable as if they had last spoken yesterday.

Her mother. What was she going to do? She stared through light drizzle that was landing on the window like mist. Back to Australia?

'Good morning.'

Emily spun back to her office, automatic smile switched on, alert to increasing bustle behind her.

Caroline, her godsend of a PA smiling in the doorway. Always a welcome sight.

'Hello Caroline. Did you have a good weekend?'

'Yes, thank you, peaceful, which was nice. Do you need anything else for Executive today? The agenda is in your folder, together with your report.' She stepped closer and lowered her voice. 'Are you ok?'

'Yes fine. Why?'

'Nothing, I just thought ... no matter. Must be Monday morning.'

Caroline always knew when something wasn't right. She'd better make sure no-one else did. How did she manage before Caroline arrived? Such a relief from the previous PA she'd inherited who was more interested in the state of her nails than whether Emily had the papers she needed.

Need to focus. Executive meeting. Emily looked at her watch. Ten minutes.

'Thank you, I think I have all I need. You look lovely today. Blue suits you.'

Caroline smiled, flicking back her smooth shoulder length hair over her crisp blue shirt and returned to her desk where her computer was already working its way through multiple start up security screens. Such an easy compliment to give. Emily smiled and nodded through the glass wall as her team began filling the stretch of cubicles outside her office; hanging up coats, turning on computers, post weekend chat.

Pushing the panic down she straightened the skirt of her new grey-green wool suit, 'shows off your green eyes', the shop assistant had said. Refreshed her lipstick in the mirror she kept in her top drawer, smoothed her dark brown bob and picked up her folder. Luckily she had nothing major on the agenda this time, just the weekly report. She forced the phone call to the back of her mind, shifting her attention to the meeting in front of her, as she walked down to the boardroom. A quirk of building design put the Chief Executive's rooms on the ninth floor rather than the tenth. Since Anthony had started in the top job, she'd noticed a momentary disturbance of her usual calm each time she walked down the stairs to his office or the adjoining boardroom. Heart beating a little faster, worry wrinkling at the edge of her brain. Too many nights watching crime shows where stairs led down to dark basements. Never good.

She put her papers down on the imposing board table that stretched almost the length of the room and poured a cup of tea from the pot on the side bench.

'What's it going to be today?' Alfred beside her.

He nodded his thanks as she poured him a cup.

'Got a kicking last week', he lowered his voice. 'But my sales figures are better this week, so it's HR's turn'. He raised his right eyebrow at her.

'I think I've been a good girl this week', she grimaced, her eyes laughing.

Alfred had the light restless energy typical of a salesman, easy to share a joke with. His bright expressive eyes, under a mop of dark curly hair that resisted attempts at control, would widen slightly across the table at her during an Anthony rant or another of David's cost warnings, causing her to drop her gaze to her papers, swallowing threatening laughter. He had been a valuable friend, lightening her mood as they struggled with the change from supportive Jeff to Anthony. Anthony had arrived to shake them out of their complacency, he said on day one, eyeballing them down the table. Here to bring them out of the dark ages of a government-owned telecommunications monopoly into a bright new world of 21st century competitive business. As usual, he was late. Not that they ever dared to be.

Still an old-fashioned room, she thought as they sat waiting, checking through their reports. Upstairs was remodelled with meeting pods, couches and coffee machines, floor to ceiling glass bringing in London's pale light. But here Anthony's speeches resounded in a room of dark wood furniture, solid chairs that they struggled to move along the thick carpet, heavy curtains that maintained a consistent gloom, regardless of the weather. Emily found it amusing when the technology faltered in these executive meetings of the 21st century, causing Anthony's fist to hit the table.

The mood tightened as Anthony marched through the door, head high, straight to his seat at the top end of the table.

'What are the results? Better than last week, I hope. David?'

Not even a "good morning", Emily sighed inside, preparing herself. David adjusted his perfectly knotted tie and began, pointing to streams of numbers appearing on the screen behind. Anthony swung his large frame around to study the graphs. Emily kept her face blank, nodding as he interrupted David, delivering the usual diatribe. Hard to concentrate today.

She walked upstairs with Alfred. Lunchtime crowds filled the walkways as people headed to the kitchens and lifts. Space and light meeting them as they neared their floor.

'Not too bad today', she said.

'We both escaped this time, watch out for next week.' Alfred grinned and half raised his hand in farewell as he turned down the corridor.

She weaved her way around empty desks to reach her office. Only William remained, eating lunch at his computer, always conscientious. She closed the door. Thank God she had kept her office, resisting the latest trend to open-plan. Her space. An hour before her next meeting. She looked at her phone, her mind snapping back to the call as she ate the sandwich Caroline had left on her desk. She couldn't have said whether it was chicken or cheese or something else.

'Emily, it's your father here.'

No acknowledgement that this was their first interaction in years. She had often wondered how he talked with patients in his surgery. Did he show care or was he formal and removed, delivering a diagnosis in that clipped voice. Perhaps it inspired confidence, the voice of an expert.

'Dad?' Her father calling her? Even knowing her phone number? Why didn't her mum ring?

'Your mother wants you. You'd better come.'

'What do you mean?'

'She's not too good. Mightn't last long. It's about time you came.'

'Is she dying?'

'Looks like it.'

Emily stood up then, her chair hitting the wall, all senses switched on.

'What? How? Is she sick?'

'Cancer. Don't suppose you knew.'

'But I spoke with her only a month ago. She didn't say anything.'

When was that last phone call?

'Where is she?'

'The Alfred. You'd better be quick. She wants to see you.'

'Yes. Of course. I'll book flights. I'll let you know.'

'Very good then.'

She had sat heavily back on her black mesh chair, returning the phone to its cradle.

What did 'dying' mean? Sometimes it took people months and months to die, in and out of hospital. What if she went back to Australia, then had to return later? Or worse, have to stay for weeks waiting. Her mother. Why didn't she know? Was that last call more than two months ago? Did she miss something? You had to read between the lines with her mother's bright quick talk. Everything always good, a happy family with much to be proud of.

As always it had started with Emily apologising for not calling, too busy at work. Irritated that it seemed to be her responsibility to call.

> 'That's fine, I know you work hard. Are you enjoying yourself? Have you been out to lunch with the girls?' No idea of the demands that filled Emily's days. She's trying, Emily reminded herself.

What did her mum talk about? A new book she was working on, a City of Ballarat commission.

> 'It was quite a surprise, I don't know how they heard of me. I've started the first few sketches, and Angus has written most of the poems, but it's hard for me to get up to Ballarat these days. The drive is tiring. I stay with George and Alice, which is nice. Dad doesn't mind too much, if I leave him his meals. It's a long way though.'

Was that a hint?

> Emily remembered to ask about her younger brother Ben, anticipating the predictable change in tone as pride in her artist son warmed her voice.
> 'He's been busy on a big piece.' Code for "I haven't seen him."
> 'Has he had any new exhibitions?'
> Emily allowed an incoming email to distract her,

one hand on her laptop on the couch, the other around the phone.

'Oh yes, last month. Marvellous, I heard. He said not to come this time. Too late for me, they had a loud band. He'll give me a private showing.'

Ben worked on the fringe. Despite some success and a reputation in certain circles, his exhibitions were not in shiny art galleries filled with people like her mum and her friends. He showed his strong works in lesser known workshops and studios down alleyways or in reclaimed warehouses.

'I'm hoping he and Natasha might have a baby soon. She's in her 30s, I think. They've been living together for a few years now. Ben says they don't want to marry, but that's not a problem these days', her mum paused. Emily tensed. 'And how about you Emily? I know you love your work, but time is ticking by. If you want to have children.'

If you want grandchildren, you mean. Her mother struggled with Emily's professional career; an executive daughter working in London was something to say on the phone to family or over lunch with friends. But they always asked when was Emily coming home, was she going to get married, have a family. As though a profession was a temporary interlude, something you did for a while until you got on with the real things in life.

'It might be a bit late for all that', said Emily, trying to sound light in this familiar conversation, not let her irritation show. She should be used to the undertone of disappointment by now.

'Oh no, I hear people of all ages are having

children. There's so much they can do these days. I would love to have grandchildren and time's running out.' She sounded despondent. Unusual for her.

Was that another hint?

Then, 'Maybe, I was wondering if, maybe, you might think of coming home for a visit?'

This was unexpected, years since she had last asked.

'Oh, um, I'm busy at work at the moment. We're getting a new boss, there's a lot to do. I'll think about it.'

Would she have gone if she'd known?

Then she remembered another strange part of the conversation, her mother's voice gaining strength as though she had prepared.

'Emily, I know you're busy and far away in London. But you know, if anything happened, please keep an eye on Ben, look after him for me.'

'He's a grown man, Mum. I'm sure he can take care of himself.'

Irritated that Ben continued to be the focus. Irritated that Ben, an adult, seemed to still need his mother's support, when she, Emily, had achieved so much alone. Annoyed that somehow, she was being asked to take responsibility.

'Yes, I know, just in case ... Anyway, lovely to hear from you. Everything's fine here. Please ring again soon. When you can. I always love it when you call.'

'Ok bye Mum.' Relief as she replaced the phone. Glad

that's done. Baby, coming home, Ben. Intrusions trying to pull her away from her life. She returned to answering her emails.

Perhaps it was four or five months ago. She should have rung more often. Emily pressed her fingers into the centre of her forehead and across to each side of her head, easing the tightness. She should have asked how her mum was, paid more attention. She could see herself only half listening, looking at emails when she was trying to tell her something. Her mum had asked her to come home, and she had pushed it aside. A picture of her in a hospital bed, a mask over her face, tubes attached, flashed into her mind, like something she'd seen on a television show

'Emily, are you ready for William?'

Startled, she jerked up to see Caroline smiling through her door, William hovering behind, folders under his arm.

'Yes, yes of course. Come in. Remind me, what are we talking about?' She reached for the printout of her calendar and knocked the glass of water over her desk.

'Oh no!' She rescued her phone and picked up the papers threatened by the widening pool.

'Don't worry.' Caroline ran in with a cloth.

'Sorry William, sorry, come in, let's sit here.'

She sat with William in the maroon leather. In role, away from family calls. Offering advice, guiding, deciding, making plans, solving problems. What she loved doing. Back-to-back meetings filled the afternoon requiring her full attention until Caroline was waving through the glass saying Emily was late for Job Night.

Not enough time to walk there. If she sped up to Moorgate station she could catch the Northern line and wouldn't have to change trains. Squeezed herself into the carriage, released a few minutes later onto a platform of queues, each stretching from train doors to the steps. Navigated through crowds coming down the station steps until she reached fresh air at the top. A short walk to the community centre, eating a prepacked sandwich she had picked up at Pret a Manger. It sounded healthy on the label, but probably made at 3 o'clock this morning in some factory. It would get her through the evening.

She turned down a narrow street opposite the estate's rows of dark brown blocks. Behind the Tate, a stone's throw from Borough markets and London Bridge, but tourists didn't venture here. She would rarely see people filling these streets near her central London office building. She ran up the rickety stairs passing the ground floor shop that seemed to sell everything, but nothing Emily wanted to buy, despite the cheap prices.

She caught her breath and smiled at Amelia, the Monday Job Night Coordinator, standing in the centre of the open room talking with a young woman who looked like she'd been sleeping rough. Straggly hair, grubby clothes, clasping a large plastic bag of belongings. Not someone Emily recognised. Amelia nodded at her, then returned to her conversation. Emily admired the respectful way Amelia talked with anyone who came in. Homeless people, job seekers, refugees, drug addicts, they all experienced Amelia's warm smile and support. Emily thought her own Monday night commitment seemed small beside Amelia's who seemed to be there most of the week. Emily waited by the small desk at the front of the room, self- conscious with her designer suit, laptop, careful makeup, sleek hair. Sometimes she considered changing before she left the office but never had time. She hoped her executive look would inspire confidence from the people who lined up to see her. Amelia gave the young woman a towel and sent her toward the showers, coming back to Emily.

'Good to see you Emily. Thanks for coming.'

'Sorry I'm late, my meeting ran over. How many tonight?'

'Well, I think five have registered.' Amelia frowned over the piece of paper she picked up from the desk. 'Oh, perhaps six, there's a late referral. Looks like a few more have turned up.' She gestured to the queue against the wall, where an older man was taking the last remaining chair.

Emily smiled, swallowing her irritation at the disorganisation she experienced every Monday night. 'Ok. That's fine. Usual room?'

Tonight would be another long one. Amelia offered so much kindness and support to anyone who walked in, but couldn't say no. The lists rarely matched the clients. Close to her mum's age but looked older, in her too-long skirt and baggy cardigan, no makeup, grey hair tied back. Her mother wore a full face of makeup and a carefully chosen outfit everywhere she went, even to the supermarket. Well, last time she saw her, anyway. She wondered whether her mother's hair was grey now.

'Hello ... good evening', she greeted those waiting, on her way to a small room at the back. Glassed in like her office but no natural light and furnished with mismatched table and chairs, well past their use-by-date. She pulled two chairs into the table, brushed a scatter of crumbs onto the floor and dropped the remains of her sandwich in the bin.

'Hi Margaret, come in. Give me a minute, I'll fetch us some water.'

She crossed the main room to the kitchen, saying 'hello' to a small group of children sitting on the worn carpet playing with toys from a basket. Two men sat in armchairs watching television, three or four people were gathered around a computer, getting assistance from a worker. The centre was clean, all ages seemed to feel welcome here, a respite from their lives outside the door.

Her earlier irritation left her as she joined Margaret in the room, pouring her a cup of water. Margaret was a regular. Referred from a Women's Refuge, trying hard to put her life back together. She liked Margaret. Similar age to herself but such a different life to Emily; a violent ex-husband, no place to call home, struggling to take care of her two children. Emily admired her resilience, her continuing efforts to look for work, to keep herself and her children neat and clean, even if it was in second-hand clothes. In the first couple of sessions, when she started, Emily concentrated on getting the job applications right. She soon discovered there was always a wider range of issues tangled with the need to find a job.

'So how did that interview go?'

Margaret shook her head, 'I didn't get there. Tom was sick and there was no-one else. I really wanted to go, I'd practiced the questions you gave me the night before but Tom had a fever, I can't leave him by himself, I never know when his father might turn up.'

'What a shame. That sounds frustrating. How is he now?' She hoped she sounded sympathetic.

Margaret rolled her eyes. 'Fine, look at him.' She pointed to the small red-headed boy sliding a truck around the floor. 'He was better in a day but the job was gone. They had lots of people applying. I'm sorry, I don't mean to waste your time.' Her shoulders drooped.

'No, no, not at all. You had Tom. These things happen.

There will be something else. Let's think what you can do next.'

By 9.30 the centre was quiet, the row of chairs empty. Emily yawned and stretched her arms up, leaning to one side, then the other. Too much sitting today. She picked up her bags and waved to Amelia, who was encouraging the last few to leave. Her energy faded as she walked down the stairs. Monday was a big start to the week with the executive in the morning and Job Night in the evening. She found it satisfying, though.

She had seen a notice asking for volunteers on her way home one evening, on the noticeboard outside the church at the end of her street. When she realised she had reread it three nights in a row, she called them. Nervous at first, wondering what to expect, would she fit in, but in her first session she discovered how much she could help and felt a growing commitment to the people she was seeing. If Margaret was in a stable job, she could find a place to rent, buy her own food instead of depending on handouts, buy her kids books for school and her self-respect would skyrocket.

Sometimes, after a busy day, she would groan inwardly at the thought of a night's work ahead, then reminded herself of the Margarets and Sharons and Stans, who were relying on her as they struggled to change their lives. She tried to tell them to make themselves the priority, protect themselves, stay positive, but there were so many more complexities in their lives and hurdles to climb over than in hers.

She walked past the overflowing bins lining the walls of the shuttered Borough markets, increasing her pace down High Street, the late hour giving a clear path to home and bed. Skirted a couple of suits trudging away from the tube and turned into her street, the blue glass of her apartment tower soaring over worn red and brown brick buildings, survivors of the redevelopment boom. She could see her window on the fourteenth floor, high enough to escape other intrusions, for now.

Emily leant against the back of the lift as it headed skywards.

"Better be quick, she wants to see you ... if anything happened ... you might think of coming home."

In the corridor, she struggled to fit her key in the lock. Why won't it go in? Eyes widening as she heard footsteps coming towards her from the other side of the door. Fuck, wrong floor. Before the door opened, she was back at the lifts, pressing the button repeatedly, watching the neon numbers as floor by floor the lift returned to her. Finally, her flat. Always a jolt of pleasure when she entered. Every time. Her space. She bolted the door against the day, the soft cocoon of her bed calling her. 'Tomorrow', she told the frown in the mirror of her gleaming bathroom. 'I'll sort it out tomorrow.' Then curled herself under the duvet, hoping that exhaustion would overcome the whirling in her mind. She protected her life, treasured it, barricaded it against disturbances, with some intensity. What if she couldn't protect it, like Margaret or Sharon or Stan?

Chapter Two

Wednesday night. After work dinner with Phillip at their favourite Italian. First visit was their second date. His choice, this Osteria down a lane on the edge of Soho, had impressed Emily. She had pushed open the door, wondering if she was too early and stepped into Europe. Subtle rather than opulent, intimate without being overtly romantic. Quality without pretension. She scanned the wine bottles lining the walls, the coffee machine polished to a high level of shine dominating the bench, white crockery and glasses gleaming on the dark wood tables. A world away from the crowds of drinkers spilling out of the pubs onto the surrounding streets. A place she would have chosen.

She wondered if Phillip often came here. She admired his ease with the regional Italian menu, his pronunciation when he ordered as though he was in Florence, a man who appreciated good food, as her first mouthful confirmed. It wasn't long before it became a weekly ritual. Always Wednesday, protected in their diaries, a chance to catch up between weekends. Only two tube stops from her work, Phillip walking to avoid peak hour. Emily enjoyed being welcomed by the staff, the same table reserved, their preferences known.

Tonight, as Emily neared the restaurant, she could see Phillip coming towards her from the opposite direction, his tall figure visible over the heads filling the narrow pavements.

She stopped at the corner of the lane, waiting for him to notice her as he hurried along, stepping on the road to avoid the tight groups of after-work drinkers, his pale brown hair pushed back by his own wind stream, thoughts elsewhere, until the warm smile she had been watching for came, as he was about to turn.

'My father called.'

Phillip looked up from the crusty bread he was munching which, as always, arrived on the table with a saucer of olive oil and a bottle of water, together with a smiling welcome from the waiter.

'Ok?'

'On Monday. I was in the office.'

'To say hello?'

'Hardly. Sorry you don't know him. It's Mum.'

Phillip raised his eyebrows. 'Is she all right?'

'No, not really.' She shifted in her seat, picked up the menu.

'Do you need to go home?' Deep brown eyes on hers.

'Well, I don't know yet', perusing the wine list. 'Just a glass for me, I've got an early start tomorrow.'

His eyes hadn't moved.

'She's in hospital.'

'That doesn't sound good.'

'Hard to know.' Emily caught the waiter's attention.

'Hello, are the scallops fresh?'

'Si Signora. Fresh in today. Luscious!'

Emily nodded.

'For you Signore?'

Phillip smiled at his enthusiasm and put his glasses on to check the day's specials on the far wall.

'Ah, my favourite, the cacciucco please.'

'Insalata to share? Your usual?' The waiter's dark eyes bright, his lively Italian face looking even more tanned against the collar of his white shirt. 'And vino? If you would like a glass, we have opened a lovely rosso, not on the menu, but you might enjoy. From Puglia. Do you want to try?'

'Thank you', they both spoke at once and laughed. 'That's a definite yes', said Phillip.

'We have become a bit of a fixture here', Emily said. 'I wonder what they think when we don't come'.

Phillip smiled. 'Conversations in the kitchen about whether the lovely couple on table 6 have broken up.' He held her eyes. 'We have been coming for a while.'

'Mmm.' Emily broke his gaze and looked around at the restaurant filling with after-work diners, lap-top bags and briefcases against the walls and under tables. More Londoners than tourists. Always busy here.

'So, your mum? Do you know what's wrong?'

'Cancer. That could mean anything though.'

'Sounds serious.'

'Could be. My father says she wants to see me. But I'm busy, it's not a good time. I've got so much on, Anthony's breathing down my neck. There's the senior leader conference, which, of course, I'm organising and it has to be bloody perfect for Anthony.' Emily took a long drink. 'He's right, this is a good red'.

'What if something happened. How would you feel if you hadn't seen her?'

'I don't know. I haven't seen them for twenty years.'

Philip sat back. 'That's a long time', his surprised eyes betraying his even voice.

'I said to Dad I'd go, but ...'

'Do you want to see her?'

'Yes, no, maybe.' She let a breath out, looked at him and then at her plate, picked up her fork and turned it over in her hand.

'That's the thing. Twenty years, I've never been back and there are reasons for that. When I think about going, all I can see is the house we lived in and my father and ... well, he was difficult.'

'It's your mum', Phillip said gently.

'I know, I know. But why would she want to see me after so long? And maybe she'll get better and there would be no point in me going. She could just be feeling lonely in hospital. And what if she recovers and then gets sick again and I'd be back and forth and ... I can't think straight. I don't know what to do.'

Emily looked down at her plate, concentrating hard on the piece of remaining bread, her eyes filling up. It felt quiet at their table, the two of them.

Phillip took her hand. 'Emily. So much going on in your head. Forget work, you'll be able to sort things out. Sometimes you have to do what's most important.'

Emily looked up at him, her forehead knotted 'But what is that?'

Phillip opened his mouth to say something, then changed his mind.

She squeezed his arm. 'I have to think about it. I could call the hospital, or talk to my brother. Dad gave me so little information.'

Phillip nodded and picked up his glass.

Back home, she busied herself organising for tomorrow. Lycra on the chair for an early morning gym class, her black pant suit with a cream silk top hung on the door handle, wash bag and towel in her backpack. Gym, shower, work. Ready. Phillip's parting comment returned. As the tube slowed for her stop, he'd hugged her saying, 'It's hard, but this might be important.' What must he think of her? He assumed she wanted to go. Well, most people would expect her to be on the next plane. Going over the dinner conversation again, it surprised her how much she poured out to him. She rarely mentioned family, never did, apart from the basics—in Australia, younger brother Ben, artists, doctor—somehow, she had said more tonight.

Emily wandered around her combined kitchen/sitting room wiping the clean bench, adjusting the stainless-steel appliances to sit in one straight line, neatening the magazines on the coffee table, rearranging cushions on the couch. Everything just where she wanted, streamlined, coordinated. A touch obsessive, she knew, but it was her place. She ran her hand over the two shelves of novels arranged in alphabetical order above the television screen. Booker prize-winners, some British and Scandinavian crime to lose herself in. A third shelf held management tomes alongside a travel and art stack. She picked up the top book, her mother's first. It arrived unexpectedly years ago, a parcel in her letter-box downstairs when she returned home late from work. Frowning, she had unwrapped the brown paper as she stood in the foyer beside the long rows of metal boxes, and there it was, *Melbourne City of Surprises* by Vivienne Green and Angus McNeill. She remembered turning the pages, going up in the lift, embarrassed that she hadn't taken her mother's artwork more seriously.

Opening it now, she was drawn to her mother's wispy delicate sketches and watercolours of Victorian era arcades, small gardens in unexpected places, an Art Deco staircase hidden from oblivious shoppers below. She had grown up with her mother sketching, spending long hours in the studio at the back of the house that was filled with pencils, sketch pads, paints. Emily had thought little of it until she opened the book. Had she congratulated her mum? Made a fuss? Surely. She snapped the book closed.

What was she going to do?

Could she ring her mum? Have a chat? Do they let you do that? What if she was too ill to talk? First step, call the medical staff, hear what they have to say, how bad things are. She would call tomorrow as soon as she got into the office.

The Doctor confirmed her father's 'come soon'. A week or two at the most, she said, closing off options to delay further. Relieved that her mother was sleeping when she called. What would she say? She buried herself in work, trying to ignore reappearing images of her mother, her father, brother, their house. Checking and rechecking her calendar between meetings, staring at her full diary.

'Would it help if I came too?'

Emily looked at Phillip in surprise. 'I haven't decided yet. I've got so much on.'

They were walking along the Thames path, a regular Sunday morning exercise. Today they had started at Westminster Bridge, a popular section for runners and walkers, straight and wide, the Londoners up early before the tourists filled the path, taking photos of each other against the backdrop of the Houses of Parliament. A morning breeze came off the river, turning the sweat on their skin to clammy damp. She should have booked her flight by now. It was close to a week since her father had called. She was usually proud of her reputation for being decisive, for getting on with things.

'Did you find out anything more?'

Emily sighed. 'Mm, yes, the hospital said she only has a week or two left.'

Phillip stopped on the path, breathing heavily. 'Emily, I'm so sorry', he rubbed her shoulder. 'I didn't realise.'

Emily looked down.

'You're going?'

'I know what you're thinking. What if she died, and I didn't go.' She pulled away from him and started walking.

Phillip broke into a jog to catch up to her. 'I mean it, I could come. If it would help.'

'No, no. You've got work. You can't just drop everything.'

Would it be easier or harder? It might help to have someone other than her family there, nice to have support. Her mother would be happy to see a man in her life. She hadn't mentioned Phillip. But him being there would create assumptions and expectations that they hadn't talked about. She couldn't trust her mother to be discreet. Then there were the family dynamics. Did she want him to see those? His presence might keep them under control, protect her. On the other hand, he might discover something different in her that he didn't like. She tried to visualise Phillip in the family house, in her child's bedroom. No.

'Shall we turn?'

The breeze became a headwind, pushing her hair back from her face. Walking harder now.

'Thank you, but you wouldn't enjoy it and ...'

'Oh, that's not it.' Phillip stopped and took a breath.

'I know, I know, you would do it for me.' Emily put an arm around his back, noticing his perspiration against her skin, and looked up at him. 'It's very thoughtful of you, a seriously generous offer, you don't even realise how generous. But I think I'd better do it by myself.'

'Well the offer stands, just ask if you change your mind.' They quickened their pace again, faces reddening in the wind. He really is lovely, thought Emily.

Then Ben rang. No executive meeting this morning. She was in her first meeting of the day going over the details of the senior leader conference with six members of the organising committee crowded into her office.

'I'm so sorry.' Caroline popped her head through the door. 'I think you'll want to take this call'. Professional calm voice, eyes telling Emily this was important.

'Ok.'

Discussion halted.

Caroline turned her attention to the group. 'It's ok. I've got you a room. Come on.'

'Thank you.' Emily looked at her gratefully as Caroline hurried them out of her office to the other side of the floor. These moments reminded her how lucky she was to have Caroline.

'Sorry, but he says he's your brother, Ben? He started crying when I said you were in a meeting. He's in Australia, isn't he?'

Emily nodded, not looking forward to this.

'I'll put him through now.' Caroline shut the door.

Emily breathed in and picked up the phone. 'Ben, Emily here. Sorry to make you wait. It must be the middle of the night.'

'It's Mum.' She could hear ragged breathing between phrases. 'Em, it's Mum', blowing his nose.

'I know Ben. Have you seen her?' Keeping her voice measured, calm.

'Of course I have. Every fucking day. I think she knows it's me. She has all these tubes. I can't lose her Em.' A choking crying kind of sound.

The solid lump that had been sitting in her stomach for the last week made its presence known, heavier, larger, harder to ignore.

'I'm sure she knows you're there', soothing.

'When are you coming? She says your name. She wants to see you. Why aren't you here?'

'Soon, soon. I just have to sort out things here.' She hadn't even booked. What was wrong with her? The inevitable decision was bearing down.

'Fuck! You left us hundreds of years ago. You have to come! Have to!' He always was emotional. Most people would be, a little voice inside rebuked her, his mother is dying. Our mother.

'I will. I will. Look, I'll book a ticket today. As soon I put the phone down. I have to go, but I promise. I'll let you know.'

She put the phone down and pressed her fingers into her forehead.

'Caroline.'

Emily moved into action. First, Caroline looking for flights, rearranging meetings. Then, down to see Anthony. Karen, his slick assistant, sighed, but squeezed her in before his next appointment.

'Well if you have to go,' lifting his eyes from the paper on his desk, 'it's not a good time, we have a lot on'.

'I'm sorry. There's nothing I can do. My mother's dying.' Surely he couldn't cause a problem over this. 'My team will take care of everything.'

'Ok then.' Dismissed.

She dropped in to see Alfred on her way back.

'Oh, I'm so sorry, that's terrible news. Sit here for a minute. How are you? Do you want a cup of tea?' His usually cheery face was all sympathy.

She sat on the edge of the chair. 'No thanks, I've a lot to do. I have to sort out the conference, finish a couple of things.'

'Don't worry about anything. Other people can do it. Go. Today.' She glanced at his family photos prominent on the desk - wife, three children, happy families.

'Thanks Alfred. Not sure when, Caroline's looking for flights. I'd better go. Lots to do.'

'If there's anything I can help with? Please, just ask.'

'Yes, thanks, appreciate it Alfred.'

She walked to her office feeling awkward. Lovely of him to be sympathetic, but he had no idea about how she felt. How to respond? How did she feel? Was she sad? She was heavy inside. Was that sadness, confusion, fear? She wasn't crying like Ben had been. Each time she told someone she felt pressured by their expectations. She would just disappear to Australia and return home, here, quickly. Only telling the people she had to. She could avoid dealing with friends' sympathy. Most wouldn't even realise she'd gone, except perhaps one or two at the community centre. She hoped Amelia could find a replacement for a week.

That night she lay poker straight in bed, staring through the dark. Suitcase standing by the front door, clothes for the flight on the chair near the bed. Change of clothes in her cabin bag, zip bag of small tubes of moisturiser and make-up.

Well prepared to manage her arrival appearance. Everything ready except her.

She woke before the alarm, restless. Watched the day begin outside her window, dawn light expanding, street lights switching off, nearby apartment lights switching on. Not yet time for the taxi to arrive, ordered earlier than needed to avoid peak hour traffic on the way to Paddington station. Once at Paddington, it would be an easy ride on the Heathrow Express. She walked through her apartment, checking. Plumping the pillows, rubbing at a squirt of toothpaste on the bathroom mirror, pulling down the kitchen blind.

She had chosen her flat after months of weekend inspections, to find an open space with windows, rejecting ground floor flats, wanting to be higher up where no-one would knock on her door. She had been lucky, got in early before Southwark prices rose. The flat opened into a combined kitchen, eating, sitting area with full-length glass at one end. She could see every space from one step inside. Compact but it felt spacious. Clean lines, coordinated creams and blues and a splash of occasional red achieved with a vase on a side table, coverings on her dining chairs. Her oasis of calm. Time to go. Bin empty, clean crockery in cupboards, everything in its place ready for her return. 'Bye', she whispered in the silence. 'I won't be long.'

Early enough for a quick check-in, but the usual chaos at security. Regular travellers with their laptops out, belts off, impatient with the inexperienced scrabbling through their bags, being sent back to take their shoes off, empty their pockets of coins. She could smell toast as she walked into the upstairs lounge. Feeling out of place today amongst business commuters crowding the coffee machine as they filled their plates and kept a sharp eye on their slices of bread in the toaster. A holidaymaker today in her capris and flats, at least not in fleeces and track pants like the queue lining up at economy check-in. She found an available armchair at a small table, reluctantly joining a man in a navy suit. Room at least for a bowl of Bircher muesli, juice and coffee. Looked better than it tasted, but it was breakfast.

'Where are you off to?' he asked, folding his newspaper.

'Australia', she smiled. 'Long trip'.

'Berlin for me and home again tomorrow. Australia would be more fun. Have a good flight.' He picked up his briefcase and left.

If only you knew, she thought. Berlin sounded good.

Her phone rang, a number she didn't recognise.

'Am I speaking with Emily Green?'

'Yes, that's me', tightening as she recognised an Australian accent, putting her hand against her other ear as boarding announcements came over the loudspeaker.

'I am Sister Anne Rogers, from the Alfred Hospital. I've been looking after your mother.'

Been?

'Yes?'

'I'm very sorry I have some bad news for you. Your mother passed away an hour ago. Your father said you were on your way to see her.'

'Yes. I'm at the airport now.'

'I am so sorry. She died peacefully. She wasn't often conscious in the last couple of days, so even if you were here, it's likely she wouldn't have been able to speak with you.'

'Was anyone with her? At the end?'

'Your brother was there. Your father was in earlier. I am so sorry you missed her.'

'Thank you. Thank you for calling me.'

Emily finished the call, stiff in her chair, breakfast discarded. Well, then. No goodbyes. Still sitting in the lounge, waiting to board a plane. Feeling sick, she sped to the bathroom and sat on the closed toilet lid, head between her knees. Gone. Too late. What kind of daughter was she, letting her mum die without seeing her. Did she still have to go? A teasing temptation to go home, send messages. Nausea easing, she lifted her head a little. She heard voices at the sinks. Should she call? Ben might want her to, but she couldn't face his grief right now. Her father? What would she say? Go? Stay? Call? Not someone who easily changed her mind once decided.

Then rescued by the loudspeaker announcement, her flight was boarding. Committed. She picked up her bag and left the cubicle. No time for calls. She would see them soon enough.

Thank God for Business Class. Relative privacy and comfort, no screaming children. She leaned back in her window seat and chose the offered champagne over orange juice or water. Too early in the day? Time had little meaning in the air. She would have welcomed something stronger, plenty of hours for that. The cabin was full, overhead lockers stuffed with roll-ons, some stretching the boundaries of allowable size. Caroline had got her the last seat. She nodded at the woman next to her and put headphones on.

As the plane started its slow trek to the runway, the stewards beginning their safety routine, she thought back to when she had left Australia. In economy, then. She and Ashleigh heading off on the big European trip. She'd been saving for years, both waiting to finish their degrees. The excitement bursting out of her. Probably annoying their neighbour in the aisle seat as they joked and laughed. Leaving, finally.

That was the last time she saw her mother. Before running through those doors at Tullamarine into customs and duty-free, she'd turned to her mum. She could see her now, standing there in her new tan and blue blouse, matching heels and bag, smiling with her hand halfway up in an uncertain wave, tears glistening in her eyes.

'Six months Mum', she'd called, waving, as she wondered how long it would be.

A decision made long before, determined to leave, simmering throughout teenage years, waiting. Even so, she didn't expect that the moment in Tullamarine would be the last time. As she remembered, she fought the urge to cry, a sharp band tightening around her forehead. Not here. The plane increased speed down the runway until the wheels lifted. She remembered the surge of excitement electrifying her twenty years ago. Anticipation of unknown possibilities fuelling adrenalin, now replaced by dread. Not something she wanted to think about. Many hours to go, watch movies, eat, drink and hopefully sleep.

Chapter Three

The hum of the aircraft penetrated the capsule that mocked a bed where Emily lay curled. Her pill-induced sleep finished. She raised her seat from almost flat to reclining and leaned forward to check the flight path, seeing the tiny plane millimetres from the coast of Australia. Slid the window shade up and pressed her forehead against the glass, staring out at the increasing scatter of islands, broken bits of the mainland sent floating millions of years ago. She stayed watching the edge of the continent come closer until the sea exchanged its characterless grey for deep blue with white tips meeting red earth. Back home. She pulled the custom's form out of the front pocket; name, address, passport number, then hesitated – 'Resident Returning Home'. Was she? 'Migrating Permanently to Australia.' Definitely not. She ticked the 'Visitor or Temporary Entrant' box.

The last time she'd crossed the country with Ashleigh she had been more interested in movies and free alcohol, paying only cursory attention to the desert vastness below. Purples, reds, pinks, white. Swirls of salt lakes, lines like contours on a map. A strange, empty beauty. Whenever she returned to London, minutes after crossing the narrow channel strip, she would see the welcoming array of small green fields, villages, larger towns, reminiscent of the jigsaws she did as a child. Signposts beckoning her home. Here, more hours of travelling across a land she didn't recognise until they transitioned to expanses of grey-green paddocks, scattered houses. A temporary green that would turn parched and brown in summer.

She flicked back to the flight path, watching their journey lengthen as she ate the final food offering, introduced as lunch. Thinking of her next meal. With her father, at the same backroom table where they had always eaten. The two of them. What would they talk about? She saw herself standing at the front door. What would she say when it opened?

The flat sprawl of suburbs came into view as they fastened their seat belts, closing in on Melbourne's cluster of tall city buildings. She tried to calm her rising agitation.

Emily joined the long queue of foreign visitors and hopeful migrants, having allowed her Australian passport to lapse years ago. She followed the barriers which forced them to turn one way and back again like folded ribbons, until reaching the immigration officer.

'Why are you here?' Taken aback by the question. She was Australian, despite the British passport. 'For my mother's funeral.' Surprised by the tears that shot into her eyes, having to clear the unexpected choke that rose in her throat to say the words. Not the answer she would have given if she'd arrived a day earlier.

'Sorry for your loss.' The woman relaxed her official demeanour to allow a look of sympathy before stamping her passport.

Still Australian, even without the passport, she thought, as she picked up her case with its priority sticker, relieved to see that it too had made it to Melbourne. Emily joined the Custom's queue behind a family with two trolleys piled with suitcases. All generations seemed to be there; grandparents, parents, children hanging off the side of the trolleys, an aunt.

She glanced at their luggage labels—Singapore. Her family, she gave a silent snort, you wouldn't have seen the four of them travelling together, let alone anyone else. They shuffled forward, protecting their place against those who tried to slide in. How inefficient sighed Emily. Why not several queues, put on more staff? Not as though planes arriving were a surprise.

Released from Customs, she emerged through the doors to an onslaught of people waving welcome balloons, expectant faces disappointed to see her. She wanted to turn around. Did anyone do that? Decide they had made a mistake and didn't want to be here? She breathed in her adult self and walked alongside the barrier, dodging a couple hugging in the middle of the space, and headed alone towards the taxi rank.

Twenty years since she had lived here. Half her life. A freeway with tolls, a bridge she didn't recognise, bright yellow and red architectural pieces sticking out of the ground like a city entrance. Through the car window, the expanse of endless blue sky caught her eyes. So different from London where you glimpsed patches of sky between buildings. Even above the river and parks it was smaller and paler than here.

She began recognising streets when the taxi turned off the freeway. Roads she walked on, drove along, tram routes to school, Saturday shopping, the train station which took her to uni, the city. Her stomach tipped as they entered her street, seconds later stopping outside her old house. Her eyes swept the neighbourhood while the taxi driver lifted her bags out of the boot. A trio of new houses on the opposite side, their tall beige walls looming over the remaining Californian bungalows. New neighbours perhaps. Not that she remembered the old ones. Taxi gone, she turned and faced their house. Same cream colour, perhaps a fresh coat of paint in the last few years. Door shut. Blinds closed. Did her father know she had arrived? Here now. Stood in the driveway, hesitating.

She didn't want her father to discover her loitering here, looking uncertain. An adult now, in charge of herself, resilient. She rolled her case around the two parked cars, guessing the smaller one was her mum's. The temperature dropped as she entered the brick and tiled porch, a later addition barricading the house against the summer sun. A body memory of cold creeping into her veins, as though twenty years ago was yesterday.

Suitcase wheels on the tiles announced her arrival. She breathed in courage and rang the bell. A visitor now. Footsteps coming closer, and then her father.

'Emily. You're here.'

An old man. Lines carved deep into his skin had altered the shape of his face. His hair now white was receding at the front, although enough remained to cover his head. A beer pot pushed his grey jumper forward. Shoulders hunched. In her mind he had been straighter, dark brown hair, smoother skin. Would she recognise him if she passed him in the street? He seemed smaller, or was his towering presence a child's memory.

'Hello Dad.'

She wondered what he was seeing. She was so young when she left.

'You'd better come in.'

No expectation to hug or kiss. She stepped inside, automatically tensing from a daily habit since she was a child. Preparing, ready.

'The hospital rang you?' as she followed the back of his head inside.

'Yes. I was at the airport.'

They passed her parents' bedroom door on the right and halted at the bottom of the stairs, halfway down the hall.

'I came as soon as I could. It was hard to get a flight.'

'Well, you're here now. Your room is still there. You can find some sheets and things.'

Closed doors enclosed the hall into a tunnel. The door at the end that led to the kitchen-living area, two doors on one side, formal sitting and dining rooms, her father's study opposite. The front door shut out the only light, filling the hall with a heavy greyness. Her heart ran a couple of beats faster. She glanced up the stairs leading to her and Ben's rooms, an escape hatch.

'Ok, thanks. I'd better unpack.'

Both awkward and uncertain. How to meet again after so long. Her mother's death not mentioned. Even when she lived there, they had few conversations. Her mother's chatter had filled the spaces.

She pulled her case up the stairs, a repeated 'clunk' on each step, breaking the house silence. At the top was a small entranceway with three doors. Bathroom in the middle, between Ben's room on the left, hers to the right. An addition to the 1930s weather-board, she couldn't remember a time before it. She paused in the doorway of her room, afternoon light flooding in from the west. She could have been a teenager again. Her desk waiting for her to start work, the wardrobe ready for her blazer. A washing basket in its place in the corner, her music stand folded against the wall behind it. She left her case upright by the door and wandered around touching the familiar furniture, running her hands over her books still in the bookcase; novels, school textbooks. Remembered spending many hours here, in her refuge. Studying at the desk with the sharp grey-green leaves of the garden eucalypts brushing the window. Lying on her bed and reading, reading, reading. Practising her violin in the centre of the room, looking across the tiled roofs of nearby houses. Little had disturbed her here. She came home to clean sheets, a pile of folded washing on her bed. Ben sometimes leant against the doorframe to chat, more often as he grew older. Her mum would call from below, on the second or third step to make sure they heard her. Everything else was a distant voice that she closed her door against. Music on, Patti Smith, Midnight Oil, Divinyls played loud.

Time to get organised. She wheeled her case over to the bed and unlocked it. Opening the wardrobe, her school uniform surprised her, hanging there as though ready for tomorrow's school day. Checked summer dresses, winter tunic, white shirts, blazer. Her mother had sent her boxes of the rest of her clothes after she got her first professional job in London. An acceptance she wasn't coming back, at least for a while. What else was still here? She opened the wide top drawer of the chest of drawers and pulled out a single long roll of paper from under navy school-issue underwear. Her eyes lit up as she unrolled the poster, revealing a woman leaning into the microphone with her ripped net stockings, too-short school tunic, dyed red hair with lipstick to match. Remembered her rock-and-roll throaty voice. She'd fantasised about being her throughout her teenage years, flamboyant, not caring what others thought. She slid it into her case.

She turned back the blue-striped quilt to find sheets already on the bed. A puff of dust floated up into her nose when she tapped the top sheet, making her sneeze. How long had it been since anyone slept here? She found replacements in the bottom drawer, not fresh but an improvement.

Showered and changed, her case underneath the bed, afternoon sun sinking below the windowsill, taking its warmth with it. Better go downstairs.

She hesitated at the door. Television buzz audible. A flick of nerves kept her there longer. Don't be ridiculous. How old am I. Her father was sitting in his usual armchair, positioned opposite the television, newspaper on his lap. He turned his head, glasses on that she didn't remember.

'I suppose you'd like a cup of tea. They feed you on the plane?'

'Yes, thank you, that would be lovely. My last meal was hours ago. I'm hoping to stay awake long enough to eat dinner.'

Professional adult Emily who could make easy talk with anyone. Her father got up and filled the kettle with water. The noise of the boiling kettle added to the shouts of the football game on the television. She'd forgotten how mad about football Melbournians were, not that she ever went. Emily sat at the corner of the table and looked around. A small room enlarged by full-length glass windows across the back wall, extending the room into the garden. She used to sit here with Ben after school, watching children's programs, warmed by the afternoon sun. Thick plastic cups of cordial and a plate of scotch finger biscuits on the coffee table between them. Their mother busy with early dinner preparations in the kitchen, leaning over the bench to chat about the day.

They always called it the back room, never the family room as a real-estate agent would. Little had changed; furnished with serviceable basics—two comfortable armchairs, perhaps new upholstery, the same wooden meals table with four matching hard chairs, an overflowing bookcase, a larger television than she remembered surrounded with boxes of videos. It struck her this wasn't a room set up for family gatherings. Apart from sitting at the dinner table, the furniture reflected or encouraged a habit of two at a time; her and Ben when they were young, sometimes her parents in the evenings, Ben and her mum when her dad was out. As she grew older, she only came here to eat.

'Milk?'

'Just a little, thanks.'

The tea gave them something to do.

'So, when's the funeral?'

'Friday morning. It's all straightforward. I made arrangements with the funeral parlour today. They said the body is available for viewing from tomorrow. You might go, as you didn't see her.'

Was that what people did? Did she want to do that? Phillip talked about the need to say goodbye, ever the psychologist. She hadn't even spoken to her, was putting that off until she arrived. Should she go? Phillip didn't know her mother had died before she left London. She missed him, wanted to talk with him, after dinner might be a good time.

'Is it far?'

'Easy drive. Up to you. Here you are.' He picked up a card from the coffee table and held it out to her. Premier Funeral Services in heavy italics across the top.

'How long are you here for then?'

'I'll need to book a flight, soon after the funeral. Work's busy. It was difficult to leave.'

Her father nodded. 'The funeral director is coming tomorrow afternoon. He said you and Ben should be here.'

Oh no, funeral arrangements. Deciding who will speak. Family discussion.

'Does Ben know?'

'You might call him, now you've arrived.'

Alert to the critical undertone. Expected.

'Fish and chips all right?'

'That's fine.' Fatty, salty, but she would eat them.

'I'll pick them up.'

After he left, she rang Ben.

'Em you're here.' Slow, slurring at the edges.

'Yes', she said brightly. 'Arrived a few hours ago. How are you Ben? This must be hard.'

'Fucking hard! She was the only one who cared anything about me.'

'She was very important to you.' Emily could have been talking to an upset employee.

'You fucking left, never came back. Dad always a bastard, there was only ever Mum. And now ...'

Emily shielded herself against the jibe, focus on the practicalities, before he burst into tears. 'Can you come over here tomorrow afternoon? The funeral director's coming. We all have to be here. Plan the funeral.'

'Oh God. There?' Ben groaned. 'Yeah, yeah, ok. For Mum. At least you're there'.

She hesitated, wondering whether to mention it. 'Dad also said people can view her body at the parlour. I don't know if you want to, I guess you saw her a lot in the last days', bracing herself for more criticism.

'Days, weeks! Every day. I was there for her. Just her and me at the end, no-one else.' Struggling to get the words out, she thought he was crying. 'Why didn't you come? She never saw you.'

'I know. I thought, well, I thought I had more time and then I couldn't get a flight. Work was busy.' She could hear the excuses. 'I guess I didn't manage it. Ben, I'm sorry'.

'She only had me. I was there. What am I going to do without her?' Weepy again.

Her dad opened the front door, a pack of white paper in his hands, fried smells of fish, salt and vinegar floated past.

'Dad's back, I have to go. I'll see you tomorrow and then we can organise to catch up, just you and me. It's at two. I'll call you if that changes.'

She put the phone down with relief.

'He's coming?'

'Yes, he'll be here.'

'Hmmph. Better come and eat then.'

They ate with the news on, as had been their pattern for as long as she could remember. Her father drinking beer. She wasn't taking in the news reports, but they filled the space. Her tired head was swimming. Ben, her father, tomorrow, Friday.

'I'm exhausted. Time for bed. If I go to the funeral parlour in the morning, can I borrow your car?'

'Use your mum's, no-one else will be. Keys're in the hall.'

She walked up the stairs; her legs moving faster as she climbed, needing to get to her room, close the door. Day one over. Much more to come.

Phillip. Her tension eased with the sound of his voice.

'So how do you feel?' he asked after she'd told him the news.

'It's all a bit strange. Here after so long. Back in my old bedroom. I've walked into my teenage years. Everything's the same as when I left.'

'And your mum? How's that?'

'I don't know. The house feels empty, just my father and me. But I don't think it's hit me yet. I mean, I haven't cried. I hardly ever cry. Actually, I will ask you something. Dad suggested I view Mum's body tomorrow. That sounds odd to me but what do you think?'

He paused. 'Well, you weren't able to say goodbye. This could be another way. It might help. Most of us need some kind of closure.'

Emily sighed. 'I thought you'd say something like that Mr Psychologist. I'm not good at all this. Oh God. Maybe I should just do it. I wouldn't have to stay long, would I?'

She could hear a smile in his voice. 'No, no. Stay only as long as you want. Give yourself some time, though. You won't know until you get there. If you want to talk to me afterwards, call anytime. I'll keep the phone beside the bed.'

'Thank you. I'm sure I can wait until a reasonable hour.'

'Seriously, I don't mind. Ring if you want to.'

She should have accepted his offer to come.

In bed, eyes open, surrounded by the shapes of her childhood, tension ran through her limbs. How do you say goodbye? To a dead body. She had never seen a dead person before. Would she look the same? Same as what? She hadn't seen her age or get sick. She liked to feel prepared but couldn't imagine what she would do there. View the body, they called it, that would only take a few minutes. Why was she going anyway? Exhaustion took over, driving her to sleep.

Chapter Four

Emily stood in her underwear in front of the open wardrobe. What do you wear to see your mother lying in a coffin? Her brain thick and sticky, her body in London-time getting ready for sleep. Tempted, she turned back towards the bed. No. Must get in the time zone. She jumped up and down on the spot, shaking her head and limbs awake, then halted abruptly, aware of her feet landing on the ceiling where her father slept. She returned to the wardrobe, shuffling through coat hangers, hand pausing on the black dress. Save for Friday.

She crept downstairs in black pants and a Liberty cotton shirt. The sounds of heavy breathing broken by snores from the front bedroom met her at the bottom of the stairs. Instead of continuing into the kitchen, she gently pushed a door into the adjoining formal sitting and dining rooms, separated only by art déco glass doors, their wood frames contrasting central lines of frosted diamonds. Emily and Ben were rarely allowed into these more impressive rooms that were reserved for visitors. Dark wooden furniture, display cabinets of small antique ornaments collected over the years, an oval teak table with matching chairs, a silver tray with bottles of Hennessy, Chivas and Penfolds alongside four crystal glasses displayed on the sideboard. Her father's wine rack, always award-winning reds, along the back wall. A three-piece lounge suite in William Morris upholstery arranged around the coffee table. Showpieces of success.

As a child, on the rare occasions when she was alone in the house, she sometimes tiptoed into this room, sat on the couch and pretended to be a lady at tea, imagining fine china, not daring to bring out the 'special occasion' sets. She would kneel in front of the cabinets to play with the delicate ornaments, replacing them exactly. Three or four times a year, on a Sunday, they all sat here when her uncle and aunt visited for afternoon tea. Slices of fruitcake from the specialty cake shop, small cream cakes. Her mother never baked. Royal Doulton cups, saucers and plates decorated with blue flowers emerged, washed that morning. Emily in her best dress, she and Ben told to sit quietly.

The visits decreased over the years. Emily rarely entered here as she grew older, moving between her bedroom and the back room, up and down the stairs. Perhaps her mother's friends gathered here when she was at school, her father at work. She realised she didn't know what her mother did during the day. Who did she see? She was the person she saw at breakfast and again when she came home.

Visitors had not been here for a long time. Morning light shut out by tightly closed curtains. Emily blinked, adjusting her eyes to the grey, her nose itching with dust. Her mother used to keep these rooms in pristine condition. Now the teak furniture sat dull and dust laden, envelopes addressed to Mrs V. Green littering the table. A pile of magazines stood high amongst the letters, bills, marketing material. *Vogue, The English Garden*, members' magazines from National Gallery Victoria, the Tate Britain, the top half dozen still in postage packs.

Cardboard boxes crowded the couch, covering the

upholstery. Emily opened one to see a framed picture of her mother holding a book to the camera, big smile, a younger suited man beside her, perhaps this was a launch of her book. She tried to recall her mother telling her about it, she must have heard, she hoped Ben and her father were there. Tumbled underneath were loose photos, many of her and Ben. She pulled one out and smiled at the two of them so young, eyes screwed up against the sun in the back garden, holding hands, Emily in a too-long school dress, Ben not yet school age. Another of her parents, her mother looking glamorous at a restaurant table, her father in his dark suit. Was that a long-ago birthday, anniversary? Emily was struck by how much older than her mother he looked, even back then. He wouldn't have expected her to die first. More boxes obscured the carpet's rich swirls of blue and rose paisley. A newish looking box with a printer's label, packed with her mother's books, untouched. Others contained a jumble of unwanted vases and ornaments, unused cards, many still in their plastic wrappers, old paperbacks. Her mother's storage area. She could imagine her father's irritation.

'This room. It's a disgrace, unusable!'
'Sorry Jack, sorry, I'll get to it soon, I will.'

Or maybe he'd given up, only entering to choose a bottle of wine or pour a brandy. She stood for a moment surveying the room, holding back a cough, dust entering her throat, nose, eyes, landing on her hair. Her breathing quickened, her forehead felt damp; she turned, propelled out, silently closing the door.

Across the hall was her father's study. Forbidden territory. She crept in without touching the half-open door. His antique desk sat beside a small window, a shaft of morning sun angling through. Underneath the window, his brown leather briefcase sagged against the wall. Did he still use it? She resisted the temptation to open it. Writing implements lined the back of the square writing area of the desk. A silver fountain pen vertical in its stand to the left, engraved *Dr J. Green*. Prominent in the centre lay a black Waterman pen in its velvet box, a card in the open lid, '*In Recognition of Services to the Medical Board of Victoria*,' written in silver calligraphy. His leather-covered notebook aligned with the front left-hand corner of the desk. She flicked through the pages, lists of things to do, the last list headed Funeral – obituary in newspapers, call relatives, order coffin, order morning tea. Items ticked. Her eyes lifted to four shelves above the desk, constructed to match its exact width. Perfectly preserved model vintage cars adorned each shelf. Positioned at angles that displayed their finer aspects. Polished. No dust. Glimmers of memories clamoured in her mind, bringing a wave of nausea. She turned away from the faint images before they firmed, putting a hand against the wall to regain her composure. She didn't want her father to find her here.

Careful to make no sound, she slid out of the room and shut the kitchen door against continuing snores and grunts from down the hallway. She leant on the edge of the sink while she waited for the kettle to fill, taking gulps of air, steadying herself. Then cleared the plates from last night into the dishwasher while the kettle boiled to its rattling crescendo. She fiddled with the radio channels, fine-tuning when she found jazz piano. Vegemite on toast, one thing she missed. She never could get used to the other versions of the thick black stuff in England.

Picking up the jar from the front of the pantry, a pile of small boxes caught her eye at the back of the shelf; Nurofen, Codeine, Panadeine, Panadeine Forte, Valium, a variety of herbal stress pills. Many packets of Valium. Sleeping tablets. Behind the tins of tomatoes, tuna and baked beans on the shelf above sat a second collection, more of the same. Certain they were her mum's, the pain killers could have been for the cancer, but the others? Was she depressed? She always sounded bright on the phone. How long had she been taking these? No Prozac or those serious anti-depressants, hard to ask your doctor husband for depression medication.

She took a deep sip of the green tea, relieved she had remembered to bring some with her. Its nurturing warmth flowed through her, helping to ease the tightness in her head, her nausea receding.

Emily wandered closer to the back windows with her cup. Remembered kneeling on the chair as a little girl, excited to see the parrots and lorikeets that came to feed from the native trees. Putting out seed for them, with her mum, attracting even more birds. She would watch from the window as they flew squawking onto the branches, flooding the room with noise. Pressing her nose against the glass she counted them, talked to them, admiring their green and red and pink and grey feathers, their bright dark eyes, and strong hooked beaks.

The garden was tidy enough now, lawn mown, bushes under control, path swept clean but missing the vibrant flowers her Mum had planted and tended. Emily remembered there were always flowers somewhere, the windows like a seasonal picture frame. She wondered when her mum had stopped working in the garden.

Her gaze returned to the room, staying for a moment on

the armchair her mother had sat in. Emily could see her sitting there in the late afternoon, when she had stopped agitating over dinner, taking a breath from running around tidying up before her father came home. Was she depressed back then? Anxious? Surprised to notice an ash tray on the coffee table. Maybe she was no longer well enough to sneak one at the back of the garden, away from her husband's criticism. Had he relented in these last months? The chair had aged with her, easing into her shape, wrinkling around her body. Cushions piled at the back and sides. Emily wondered how fragile she was after getting sick, how much support she needed. What she looked like. She would soon see.

She jumped with the squeak of the kitchen door opening as her dad shuffled in, still in his striped pyjamas.

'Good, got tea and toast there?'

He sat down at the table. Seemed that providing breakfast was her job.

'What's that music? Put on the ABC will you.'

'Yes, of course.' She realised the cup in her hand was cold, her toast still in the toaster. She started the kettle again and pulled more bread out of the bag. Found ABC Morning. News and talk.

She glanced at him waiting, his face impassive. He's an old man who has just lost his wife, she reminded herself.

'How many Dad?'

'Two thank you. One Vegemite, one marmalade.'

'Coming up.'

'How did you sleep?' she asked.

'Well. You find everything?'

'Yes, no problems. I thought I'd go out to the funeral parlour this morning.'

'Right then. Be back by two for the meeting. Your

mother's car hasn't been driven for a while. Should be all right. I started it up last week.'

She wondered how long it had been since her mother was driving around, doing the things she enjoyed. She knew so little but didn't want to ask.

Emily made herself concentrate as she drove east on Maroondah Highway, aware she hadn't driven for at least a year when she'd last hired a car. Like riding a bike, she thought, or swimming. Seeing the 'Premier Funeral Services' sign prominent on top of a brown brick building, she turned left, following the arrows down the side to the expanse of car park at the back. So, this is where it will be. Relieved to see only two other parked cars, she wouldn't have to navigate around the grief of another funeral's mourners. A large flowerpot filled with funeral-appropriate white crocuses marked the front door.

'Ah yes. Emily. Welcome. Your father said you might come.' A middle-aged woman smiled over the counter, dressed in a navy suit that looked like a uniform. A narrow white badge with matching navy lettering on her jacket; Anita Renfrey, Premier Funeral Services Officer.

'I'm so sorry for your loss. I hear you've travelled a long way.'

'Yes, thank you.' She would have to deal with a lot of this.

Anita left the counter and reappeared through a door at the side. 'We laid out your mother in a room at the back. Would you like a cup of tea first?'

'No thanks. I won't be long.' Let's get this over with, her stomach churning again. What was expected of her?

'You take as much time as you want. No-one will disturb you.'

Emily felt irritated by her sympathetic niceness. Unfair,

she knew. She followed Anita along a carpeted corridor to the back of the building, accompanied by gentle background music from the ceiling's loudspeakers. She wrinkled her nose, some kind of perfumed air freshener. Inspiring pictures lined the walls – meadows of flowers, birds soaring, seascapes, with innocuous phrases, "may every sunrise offer more promise, every moonrise offer more peace," "beauty at peace." How she hated sentimentality.

'Here you are then, please take your time. I will be in the office if you need me', opening a door on their left.

Emily looked at the half-open pale apricot door and then back down the corridor at Anita in her low-heeled court shoes, returning to reception. Why am I doing this? I could just leave. Hearing voices near reception, she pushed the door wider and entered.

The coffin seemed to fill the plain room. A single cross on the wall, the only decoration. Her gaze fixed on the coffin, she stepped backwards against the door until she heard it click. The music stayed in the corridor, leaving Emily and the coffin in silence. Distant sounds of a lawnmower, the only sign of life outside the room, magnified the silence inside. She took a step away from the door and lifted her eyes above the edge of the coffin and saw her mother. She breathed in sharply, her stomach contracting. Lying on white silk, wearing a navy dress as though she was going out for dinner. Her father must have picked it out for her. How did he choose? His favourite? The first thing he saw in her wardrobe? One he thought would be suitable? What is a suitable dress for lying in a coffin? She took another step. No longer the bright face that waved her good-bye at the airport. Make-up didn't hide the dark shadows under her eyes, skin sagging from her cheek bones, lines tightening her mouth. A pink lipstick colour she would not have chosen. No dye left in her mottled grey hair. An old woman. More like eighty than early sixties. What had happened to her in twenty years? She looked stiff in death, rigid, harsh even. No smiles now. At peace?

Emily stared for a moment, nervous, not sure what she should do. She moved a step closer, her stomach knotting.

'I'm sorry, Mum. I tried to make it. It was just difficult for me. I ... I don't know. It's been so long. I know you wanted to see me.' Tears choked in her throat. 'I know ... you ... asked me to visit ... I didn't realise ... I was going to call you but I thought I'd see you ... I was too late ... I'm sorry, I'm so sorry ...'

She struggled to quell the sobs that rose in her throat. The emotion she'd kept under control since the airport lounge thousands of miles away surged. A tidal wave poured through her reinforcements, sweeping her usual constraints aside. She turned away until she could find her voice again. She paced up and down alongside the coffin, eyes on the floor, taking gulps of air between choking sobs.

'Maybe we didn't know each other that well. I know I left ... but you had Ben ... I couldn't stay ... I had to get away ... you must have known ... I thought it would be all right ... no-one bothered about me anyway. Did anyone notice? Were you proud of me? I didn't get married, I know you wanted grandchildren, but I've done so much. Did you realise ... I have a big job ... I did it on my own.'

Her tears became a harsh, angry crying. Her body shook, engulfed by anguish.

'You were always looking after Ben ... What about me? Ben. Ben. Why didn't I matter? And Dad!'

She stopped pacing, stood at the foot of the coffin with

her eyes raised to the cross on the opposite wall, folded arms holding herself tight.

'Dad. Controlling everything. Shouting. None of us were good enough. You kept pretending we were fine. Normal middle-class family, two children, private schools, wonderful life, fucking happy families. We were never happy. Always scared, scared to come home, scared to come downstairs. That fucking horrible house. Couldn't you have done something? Why did you put up with it? How could you let it get so bad?'

Crying and shouting. A voice she didn't recognise pouring out a confused dark stream of anger and loss. A flood that had been kept hidden, even from herself. Out of words, she sat on one of the hard-back chairs at the side, arms wrapped around her stomach, bent over, crying until her head pounded, crying well after the tears dried up with a deep guttural wail that left her throat scorched. Subsiding until it was over. Quieting to an even breath.

Emily lifted her head, almost surprised to find herself still here. She found her bag beside the door where she'd dropped it. Fumbled for tissues. She blew her nose several times, using the last tissue to wipe her eyes before putting on her sunglasses.

She looked down at her mother, at the wrinkled face, the grey hair.

'And what about you Mum?' She shook her head. 'Maybe you just couldn't do any more. I guess I'll never know now. Bye Mum. Bye'.

Before tears spilled again, she turned and hurried out of the room, not looking back as she shut the door. Disoriented for a moment amid pastels and soft music, her eyes darted round the empty stretch of carpet, wondering if anyone had heard her outburst. Thankful to see a fire exit she went through it, running down the concrete steps, praying they would lead to the car park. Opening the door at the bottom, the sun's sudden glare met her, bouncing off the bitumen, burning into her skin, her eyes blinking raw behind her sunglasses. She ran to the car and sat with her hands on the wheel, head dropped, unable to turn the ignition on. Just breathing. Drained. Bare bitumen stretching out behind. What was that all about? Those anxious years of growing up. Always on alert. Thinking this was normal. Loss of a life she never had. Emily was ok, Emily was doing well, Emily could manage. Emily left alone. A deep resentment and a loss she rarely let herself go near.

Coffee. She parked on the side road, beside a group of tables with umbrellas. Checked her face in the narrow car mirror, not at her best, sunglasses would cover those patchy red streaks. Emotion still clouding her head, she hesitated at the door of the bustling café. No one took any notice.

'Large skim milk latte, extra strong please.'

Emily sat at the bench, staring through the window, oblivious to children's voices and coffee machine hisses and bangs behind her. She ran her spoon slowly between the cream latte top and the glass rim, visualising shutters sliding along the length of the coffin, pulled down on the door of that room, padlocked. Caffeine seeped into her veins, opening a space in her muddled brain. She had to pull herself together for this afternoon's funeral meeting. When had the three of them ever discussed anything? Certainly never made decisions together. Did Ben and their father talk, at all, these days? And then there was herself, who had left, who came back too late to see her mother. How to keep it calm, without eruptions. She could manage difficult work meetings. This was similar. Maintain a focus on what was needed, stay practical to get through. Before, there was always Mum, running between them all, trying to keep things together. Now it was just them.

Chapter Five

Emily made tea. Black tea in a large white teapot. Small jug of milk, sugar bowl, cups and saucers, a plate of assorted creams she had found in the pantry, placed on the table in the back room where her father and Peter Ash sat. Peter with his close-shaven face, a subtle hint of after-shave, again a navy suit with a badge; Premier Funeral Services Senior Officer. His smooth voice a background hum as she waited for Ben.

At the first note of the doorbell, she hurried up the hall. She felt a rush of warmth for her brother standing in the porch, hands in the pockets of his worn black jacket. He was still attractive in an unkempt artist kind of way. Age hadn't fattened him, no paunch, his tall body seemed to bend and sway, like those slender gum trees you were never sure if they would stay in the earth. He shook back his shoulder-length hair that had hung around his sensitive face since his late teens. Their mother's pale skin stretched across his cheekbones. Where did that beanpole length come from? Somewhere in the genes.

'Em.' He smiled, head tilted and gave her a long hug. She could smell a mix of alcohol, cigarettes and after-shave. Too much after-shave.

'It's good to see you, bro.'

And it was. It had been several years since he and Natasha had visited. Maybe ten? In one of their together periods. Two hippy artists travelling on a shoestring. Her place was a luxury stop. Ben flaunted their open relationship, presenting it as freedom, none of that limiting middle-class coupledom. But he always seemed happiest when they were together. Emily would often get a phone call when Natasha had gone off with someone else, sensing his unspoken loss. She had been excited to see them, then relieved to say good-bye after a week of their dishes in the sink, cigarette smoke hovering, washing drying over chairs, bedding taking up the floor space in the sitting room. After they left, she spent a weekend restoring order, scrubbing, vacuuming, wide-open windows.

Emily kept one arm on his shoulder as she examined his face. He had deteriorated since that visit. If ever she felt a moment of regret about leaving, it was Ben she thought about. He was more lined, hunched, somehow worn. Was that age? Grief?

'You're here. We can start now.' Her father nodded at Ben and turned to Peter who was sitting back down after shaking Ben's hand.

Ben sat on the seat nearest the door. Emily and Peter at the long edge of the table. Her father opposite Ben. Emily poured tea, offered biscuits.

'Let me say how sorry I am for your loss. This is such a difficult time for you', Peter began.

A practiced look of deep sympathy, just the right tone of voice. She wondered if he had been at the funeral parlour this morning, whether he had heard her through the door, shouting and crying. She tensed, ready, in case he might mention it, ask how she was.

'This is a difficult but special time for the family, for Vivienne's loved ones. Today we want to plan a service that remembers your wife and mother and supports everyone as they say goodbye.' Peter nodded at each.

Usual patter, thought Emily. At least he appeared able to manage the meeting.

'So perhaps if we could start by talking about her life, childhood, her achievements, memorable experiences, people important to her.' He scanned his eyes around the table, looking for who might respond.

Her father cleared his throat. 'Well she was born in ...'

A chronology of major events followed, a timeline of her mother's life. Her external life. Peter taking notes, asking questions, Ben's head drooped. Emily realised she didn't know much. He would see so many families. Did others share memories? Laugh, cry? Dwell on special moments? Perhaps some fought. At least they kept themselves back from that.

She refocused as she heard, ' ... and then we married in March 1972 ...'

What? Only five months before she was born? Why didn't she know? Was she the unwanted, shameful baby? That explains something. What a great start! Why the secret? What else had they hidden from her? She switched her attention back to Peter's voice now, a little louder.

'So, she was an artist?'

Her father must have mentioned it. Peter seemed pleased to get more than a list of birthplace, school, marriage, children. He turned his head towards her and Ben. Ben lifted his eyes from the table and leant forward, fixing his gaze on Peter. His turn.

'Yeah Mum was an artist. She encouraged me a lot.' A flicker of an eye towards his father and back to Peter. 'She was fantastic, published two books of drawings with poems, was working on a third when she got sick.'

His eyes brightened as he talked. He got up and brought the Melbourne volume to the table. Emily made a space for him next to Peter as he took him through the book, pointing, talking. Then into the studio, bringing back a sheaf of watercolours, spreading them out in front of everyone.

'See here, these are wonderful. Serious talent. She had enough for an exhibition, she should have had one. Too late now.'

Peter taking more notes, her father turning sideways, staring ahead to some blank space. It surprised Emily how much Ben could talk once he started. She would have struggled. He spoke with a strength and passion she rarely saw. Was he promoting or defending their mother? Emily reflected she never had a bond with her mother like Ben did. Ben the artist, the young son who needed all his mother's love and protection. A disappointing daughter, deep in her books, clever at essays but no artistic ability, no husband or children, just a job her mother didn't understand, far away.

'Is there someone who would like to speak about Vivienne?' Peter again.

Ben was back in his seat, returning his gaze to the table, his face flushed.

'Someone who might talk about your special memories of her. It is a way of offering a tribute, to express what she meant to you. One of you, her immediate family? Or if you'd prefer there may be another family member or a close friend.' Peter looked around at each, trying to gather them all into the planning, that serious sympathetic look again.

'No good at public speaking', her father grunted, swiveling back to the conversation. 'You're the oldest Emily, you'd be used to it in your job, wouldn't you? Though it is a long time since you saw her'.

Emily's heart sank. No, not her. The daughter who ran away and never returned, then arriving to speak at the funeral. Emily the executive could present at conferences, employee forums, be confident in front of hundreds of people, but Emily the daughter? Her father must have had to make speeches before, those committees he was on, couldn't he do it?

'I will,' Ben said, looking at Emily, 'for Mum'.

'That would be great Ben, you were close to her', relieved. She hoped he could manage; at least it would be genuine.

'Hmmph', her father.

The three of them stood in the back room, awkward together. Then finally, handshakes on the porch, Emily avoiding his sympathetic eyes, and Peter drove away in his shiny black car. We got through that, she thought. Not that I did much.

'Well, is there anything else we need to do before Friday?' Emily in management mode, looking at her father.

'Everything's done. Up to them now.'

Emily remembered the ticks in his notebook; he'd prepared, good at organising, that's where she got it from.

'Yep, ummm ... I've gotta go but ...' Ben put his hands in his pockets and took a breath, looking at Emily. 'I'm going to be a dad'.

'Ben', she hugged him, 'that's wonderful. Congratulations! When?'

Ben smiled and puffed his chest out a little. 'September.'

'Oh Ben', she touched his arm. 'Mum ....'

Ben nodded. 'I did tell her. Near the end. I hope she heard.'

'So, Ben, don't suppose you will get married', their father's voice came from the side of them.

'No need for that.'

'Do you have a job?' Closer, chin out.

Emily could hear it coming, the too familiar dynamic, heat rising, diatribe starting, on repeat from teenage years, childhood years. She tightened inside, preparing.

'Got some work.' Excitement fading from his face.

'"Some work". Listen to me, Ben, being a father brings responsibility. You have to provide. "Some work" won't be enough.'

'We'll be ok. We don't need much', eyes on the ground, shifting around.

'So you say. Time to stand on your own two feet. God knows you're old enough. Don't you come running to me'. Louder now.

'I won't be', taking a few steps back.

'You've never taken responsibility, that's your problem. Nothing changes. No job, still playing with a bloody paintbrush.'

Emily could see the veins in the side of her father's face swell as his skin reddened. She looked towards the door, wanting to leave.

He kept on. 'Wake up to yourself, Ben. Time to grow up. Stone the bloody crows. I can't believe I'm saying this to someone as old as you. At your age I had a career, owned a house, supported a family. Hard work got me there. Work's not something you understand. You've had it too easy, Ben. Life isn't a picnic. Time you realised that.'

Ben edged away from his jabbing finger, from the voice filling the room.

'Gotta go', he mumbled and turned out into the hall. Emily followed.

'Wear something decent on Friday. Have a wash! Don't be late!'

The shouted instructions resounded after them as Ben

stumbled out the front door, slamming the fly wire back against the house. Emily close behind him. Ben fumbled in his jacket pocket, finding a cigarette, hands shaking as he lit it. Sucking hard as they stood at the letter-box.

'Always a bastard! I give him this great news, he's going to be a fucking grandfather for chrissakes and he can't even be nice about that. First grandchild. I can't do anything right, apparently. Why the fuck did I ever think, for one minute, that he might say congratulations.'

Emily shook her head. 'What gets into him?' Her heartbeat slowing to a normal rhythm.

'Well, he won't be seeing my child, that's for sure. My child won't go through what I did. Fucking bastard', kicking the pole that held the letter-box high above the fence. The metal clanged as it shuddered.

'Forget it, Ben. Just think about Mum. We're saying goodbye. She'd be so happy that you're going to speak. Don't let him spoil it. Let it go.'

'Yeah, yeah, ok. I'm going now. I need a drink after that.'

'Let's get together before. How about dinner tomorrow night?'

There wouldn't be much chance at the funeral to talk. They were so different. She would never see Ben in her world, or herself in his, but she had to admit she missed him.

'Hey, just before you go. Did you hear in there that they were pregnant with me when they got married? Did you know?'

'No! The old bastard! He's always fucking carrying on at me about doing the right thing. Who gives a shit anyway.'

'Dad's always been a bit old-fashioned. He's older. Probably felt responsible. You know him, always on about responsibility. It makes me wonder though. Would Mum have married him if that hadn't happened? They weren't especially happy.'

'Happy!' Ben's face twisted into a scowl. 'As if! Poor Mum. How did she put up with him? No wonder she got sick.' Ben banged his fist on the top of the letter-box.

'But it was cancer?'

'Yeah, but you never know. I reckon she'd had enough. And where were you??? In fucking London.'

'I know, I know. I'm sorry.' Would this ever stop. At least she was here now. 'So tomorrow?'.

'Yeah, let's get drunk and drag up all our horrible family history. Come to our place and you can see my work. 'Tash might be there.'

He leant down and gave her a smoky kiss. Emily watched him walk down the street, hunching his shoulders, one hand in his pocket, cigarette in the other.

Chapter Six

One small click to shut the front door, inaudible beyond the hallway. Emily hesitated at the foot of the stairs, hearing the television. Then straight up into her room, and sat on her bed, expelling a deep breath as though she had forgotten to breathe. Any possibility her father had mellowed with age, might have wanted a relationship with his remaining family, wanted to put those horrible years behind him.

Nothing had changed. Thank God she didn't live here anymore. She thought back to the morning, to her mum, aged and worn in the coffin. What was it like, after she'd gone, the two of them here? Would it have been any different for her mum, for Ben, if she'd stayed in Melbourne? She pulled the blind against the intense western sun coming through the window. She had never spoken up when she was here, never protected, supported, just kept away. Not that he focused on her. She lived in the centre of their whirlpool, spinning around her; caught in a spiral of tension, aggression, fear.

She drank the remains of last night's water and went to refill the glass in the bathroom. She paused and opened Ben's door with her free hand. Hers the master bedroom with a double bed, surrounded by space and windows, Ben's a child's room. A few steps in and you bumped into the single bed, a narrow gap between its foot and the desk against the wall, a wardrobe opposite, one small window looking out to the roof next door. Like hers, it hadn't changed since he'd left, though cleaner and neater. The sheets looked fresh. Had her mum been hoping he'd come back?

She put her glass down on his desk and flicked through a sketchbook. Pages of faces, no-one she recognised. She saw a basketball under the desk. Remembered going with her mum to see him play at a final, cheering him on as he revelled in his height, easily getting the ball into the hoop, the team ecstatic as their score skyrocketed. She rolled it around under her foot, letting a short laugh escape as she caught sight of the model aeroplanes on the shelf above his desk. So like Ben. Not for him the meticulous attention of a model maker replicating the designs of German or English war planes. She assumed these hobby sets came with instructions, correct colour paints, stickers. Ben, of course, made different decisions.

She smiled at the thin rainbow stripes covering one, small red spiders crawling over the wing of another, she picked up the largest, dropping it back on the shelf, disturbed by the miniature broken human body parts painted on the wings, the staring faces on each side of the plane. Turning away, she noticed a wardrobe door swinging open, glimpsed his school uniform inside. Curious, she opened it wider. Once, she'd come in to borrow something and found him sitting in the wardrobe, behind the hanging clothes, knees pulled into his chest.

'Go away', he had grunted, and she did.

She saw the edge of a manila folder, under a pair of scuffed school shoes at the back, and pulled it out. A sheaf of drawings. Cartoon-like. On top, a pencil sketch of a school boy, big and fleshy with exaggerated ears. On his knees, his blazer splattered with dirt, a shiny bruise on his head, tears falling on his round face as he looked up to easily-recognisable

Ben looming over him. Ben was standing tall, hands on his hips, a confident smile.

Superman Ben filled the next page, bulging muscles, lifting his terrified father up by the throat, legs dangling and looking ridiculous with his tie hanging from his neck. A wide grin spread across Ben's face as he saved the world from evil. She wondered how old they were then. Maybe early high school?

She sat on his bed, sipping water, the drawings in her lap. Back in a school day, sitting on the stairs that led to her and Ben's bedrooms, high up enough to stay hidden, low enough to hear. Her too-long school dress tucked between her legs, arms in her blazer and wrapped around her legs, chin on her knees. Listening, listening, not wanting to hear.

She was in Maths, period five, when a voice came over the loudspeaker for her to report to the office. Bring your hat and bag. She exchanged glances with Linda sitting next to her and shrugged. Puzzled, she got her things from her locker, alert when she saw her mum at the end of the corridor, on a visitor's chair. She jumped up as Emily approached, quick steps towards her, tap, tap, tap.

'Mum, what are you doing here? What's happened?'

Worry turning into annoyance with her mum's reply.

'It's Ben. He wasn't at school this afternoon. They rang. We have to find him.'

Ben again.

'Why do I have to come? I missed the last bit

of Maths, and I was going to catch the tram with Linda. I won't know the homework now.'

Emily jammed her school boater on her head as she followed her mother out of the building, along the path to the car park, tucking her dark hair up into the hat, a regular habit. Why can't she find Ben herself?

'Your dad's home. He's not happy.'

'Oh? What's he doing home?' Emily knew that meant trouble, at least for Ben, but they would all be caught up in it.

'Please help me, we have to find him.' Head down over her bag, hands busy searching for her keys.

Emily sighed, standing by the passenger door, wishing she would hurry so no-one would see her. Surprised to notice her mum out with no make-up. The lock clicked open, and she swung into the front seat, hers by birthright, well understood by Ben. She sunk back and stared through the windscreen, bag at her feet, keeping her hat on until they turned out of the school grounds.

'He's probably at his tram stop. Just go there', Emily said.

Resigned to the task she looked along the streets as they drove, her green eyes sharp and alert, closing her ears against her mother muttering 'We have to find him, we have to find him'.

'There he is.' She saw a thin figure, tall for his age, cap in danger of sliding off his head, eyes to the ground, on the verge of running towards the tram stop. She rolled down the window. 'Ben! Over here!'

Ben looked over his shoulder, a momentary look of panic turning into a smile and a wave as he recognised the car.

'Thank God. Open the door for him Emily, quickly, I shouldn't stop here.'

Ben climbed in, throwing his school bag ahead of him. 'Hey, great. A lift', surprised pleasure fading to characteristic unease, anxious as he saw their faces.

'Ben, where have you been?' His mother looked over the back seat. 'You're so dirty.'

He was. He rubbed his knees, causing small pieces of gravel to fall onto the carpet. His blazer, black that morning, had turned grey with swathes of dirt and dust. Patches of dirt on his face, broken by greyish spaces where he had tried to rub it off.

'What's that cut on your head?' She reached her hand to him.

'Nothing.' He pulled back and straightened his cap low over his forehead.

A car beeped behind them.

'Mum we have to move.' Emily staring straight ahead.

'Yes, of course.'

The click, click of the indicator as they rejoined the stream of traffic.

'Where have you been, Ben? We've been looking for you', her voice wavering, anxious, flicking her eyes to him in the rear vision mirror.

'Just school.'

'Ben, they rang. You disappeared after lunch.'

Ben slouched down in the seat.

'Dad's at home. You're going to get into trouble now.' Emily's clear older-sister voice.

Ben tucked his hands under his legs.

His mum turned into a side street and stopped, a sharp creak as she pulled up the handbrake hard. She twisted around to look at Ben, her face full of concern.

'Ben, your dad took the call from school. Tell me what happened. Let's try to sort it out before we get home.'

Ben met her eyes briefly before dropping his head again. 'Stephen and all them were at me at lunchtime. William was sick and Paul left early to go to the dentist. So it was just me', mumbling.

'Ben! Did they hurt you? Oh, the cut. My poor boy.' It was all becoming clearer now. 'Did you tell the teacher?'

'No, no, can't do that, they'd only get me again.'

'So, what did you do?'

'I ran to the park. The one near school. No-one saw me, there's a gate. I'd get into trouble if I went to class dirty. And they'd be there. There was a whole group of them and they tripped me up as I was going to the library. I was just walking, eating my sandwich and they came around me,' the words were tumbling out now, 'and they pushed me and I fell and they kicked me and were saying stuff'.

'Oh, my poor darling. I'll talk to your teacher tomorrow.'

Ben raised his head in horror. 'No Mum, you can't do that. You can't say. No, please Mum, don't do that.'

'Mum, the air-conditioning, I'm sweating.' Emily nudged her.

'Yes, of course, sorry. There, that's better.'

The cool air blew with a rattling force from the vents, pushing the heat aside.

She turned back to Ben. 'Ben, we're going to have to tell your dad what happened. I'll help. I believe you', she smiled. 'We'll do it together', running her hand through her hair, her eyes anxious.

Silence as they drove in after-school traffic, stopping behind trams, waiting for cars to turn into their steep driveways, houses hidden from the road by high fences. They could see their father's car jutting out of the driveway when they turned into their street.

'Ready?' their mum smiled at Ben. 'Come on now, you'll be all right, straighten your tie. Let's brush that dirt off'.

'Ben! Come here!'

It started as soon as they opened the door, their father's voice travelling from the back room, louder and stronger than her mother's wavering voice beside them. Ben hung behind his mother.

'Emily, upstairs', her mum whispered, shuffling Ben forward, brushing at the dirt on his jacket and legs as he walked.

Emily ran up the stairs and slid her bag along the floor into her room. Tip-toed back down to the second stair from the top. Her father's voice came clearly through the closed door, she strained to hear her mum's occasional words and Ben's small high voice. She imagined them in the room. Her father standing with his back to the windows, blocking the afternoon sun. He would have his hands crossed behind him, pushing out his chest. Ben and her mum at the edge of the room. Maybe her mum's hand on Ben's shoulder.

Exaggerated politeness at first. 'The principal rang today. Apparently, you weren't there. Where were you?'

'I was there.' Good try Ben, thought Emily.

'The morning only, they told us.'

'Well I felt sick.'

'They checked the sick bay.'

'I was in the toilets.' Ben was struggling for answers now.

'Don't lie to me, you little idiot!' the veneer of polite questioning broken. 'Where. Were. You?' Each word defined.

Did Ben reply?

'Why are you so dirty? Were you fighting?'

'No, the other boys ...'

'Did you fight back?' his father interrupted as Ben trailed off.

'There was only me and all of them'.

Silly Ben, thought Emily, he thinks that will save him. She twisted her ponytail round and round.

'Of course you didn't', his father said in disgust. 'Of course you didn't fight, you little wimp. And then what?' Sarcastic now, slowing his voice, making every word count, volume steadily increasing. 'Couldn't face the music, couldn't stand up for yourself. You ran away. Stone the bloody crows, what a weakling. What kind of a son have I got!!'

Her mother pleading, 'Jack, they hurt him'.

'You keep out of this', he growled.

Emily imagined her father's face getting redder, his eyes harder, his face screwed up.

'So, where did you run?'

'Nowhere.'

'Where did you run?' Her father was shouting now. 'Where did you go?'

'Just the park near school', Ben's thin voice one decibel higher.

'You decided to hide in the park instead of going to school.'

'Jack, he was scared, those boys.'

Emily knew this scene; her mother, trying to protect, begging with a voice that held little confidence of being listened to. She closed her eyes, waiting for her father's predictable response.

'Shut up! You're half the problem, babying him! Well, let me tell you, no son of mine skips school whatever happens. Is that clear?' His rage building.

'What was that?' Was he talking to Ben or her mum?

Then 'Yes', from both. 'Yes, yes, of course, he has to stay at school. You won't do it again will you Ben.'

'I'll make sure you don't!! No son of mine lets himself be beaten up, by anyone. My son does not run away at the first sign of trouble. I never want the principal to ring me again because you have run away. Do you understand?'

There was a thump. Emily jumped. Was that a

fist? On the table? On the wall? Then something cracked.

'I've got a good mind to give you a beating you won't forget. Time you toughened up. See this belt.' The cracking sound again.

'Jack, no, he won't do it again.' Pleading, quavering.

'Get out of the way!'

Footsteps stumbling, her mother's gasp. Emily hummed inside her head.

'Come here boy!'

Ben whimpered, 'No Dad, I'll be good, I will'.

Another crack.

'You'd better not let this happen again. Now get out of my bloody sight. You've escaped this time, it will be worse next time! And clean up for dinner!!'.

That was the moment. In that split second before the door opened, before Ben and her mum spilled out of the room, before she jumped up and ran back into her room, closing the door, heart thumping, she knew she had to leave.

She lay on her bed, hearing Ben sobbing, her mother's soothing voice in the next room. She would leave. Not now. Far too sensible for that. She would put her head down, work hard at school, keep out of his way, give him no reason to pay attention to her. One day though, she would go far, far away and never come back.

Her decision never left her. It sat hidden in the layers of her mind, coming to the fore and then receding before the next occasion. When she heard the heat rising downstairs, she closed her bedroom door, put headphones on. When her father's frustration boiled over at Ben, the jobs he hadn't done, his poor marks in maths and science (art distinctions irrelevant), his failure at cricket or football (basketball was a 'girl's game'). When he shouted at their mother at dinner, for running out of the housekeeping money, forgetting his dry cleaning, her and Ben keeping their eyes on their plates, as she explained, apologised, her faltering voice flattened by his anger. There was always something. When it started she would gulp her meal down into a lump in her stomach, clear the dishes, avoiding looking at anyone and run upstairs muttering 'homework'. Head down, music on, counting the years.

She took the drawings into her room and curled up in bed. She could do without dinner tonight.

Chapter Seven

Lunch with Ashleigh, one good thing about being in Melbourne. Light-hearted as she turned her back to the house, walking down the hill in the sun to the train station. Signs met her, 'Touch on and touch off with Myki'. Like an Oyster card? She sighed to see the queue, all without Mykis. One train arrived and left as the single person at the counter worked his way through the line, unaffected by crossed arms, watch checking, craning necks and grumpy asides.

'Next?' A gruff voice came from under a cap.

'Err, just a ticket into the city, please.'

'No tickets anymore.'

He looked up, squinted at her through the glass barrier. Was it there to protect him from her, or her from him? Faded eyes in his wrinkled face, must have worked here forever.

'You a visitor?'

She could hear a sigh behind her. She'd used this station hundreds of times, but yes, now a visitor.

'Lucky you're at this station; they got rid of most of us.' He handed her a narrow card. 'That'll do you for today. Use it on trains, trams, buses. Best go to a shop next time.'

She ran down the slope as she heard a train approaching. She delighted in being above ground, seeing where she was going, fresh air coming through open windows, instead of the Tube's hot claustrophobia. Passing rows of narrow older houses that lined the tracks, soon changing into new sporting arenas by the river, more the size of a canal by English standards, then familiar Flinders Street station.

Sleek, smooth-riding trams with doors that closed were a surprise, twice as long as before. She almost missed the rattle and lurching of the old trams as she travelled through the city up to Brunswick. She felt conspicuous, a tourist, working out how to use her ticket, examining the map posted at one end. While other passengers had their heads down in papers and phones, she fixed her eyes on the passing view, taking in the changes and searching for familiar landmarks, that central corner of the GPO, Bourke Street mall, Myer, all still there.

They left the wide boulevard and parks of Parkville, squeezing into narrow Sydney Road, the driver slowing and ringing the bell as they competed with traffic. She jumped up, recognising the restaurant's bright colours as they passed. Ashleigh's suggestion, 'Let's go to that Turkish place, remember our regular haunt?' Walking back from the next stop, she breathed in the smell of kebabs and fresh bread on her right, diesel fumes on her left. She was a uni student again, going to exotic places faraway from suburban middle-class Camberwell.

A few minutes early, she sat at the side and leant against the fake wooden panels to survey the restaurant. The same tight table of older Turkish men, there every time she visited, shoulders almost touching, deep in conversation over tiny cups of strong coffee. Smells of bread, meat, onion, spices took her back to meals with uni friends, talking and laughing as they filled up with rounds of bread, dips and kebabs. The food hadn't changed, her mouth watering as she watched trays of Turkish breads and laden pizzas slide out of the stone oven. Rotating lamb still displayed in the front window, glistening with running juices from hours of cooking. Nor had the clientele changed, a group of young westerners who could have been her, alongside women in headscarves with their pre-schoolers. And always the swarthy men. So familiar she fantasised that the waiters would remember herself and Ashleigh. They mightn't be as keen to chat to forty-year-olds as they were to eighteen-year-olds.

And then there was Ashleigh. Ashleigh with her long curls at the door, running between the tables towards her, enveloping her in a tight hug.

'Emily. I've missed you sooo much.'

Close to tears as Ashleigh's warmth reached into every part of her, easing the tightness in her head, releasing her muscles. Everything was better with Ashleigh here. They sat grinning at each other across the table.

'It's been a while.' Emily spoke first.

'Way too long. Not since the twins.'

'You were with me in London, when you found out you were pregnant', Emily laughed. 'I remember those calls to Simon.'

'And I didn't even know it was twins then. Sadly, that was my last trip.'

'I guess life has changed a bit'.

'Tell me about it. All those cancelled Skypes. Those two baby girls have consumed me.' Her eyes brightened. 'Not that you came.'

'Yes, well ...'

'No, no, it's ok. But today. Here we are. Both of us. So good. Twins in child-care, told work I'm sick. I'm a free woman, for a few hours.'

We've both aged, thought Emily. Shadows under her eyes but Ashleigh's vivacious warmth still glowed around her. The same energy that attracted her when they met signing up for first year history tutes. Ashleigh borrowing her pen, laughing at coming to sign up without one. Life seemed so easy, so enjoyable. Despite distance, our lives so different, she is the one I turn to.

A plate with three dollops of dips and hot Turkish bread arrived on the table. No menu.

'This could be twenty years ago. I always loved this place. Brilliant choice, takes me back.' Emily scooped up the garlicky babaganoush with the steaming bread. 'I could eat this all day.'

'I haven't been here much either. Simon and I came with the twins once. Lucky it's a noisy place', Ashleigh laughed. 'Such a mess!'

'Remember we used to come on the way to Ben's warehouse. Cheap food to soak up the alcohol.'

'Yeah, further up the road wasn't it. They had the best parties. The groovy arts crowd. I was the friend of the sister of the brother, my entry card.' Ashleigh grinned.

'Mmm. He certainly was Mr Cool in those days. What about some wine? Is it still Chateau Cardboard here?'

'Bottles now, upmarket.' Ashleigh waved at a waiter.

She turned back to Emily. 'Your mum.' Reaching out to hold her arm. 'So sad.'

'Yes. Thanks. Please don't say, "I'm sorry for your loss." I should make a CD where I can press play to reply.' I couldn't say that to anyone else, she thought.

'You didn't get there in time?'

'No, I was on my way. Pretty hopeless really. I don't see her for twenty years and then I can't get back in time.'

Emily filled their café glasses with red wine.

'Don't beat yourself up. You tried.'

'Well, not hard enough. I kept delaying, hoping that it

would all just go away. And now I'm here and she's not. I don't even know what I'm doing here.'

Emily shook her head and sipped the wine. 'Mm you're right, better than it used to be.'

'I bet Ben's glad you're here.'

'I got a good welcome. It's harder for him, they were close. Two artists, mother and son, all that.'

'Even for you. You've lost your mum.'

'I haven't seen her for so long. I didn't think it would matter too much. But I went to the funeral parlour yesterday. View her body. God knows why. And found myself crying. A lot actually.' A flicker-memory of the coffin, seeing her own bent-over figure, crying herself dry.

'Good to let it out.' Ashleigh's large eyes intent.

'It didn't feel good. Strange. We never connected that well, not like Ben.'

'How's he doing these days?'

'Hard to say with him. Upset, but not sure more generally. We're having dinner tonight. They're pregnant though.'

'Wow, that will be a change. As I've discovered. Does he know what he's letting himself in for? Tell him he can come and practice with my two anytime', she laughed.

'Well, you've met my brother, caught up with the emotion of it all, never practical.'

Ashleigh looked more closely at her. 'So, what's it like being back with your dad?'

Emily rolled her eyes.

'Is he a grumpy old man?' Ashleigh chuckled.

Emily's face tightened. 'Grumpy is too kind for him. He let off at Ben yesterday, just like he always did. You remember. We never had much to say to each other and now it's only us, without Mum.'

'Is he ok with you?'

'Polite. In his way. Critical of me being away, a comment or two, nothing direct, but the message is clear. Why would he care?'

'For your mum?'

'Doubt it! Oh, perhaps when she was sick. To be honest, it is hard to be there. I mean, not like it was, but I'm tense all the time. As though I haven't grown up. And it's empty without Mum. I used to get irritated with all her chatter, but it's eerily quiet now. I guess I miss her. Anyway, enough about me, how about you—the twins, Simon, work—how's it all going?'

Emily scraped up the last of the dips, combined into a mushy blob.

'All fine, super busy, juggling home and work. I love it all, the girls are gorgeous, but I'm happy to be working again. Simon's good. More time to myself would be nice. Like today!' She raised her glass. 'To us and more lunches!' they clinked.

'I admire you. Not something I could do.'

'You won't have kids?'

'I'm already on the wrong side of that biological clock. But I never planned on children. All too hard. I've always been a career girl.'

'It would definitely disturb your lifestyle!' Ashleigh laughed. 'So what's happening on the man front? Is Phillip still around?'

'Yes, yes, he is.' Emily spoke slowly, 'I've been with him quite a while now, longer than anyone else. Not quite a year'.

'He must be nice. Wasn't there an Andrew a while back? When I was in London? Not that you ever introduced us!'

She made a face and punched Emily on the arm.

'Mmm, I finished it with him. He was heading down the marriage and children path. Not what I wanted. I mean he was fun, but that was all, for me.'

Like most of them, she thought. Aware she kept men at a manageable distance; interested at first, enjoyed going out, dinner, sex, then she would notice herself withdrawing. She wouldn't have said threatened, but noticed a rising tension, realised she was finding excuses not to go out, letting it fade before it became something. She had been careless with Andrew, let it go on. He was fun to be with for a while, but never long-term in her mind. Then as the months progressed, he wanted to spend more and more time together, stay over for longer, talked about moving in. She felt pressure building that he was trying to insert himself into her life or take over. When she ended it, his sadness surprised her. Didn't expect him to care as much. She didn't know how to respond to his weepy pleading calls. Wary of being trapped into starting it again, she stopped answering. By now she expected he had found someone desperate to marry the successful executive.

'So, what about Phillip? Is he different?'

'Must be, I guess.'

Ashleigh laughed. 'Don't sound so enthusiastic!'

They were tucking into the charcoal-grilled kebabs. A pile of blackened chicken and lamb skewers on a hot griddle in the middle of the table. A side plate of shredded lettuce and onion. Emily finished her mouthful, laughing.

'No, no. I do like him. I feel very comfortable with him. He doesn't push. He seems happy to take it slowly, enjoy our time and see what happens. A touch older, divorced. Nothing too traumatic. From what I can gather they got together too young, then she wanted to move to the country, have children and keep chickens. Don't know what she thought Phillip was going to do. So, no red flags there.'

'What do you like about him, apart from not challenging the ice queen?'

Emily screwed up her nose at her. 'Hard to say. He's attractive, not in a magazine kind of way. A warm intelligent face. He's his own person, at ease in his own skin, manages himself, not dependent on a woman to enjoy life. You'll laugh—he's a psychologist, works in executive recruitment, which is where I met him. He seems to care about me, which is nice. Very nice, actually. What's different is that he gets to me emotionally; I can't describe how, he's the only man I've ever met to do that, and I trust him. I'm not sure I've trusted any other man.'

'That sounds good. So what next? Would you move in together?'

'That's a big step. He mentioned it once.'

'Do you mean he asked?'

'No, no. Just let it float. I don't need to give him an answer. Yet.'

'So, what do you want?'

'Oh God, I don't want to decide. That's what. I love my own space. The thought of entwining my life so tightly with someone else—it's scary, to be honest. Was it hard for you to make that decision?'

'No, you know me; I dive in quickly. I fell madly in love with Simon. Straight away he was the one for me. Took me two minutes to decide. But you, why not? It might be nice?'

'Maybe, but what if it isn't?' Even talking to Ashleigh about it was making her feel nervous. Phillip casually mentioning the idea meant more, she knew.

'You make me laugh. You've always been the strong one.

You stayed in London by yourself after our amazing Europe trip, with only a waitressing job, while I ran back to my family. You set up a life far away from everyone when you were so young. I was still a child. You're so much braver than me.'

'It was just exciting, and I didn't want to go home. Running away isn't so brave. You had something to come back to.'

Running away. That's what I do. Whenever anything gets too hard or too close. She liked to think of herself as strong independent Emily but ...

'This is all new for me. Only you would know this is my first proper relationship, discounting Andrew. Embarrassing at my age.'

'Could you lose him if you keep that famous distance?'

'I hope not. I'd like to just continue. We do spend most weekends together. Stop smiling at me!'

'Well my friend, you have a smile on your face when you talk about him. He sounds lovely.'

'Oh, I miss you. Why don't you live in London?' None of her other friends came anywhere near Ashleigh. No-one else understood her so deeply, without explanation. Something about long-term friendships.

'Finish the wine, I'm driving.'

Their lunch ended abruptly when Ashleigh checked her watch.

'I have to pick up the kids. Come with me and meet my gorgeous darlings.'

Emily peered through the windscreen outside the Child Care Centre, watching Ashleigh emerge, a toddler holding onto each hand, Ashleigh's large eyes in small faces.

'This is my friend Emily ... that's such a lovely drawing ... You were on the swing ... you didn't like lunch today, I hope you ate it anyway … just put your arm through here, that's right …'

'This is why we went out instead of you coming over', she grimaced at Emily as she strapped her two girls into the car.

'You're amazing.'

Emily thought of her quiet ordered apartment waiting for her after work each day. Could this ever have been her? Relieved that decision was behind her.

Late afternoon, peak-hour building as she navigated the trains again to Footscray. Couldn't recall having been to this suburb before. No-one at school or uni had lived here. Only heard of suburbs in the west as Melbourne's industrial area, stories of pollution, smells from the abattoirs, blood in the river. 'Full of druggies and no-hopers,' her father had snorted, when she said she was going to Footscray to visit Ben.

Out of the station, head bent down over the directions she'd scribbled that morning from the maps in her father's Melways; left, right, left into Ben's street. A long row of narrow single-storey terraces. She walked past a couple of renovations, new French doors opening onto a porch, heritage paintwork, boxes of vegetables growing in the front yard of one, a native garden in another; the trendies were moving in. Not his place. An iron gate half off its hinges scraped along the concrete path in a well-worn groove as she pushed it open. A box of empty beer bottles beside a broken couch that took up the rest of the veranda. A full ashtray on the ground. Somebody spent time out here.

'Hey.' A warm smile greeted her as Ben opened the door. 'Come down the back. There's a painting I want to show you.'

Emily followed him down a hallway with paint peeling off the walls, into a room where a table, a few chairs and a couch were interspersed with pots of paint, glue, a collection of branches Natasha had collected for a sculpture.

'Sorry, 'Tash is at work. You'll see her tomorrow. Hang on, let me find it.'

She moved a pile of paper off a chair and sat, scanning the room as Ben shuffled through the pile of canvases. It looked as though this was the only living area in the house, a bench at one end separating the kitchen; seemed more like an artists' workshop. Noted an open bottle of whisky on the table, she hoped he would be all right for the funeral.

'Fuck.' Ben turned and scratched his head. 'Sorry, I left it at the studio, I'm still working on it.'

'No matter. Next time', she smiled. 'Where will we eat?' Glancing at the kitchen, no signs of dinner preparation.

'There's great Vietnamese food round the corner, super cheap.'

They walked down a street that looked like scenes of Saigon in films, without the rickshaws. Vietnamese grocery stores, restaurants, clothes shops. Shop names in curvy script.

'In here.'

Ben stopped outside a blue painted restaurant and opened the glass door to a room of laminex tables, looking like a kitchen from the sixties. She glanced around, relieved to see a few westerners scattered among the noisy Vietnamese families eating an early dinner. Cleaner than Ben's place.

'What's in this?' She picked up a red thermos.

Ben laughed. 'Tea, have some.' He poured the light-coloured liquid into two small cups which had arrived on their table with the menu. 'Jasmine.'

She nodded and sipped. 'Not bad. You order. I don't know Vietnamese food, they haven't moved into London yet.

Butter chicken is taking over from spaghetti bolognese as the Brit favourite. Noodles is the closest we get to Vietnamese.'

The beer came first.

'So, tomorrow', Emily grimaced.

'Mmm.' A gulp of beer.

'How's the speech going?'

'Yeah, fine, I'll get there.'

'George is speaking too, apparently.' Her mother's brother.

'Christ! Such a pompous bastard. My speech will be a lot better than his!' His tone softened, 'It'll be awful though. How can I say goodbye to Mum?'

'It'll be tough. We'll get through. Just a few hours.' Please don't cry here, she silently begged.

Several waiters interrupted them landing bowls and food on the table; some kind of chicken, spring rolls, a plate of vegetables with a pile of lettuce, bean sprouts and long strands of mint on the side. Good timing. She didn't want a grief laden conversation.

'Do they have forks?' Emily eyed the chopsticks.

'Sure, I'll get you one. These are easy - you do this.' Ben wrapped a spring roll in a lettuce leaf, dipped it in a bowl of sauce and took a bite.

'Yum.'

'I found these.' Emily took the drawings out of her bag and passed them over.

Ben spread them out on the table, frowning. 'That was a terrible time.'

'Looked like it.'

Ben finished his beer. 'Bullied at school, bullied at home. That was life for a while. If it wasn't for Mum ...'

'I saw a bit, but I was young.' And unnoticed, thought Emily. All that attention on Ben. 'I kept busy.'

'Yeah, you were always busy.' What else was she going to do? Always laying the guilt on. She let it go. No arguments today, this might be her only chance to spend time with him.

'But things changed, hey?'

'Found a few friends. Discovered art. Got taller, that helped the most when I think about it, got me playing basketball. But home ... Dad never let up. I couldn't do anything right, continually telling me how useless I was. His long list of jobs I hadn't done, no good at maths or science, top marks in art didn't count, hopeless at cricket which, apparently, is a superior game to basketball. He terrified me. I wet the bed for years and that set him off, more signs of my failure as a human being. Mum would try to hide it, until thank Christ, I grew out of that. He still thinks I'm a worthless piece of shit. You heard him. He has never, ever come to one of my exhibitions. Not once. Never.' Ben stabbed his chopstick into the chicken. 'It shits me that I care. Such a bastard. I couldn't believe how amazingly fabulous life became once I left.'

He stared down at the plate. Emily told herself off for her jab of resentment. Ben had a harder time than she did.

'I haven't thought about this stuff for ages. He ignored me, but it was still difficult to be there. All of us were tiptoeing around, scared of getting him angry, even Mum. Then you left me there! Off to your bohemian warehouse'.

She punched his arm.

'Hey!' Ben rubbed his shoulder, 'At least I only went to Brunswick.'

How many times does he want me to say sorry?

'I wonder about Mum. She put on a positive face, but not sure I believe it. I found boxes of Valium in the pantry.'

'How could she be happy living with him.' Ben shook his head, opening a second bottle of beer. He rolled up the drawings.

Emily poured more tea. 'So, what are you doing now?'

'Painting. Remember, I'm an artist. A couple of pieces to finish for an exhibition coming up.'

'Hey that's great.' Why did he need to be defensive with her? 'Anything I've seen?'

'Hmm, I might have sent you a photo of the Vietnamese woman in the war. It's old, but it didn't sell so I'll put it in.'

Ben painted confronting pictures. Faces clearer than photographs, large and detailed. Emily did remember the Vietnamese woman dominating the canvas, surrounded by chaos and violence. Something in her eyes compelled you, reluctantly. Many of his works were about war or conflict of some sort. They were hard to look at. Fear or anger jumping out of the canvases. Caught by the fear in the painting or wanting to move back from the aggressor coming out of the frame. Difficult to hang in your lounge-room.

'What about money? How do you manage?'

'Occasional sale. I pick up work here and there. And there's the generosity of our benefactor government. I get by. 'Tash has a job.'

A shot of irritation. How old was he? Sometimes she understood her father's frustration.

'Well I guess if it works for you. Things might change with a baby.'

'We'll be right.'

The restaurant was emptying, chairs being put up on tables around them. Their waiter was mopping the floor, coming closer.

'Looks like they want us out of here. Think I'll go. Big day tomorrow.'

Emily hailed a taxi, a little nervous in these streets at night. Tomorrow looming. Back to eastern suburbia with leafy European trees, men in suits late home, turning keys into their well-maintained houses. What goes on behind those doors?

Chapter Eight

Two hands curved around a cooling cup of tea, eyes fixed on the small window opposite, not seeing. On the same stool at the kitchen bench where she had sat with Ben eating breakfast every morning before school. Her father gone for the day, her mother in her dressing gown handing out toast and making sandwiches, radio on.

Today only the fridge hum broke the silence. Readying herself. Black wool dress, silver and pearl necklace, earrings to match. Respect for the occasion. Professional. A message she was doing well. Successful Emily returns. She would need all her strength to get through the day. No repeat of the scene in that small back room with the coffin. Conversations with people she hadn't seen for so long. Relatives, her Mum's friends. What to say? What did they think of her? She had only been to staff funerals before. What would this be like? She would hold herself tight. Hoped Ben would be ok.

Emily heard the bathroom door close and took a sip of tea, throwing the rest in the sink. Checked her watch, two hours to go. She leaned across the bench to switch the kettle back on. Hearing footsteps she spooned leaves into the teapot and was pouring the boiling water when her father entered the kitchen; navy suit, jacket already on, his pale grey tie in a perfect knot. He nodded at her and took his seat at the table. He drank from the cup Emily put in front of him.

'George and Alice and maybe Bill might come back for a drink afterwards.'

'Oh. Ok,' Relatives. She hadn't thought of this possibility. 'We'd better get food. I'll go up to the shops. What about your brother? Is he coming?'

'No. You got toast there? Another cup?'

No-one had mentioned her uncle's name for years in her hearing. Nor her cousins; Susan who was somewhere around her age she thought, and whatever her brother's name was.

'Sure. How about we take Mum's books to put out? Maybe those water colours that Ben was showing the funeral director. And what about photos?'

We should have organised these days ago. Irritated with herself. Not on his list.

'If you like.'

'Well, do you want to choose?'

'You decide.'

How would I know which ones are important? Maybe he doesn't either. Difficult for him too, she thought, looking across at him, stiff in his suit, concentrating on his toast. What does he feel? Does he know?

They left early, a box of books, paintings and photos on the back seat; unframed, but still, they were her mum's. Her father had refused the offer from the funeral parlour to pick them up in their black car. in her memory he'd never let other people drive him anywhere. Driving up the highway again, post-peak but four lanes busy with fast moving traffic. Was it only two days ago that she had turned down the side of this brown brick building? This time there were several cars scattered across the wide spread of grey bitumen. She hoped they weren't early guests. As they parked she could see the small window in that back room. How long did her mother stay there? When did they close the coffin?

Anita Renfrey and Peter Ash met them at the door in their neat blue suits, offering to lay out the books and paintings. As they smoothly managed their tasks, Emily felt she had stepped into a process that would move her along until she came out the other end. For once, relieved to let others manage. She stood next to her father in the foyer, greeting people as they arrived.

'Oh, you're Emily.'

'Emily, so long since we've seen you.'

'Emily, good to see you back again.'

'A terrible loss.'

'So sad.'

All she had to do was smile, shake hands, and thank them for their condolences. Where was Ben? She continued to greet the people coming in while glancing to the door for Ben. George, Alice and Bill arrived, hugs, kisses on her cheek. Relieved she recognised them. Her mother looked a little like Bill but hard to see the resemblance in George. Alice looked up with warmth in her eyes,

'Emily, lovely to see you. So sad that you missed her. It'd been such a long time.'

She thought her mum might have been close to Alice, similar age even though married to her older brother George, perhaps easier to talk to another woman in the family, rather than her brothers. Then Ben and Natasha. Emily was relieved to see his white shirt and jacket over black jeans. Not what their father would think was appropriate but clean, ironed. As they hugged, she could smell alcohol through the layers of after-shave, but he looked clear eyed.

'You ok Ben?'

'Yep. I'm ready.'

'Natasha', hugging her again. 'London was a long time ago. Good to see you. And congratulations. Very exciting news.'

She was still an attractive woman; reddish curls lengthening below her shoulders, tall and slim, strong looking. Pregnancy not obvious under her loose dress.

Ben nodded at his dad. 'You remember Natasha?' She shook his hand. 'Hello Jack.' So, they had met.

'You got here. We're in the front row.'

They sat there in a line, the grieving family, Emily between her father and her brother. Surrounded by pale apricot walls with more of those pictures; birds, flowers, seascapes, mountains. Emily stared at the coffin looming on the small stage, closed now. She visualised her mother inside, lying on the white silk in her navy dress, ready to go. Remembering her surge of anger in that small room as though it was someone else. Tears threatened as she lingered on her mother's face, smiling at her from the leaflet on her lap. Much younger. She tensed as they waited, a tight band across her chest, protecting her emotion. Rustles around her as people entered, laid bouquets in front of the coffin, nodded in her direction. Whispers from her relatives in the row behind. She couldn't remember another occasion when she, Ben and her father had sat together outside the home. She didn't go to her graduation ceremony, she'd left the country by then, gone before Ben graduated. She went with her mother to his end of first year exhibition, her father didn't come. Only her mum went to her father's work functions. Was this, her mother's funeral, the first time?

The music faded, Peter speaking at the lectern, looking sympathetically at the front row at regular intervals, no doubt as someone trained him to do. Emily squirmed inside. He recited the facts of her mother's life accompanied by formulaic phrases useful for any funeral. I suppose we didn't give him much. Except for Ben. There was no singing, one thing they all agreed on. It became more personal when George stood up. A large man, his tailored pin striped suit just covering his paunch. He spoke with a lawyer's confidence. Attempting to be light-hearted, maybe he imagined warm, but his funny stories painted a picture of a silly woman who couldn't get anything right. Jokes about her cooking, always late, never meeting deadlines. Yet another way of reminding us all how much more sensible and successful he was than his younger sister. Emily wondered if her mother knew how her brothers talked about her.

Emotion seeped out of Ben as he faced the gathering. He took his notes out of his jacket pocket and stood for a moment, looking away from the rows of faces, swaying slightly. The room silent, caught by his loss, even before he spoke. Emily tensed, eyes on his pale face, watching him swallow hard. Then a deep breath and he lifted his head to begin. Not a well-structured speech like George before him: a meandering flow; pride in her achievements; gratitude for her love and support. A despairing sadness, interspersed with swallows, breaths to regain composure. The depth of his emotion took her aback. It was like he had lost a core part of himself. She wondered what she would have said. No memories of important moments of support from her mother, valuable advice, special experiences. Did she only have enough energy for one of them? And chose Ben? She had never felt the close, loving relationship that Ben did. She told herself off for a rush of resentment, Ben needed his mum's support. Underneath layers of resentment, anger, abandonment she knew her mum loved her, maybe she did what she could. Would she miss her? Hard to know. Phone calls had been a duty she couldn't quite leave behind, listening to her mother, trying to think of something to say, managing her voice to screen out her irritation. Somehow, hoping for more. In one sense already living with loss, now strengthened with this finality.

'Well done Ben', she whispered as he sank on the seat beside her. A slight nod, his eyes wet, he crouched over his knees and blew his nose. Echoed behind them. Natasha put her arm around his shoulders, leant close.

Then it was time. Peter standing aside, head bowed as curtains drew around the coffin. Emily held Ben's arm, tightly, as they heard the coffin sliding away on the rails. The last goodbye. Peter came down the steps and stretched out his hand as he reached the front row. She kept her head down, focusing on her father's shoes in front as they walked up the aisle, still holding onto Ben, Natasha on his other arm. George, Alice and Bill following. The aisle seemed long. She was aware of people standing as they passed. She realised she didn't know whether her mother had many friends, a few friends, she knew so little about her life. As they neared the last row, Ashleigh ran out into the aisle and hugged her. Tight. Bringing tears close to the surface. 'Oh Emily.'

Instead of heading into the refreshments room, she turned right and stepped outside, taking several deep breaths. Don't cry, don't cry. Released from the closed atmosphere of the last hour, she welcomed the fresh air in her lungs, on the skin of her face offering a kind of relief. She moved away from the door to stand alone between a row of knee-high bushes marking the boundary between the brown brick building and the busy highway a few metres away. The few remaining summer splashes of red and orange drooped on the bushes in front of her. Pull yourself together. She had more to get through.

'Glad that's over.' Natasha was beside her, lighting a cigarette. 'Just one, I shouldn't do this.'

'One won't hurt. How have you been?' Emily watched her draw on the cigarette and almost wished she smoked. Pulling on a cigarette looked appealing today.

'Yeah, ok. I've been throwing up as everyone does, but I'm over that now. Pregnancy isn't fun, but if I want to have a baby, I can't put it off any longer.'

'How will you manage?' Emily thought back to the chaotic house.

'Money-wise you mean? I'm not sure. I'll have to stop working for a while. Ben will have to get his act together. Earn some money. Sorry, this isn't the best time, but to be honest I am worried about him. I don't know if you've noticed, but he's drinking a lot more. I think since he realised his mother wouldn't survive. He's not painting as much; he seems to have lost his drive.'

'I had wondered.'

'Look I'm no puritan, but things have to change with a baby. I'm hoping that the baby will help him, give him some focus. Help him get through this.'

Natasha had always seemed the strong one. Independent, had looked after herself for many years, maybe Ben too. She suspected Ben depended on her more than he would want to admit.

'Here he is now.'

Ben was coming towards them, taking a quick gulp out of a silver flask he pulled out of his jacket pocket, flat enough to stay hidden.

'Want some?' He held it out to Emily and Natasha.

'No thanks. I'll need a clear head for this. I'd better go in. See you in there.'

Emily stopped for a moment outside the room, an indistinct murmur of voices coming through the open double doors, an expanse of greys, blacks, navy. Then straightened her back, gripping herself inside and walked in, unsure if she should recognise any of the faces with their cups of tea and plates of triangular sandwiches and cakes. Not hungry, but holding a plate and choosing a sandwich gave her something to do. Relieved to see Ashleigh's head amongst the grey groups, she headed towards her when a man closer to her age in a sharp black suit touched her arm and introduced himself as Christopher.

'You must be Emily. I'm your mother's publisher', he explained, the skin of his hand smooth against hers in a firm handshake.

'Yes. Good to meet you. You have done a lovely job', recognising him from the photo.

'Thank you. But it was all Vivienne and Angus. Such beautiful work and quite unique. Here's Angus now. Have you met each other?'

Emily shook her head and held out her hand to Angus. Her mother's vintage. Greying beard, peppering the ginger. Looked a creative type, she thought. Tweed jacket, scarf around his neck, cravat he might call it, black hat in his other hand.

'Emily, at last. I've heard so much about you.'

'All good, I hope.' Emily smiled nervously.

'Oh yes, Viv was very proud of you. She missed you, though. Viv was so lovely, she was an important friend to me and wonderful to work with. We had such a symbiotic relationship, my poems, her artwork. A special connection in my work, my life. She was so young. I don't know what I'll do without her. A big hole in my life.' He turned away and pulled out a colourful hanky.

Christopher looked at her intently. 'Your mother was seriously talented you know.'

'Yes, ahh, I, I live overseas.'

'I hope you don't mind me saying', he lowered his voice, leant in a little closer, his after shave touching the edges of her nose. 'That speech from her brother annoyed me. He made her work sound like a hobby. I realise now what Vivienne was up against. She could have done so much. If only she had believed in herself just a little more. I did, it's why I stayed with her. She didn't bring in significant income, but I knew she had potential, I had to keep encouraging her to get as far as she did, Angus and me both, most likely we were the only ones, and your brother I guess. Sorry, I'm sure you were a significant support too.' He glanced at her.

'Not enough, too far away.' Emily struggled, what must he think of them? Only Ben respected her as a professional.

Christopher wasn't listening. He ran his fingers through his hair. 'If only things had been different, and now no more. Gone. 'Hey Angus.' He held an arm out to Angus who was hovering nearby. 'We'll miss Vivienne, won't we?'

Angus rejoined them. 'Oh yes, yes, so much', sniffing.

'We must leave you to others, I'm glad to have met you.' Christopher shook hands again, warmer this time. 'Here's my card, in case you need to contact me.'

Angus surprised her with a hug. She watched the pressed black suit and the tweed jacket weave through the talking clusters and slipped the card into her bag. Was she that selfish, so intent on progressing her career, proud of her own achievements, grumpy about not getting enough attention, and not recognising what her mother was trying to do. She knew her dad had traditional ideas about family, what he expected from his wife, but she, Emily, who called herself a feminist, she could have supported her mother, helped her. She scanned the crowd, where was Ashleigh?

Then Alice was coming towards her. Emily had dim memories of her at Christmas gatherings, those occasional Sunday afternoon teas when she was young. A tiny woman, short and thin with a determined look about her that made Emily feel nervous even before she spoke.

'So, Emily it's been a long time', tilting her head to look into Emily's face.

'Yes.' There was something coming.

'Your mother missed you, you know.'

She had reacted to Angus's comment with guilty warmth. With Alice her defences were up.

'We talked on the phone; I have a busy life.'

'Yes, she was proud of your success.' So she kept hearing.

'Your mother and I talked a lot. I will miss her more than anyone realises. Look, let's move somewhere we can talk.'

Definitely something on her mind. They stood against the wall, away from the food and the tables of books.

Alice turned towards her and lowered her voice. 'I don't know how much Vivienne said to you, knowing your mum, very little, if anything, but I think it's important that someone in the family understands what was happening for her and you're my best bet. I can't keep it to myself anymore.'

'What do you mean?'

'Your mother liked to keep a good appearance. She hid her problems.'

Emily thought of those bright conversations, how well

dressed she was, how everything was always fine. The pills in the cupboard.

'The reality is she found life difficult. Her art saved her, kept her sane. To be honest, she struggled with your father.' Surprisingly straightforward.

'I know he was hard on Ben.'

'She was absolutely distraught about the way Jack treated Ben. She spent her life trying to protect him. But that was only part of it. It wasn't just Ben. From what I can gather you were ok, but he didn't treat Vivienne well. Sounded like he ruled the house, extremely controlling, including Vivienne. You might have seen some of that?'

Emily nodded, her stomach tightening.

'She would ring me in tears many times; perhaps I was the only one she could do that with. He was often angry with her, aggressive, she felt she couldn't do anything right. He kept a tight rein on the housekeeping, he'd hand it out and if she ran out he interrogated her, for God's sake, like a principal with a naughty student. I'm not telling you anything new when I say what an old-fashioned man he was. Is. With all the expectations that go with that, for his wife and especially for his son. As you know Ben was different, nothing like what Jack wanted, expected. He blamed Vivienne for encouraging him. He wanted a middle-class housewife but Vivienne was an artist.'

Alice waved her arm towards the tables of books and prints. 'Beautiful work, it was her lifeblood, but it could have been so much more. She kept it small, made it seem like a hobby, never a profession. If she stepped across that line, she knew there'd be trouble. Jack had to come first, had to do things his way, she tried so hard, but it never satisfied him. In the early days this older, successful doctor dazzled her, she looked up to him and blamed herself when things weren't going right.' Alice nodded. 'You know what I'm saying.'

Emily leaned her back against the wall trying to avoid Alice's penetrating eyes. She couldn't remember Alice saying much at all to her before and now a downpour, like there would never be another time.

'I guess I ... well, as you say, Mum didn't say much.'

'No, she wouldn't have. I don't think she talked to anyone. I heard a little, enough. Not George, this family doesn't talk. Now she's gone I am not betraying her confidences, I think you should know.'

If her mum had said this much to Alice, she was sure it was true. Had she seen anything? The years away had faded her memories to a dim outline. They all experienced that apprehensive fog as they stepped through the front door; she had felt that again this week, so many years later. Ben, yes, she knew he'd suffered, but she'd thought little about her mother. Or hadn't wanted to.

'And the thing that annoyed me the most,' Alice's eyes flashed, energy rising, 'was that she thought she just needed to try harder. As though it was her fault. I guess we women think we have to put up with it. That we have to do something different, that we have to fix it. Sorry to say Emily, she should have left him years ago. He absolutely stifled her. But that's difficult to do. How would she live, she hadn't worked for years, he made sure of that. We talked about it, once or twice when she was particularly down, but it was too hard. Even these days, in that circle, it was too big a step. She'd tell herself it wasn't too bad, she could manage'.

Emily looked across the mass of heads. She glimpsed her father on the other side of the room talking to an elderly couple. It surprised her to see him deep in close conversation.

The woman touching his arm. Patients? Friends? She turned her head away from him, scanning the room until she saw Ben and Natasha, opposite, talking with Ashleigh, sharing a plate of food.

'Maybe Ben knew more than me? They were close.'

'Perhaps. You can't imagine how hard she tried to create a good normal family for you. I think it calmed down a bit in recent years, to be fair I have to say he took care of her when she got sick, I guess being a Doctor. But those earlier years ...'

Good normal family, thought Emily, well that was a failure. I wonder if she seriously considered leaving, more than what Alice realised. Did she look at rental prices, save money, open a bank account? Could she, Emily, have done anything? She'd kept herself at a distance, waiting for the moment to leave. Because she could, the thought struck her, she could leave. And her mother couldn't.

This was a different Alice from the hostess or the helpful visitor that Emily remembered. Welcoming, smiling, organising food, making sure everyone had drinks. Not this direct, strong little woman. At least her mum had someone to talk to.

'Well, ah, this is all pretty awful.' Emily found it hard to speak. Whirling inside. She'd abandoned Ben and her mother, distancing herself from their struggles. She fought a desire to run from the room. Where was the bathroom? George's booming voice coming towards them saved her.

'Alice, come and talk to Jennifer over here, you remember Jennifer', glancing at Emily. 'Sorry Emily, if I can just borrow my dear wife', as though he was at some networking event.

Alice gave Emily a quick nod as she followed George. Back to role.

Could she sit in the car, get a taxi? Too many people still

here. Not the right thing to do. She looked around for Ben who had moved to the table spread with books and photos, bending down talking to two older women, three heads looking through the books. She didn't want to be dragged into that conversation. Natasha leant against the wall beside them, eyes closed. She saw the staff bring in fresh tea and went to get a cup.

'There you are.' Ashleigh beside her, arm around her shoulder. 'How are you going?'

'Oh Ash, God, I don't know how much of this I can take.'

'Let's take a breather, come on.' Ashleigh inclined her head to the exit, taking her arm. Before they reached the doorway, a woman's voice beside her.

'Emily, sorry, are you going? I wanted to catch you.'

Emily turned to a woman in a navy suit and pearls, ready with her practiced smile. 'No, no, that's fine.'

Ashleigh hesitated. Emily glanced at her, please stay.

'I don't mean to keep you but wanted the chance to say hello. You may not remember me. I was at school with your mother. Janet.'

'Hello, good to meet you, I'm sure I've heard Mum talking about you. This is my friend Ashleigh.'

Janet nodded to Ashleigh. 'Lovely. Emily, so good to see you. You were just a young girl when I last saw you, now look at you, so grown up. Working in London I hear.' Emily smiled, Janet continuing before she could think of a reply. 'I can't believe Vivienne has gone. It must be terrible for you to lose your mum so early. I know you've been away for a long time, but still, your mum. We live down the coast now, so I didn't see her as much in the last few years. I missed her. She was such a wonderful friend. I wish I'd seen her more often. The phone's never as good. It was quite a shock to hear she was ill, so young. And hard for your dad too. He must have expected he would be the first to go. What will he do without her? I didn't know him that well, but a fine man. I remember hearing so much about him when they were getting together, older but so handsome and a doctor. We were all envious. Such a splendid match. I was at their wedding, you know. Then you came along, a little early of course, but these things happen, and then Ben. Viv was so lucky to have you both. Sadly, I wasn't able to. I always admired her, two lovely children, those beautiful books, such an achievement, and she always looked wonderful when I saw her. I couldn't believe it when I heard the news, not Viv, I came up to see her before the end. It was terrible to see her like that.'

Janet stepped closer and put her hand on her arm, looking up into Emily's face. 'She missed you, you know. She loved you, was immensely proud of you, was always talking about you and Ben. Ben's a bit different, the artist temperament. You sound like the strong one. He might need you now. Viv was a great support to him, and he to her from what I can gather.'

Emily nodded. Always Ben.

'Well, I must go. Lovely to see you Emily. If there's anything I can do I'll just see your dad before I head back home.' Janet pressed her soft cheek against Emily's for a moment and disappeared into the crowd.

Emily rubbed her forehead at a growing headache. She thought again of her mother lying in the coffin, how much older she had looked, her shock at seeing her. The piles of pills in the cupboard.

'So confusing', Emily muttered to Ashleigh, watching Janet as she joined the group surrounding her father.

'What do you mean? She seemed lovely, hardly drew

breath though.' Ashleigh gave a slight smile, uncertain about humour at a funeral.

Emily shook her head. 'Mum – what the hell was going on, her friends thought she had this fabulous life.'

Ashleigh looked at her questioningly.

'Not here. Too many people. Have you seen Ben?'

Ben squatted next to Natasha, who was sitting on a chair against the wall. The two women gone. Emily weaved her way through the remaining people over to them, avoiding eyes, Ashleigh following.

'How you doing Ben?' He looked up at her, face grey and strained.

'All right. I've had enough of this though. Natasha's tired.'

'Me too, hopefully not too much longer. The food's nearly finished.' She gestured to the photo table. 'We could pack that up, people are going.'

Ben looked at Natasha. 'Yeah, we're gonna go.' He straightened up, uncurling his long lanky form. Natasha got up, the top of her head just below Ben's shoulder. Tired, smaller but definitely stronger, Emily thought, he'll be all right with Natasha.

'You're not coming back to the house? The uncles are coming for a drink.'

He screwed up his face. 'You're joking. After the other day?'

Maybe it would be easier without him.

'We'll catch up, hey? I'm going back soon though.'

'Of course you are.' He rolled his eyes and gave her a quick hug, started towards the door.

'See you Ash.' He waved towards the table where Ashleigh was piling photos and books.

Emily smiled at Natasha. 'Take care; I want to hear the

news.' Lowered her voice, 'I'm sure Ben'll be ok, once he's over all this'.

'I hope so.'

She watched them leave the emptying room, noting Ben on his way out nodding at their father from a distance.

'I'd better go too, I need to pop in at work before picking up the girls. Try to sleep tonight. I'll call you tomorrow.'

'So good to have you here. You're my best support, only support.'

Ashleigh hugged her tightly. 'And you're my dear, dear friend.'

Emily could hear a little voice inside her crying, "don't leave me". She mustn't fall apart.

Ashleigh was saying something. 'That man of yours sounds pretty good too.'

'Nothing like you Ash.' Back under control.

Near the door she saw Ashleigh shaking her dad's hand. They seemed far away. Glimpsed George, Alice and Bill grouped with their bags and coats waiting, staff unobtrusively clearing plates, half-drunk cups of tea. She stood alone in the space, watching the remaining guests farewell her father. Onto the next thing, she took a deep breath, picked up the pile from the table and walked over.

Her father glanced at them. 'That's it then. Time for a proper drink. Come on.'

They headed down the highway, lines of traffic in front, alongside. George following in his BMW behind, Alice's head low beside him, sunglasses on, Bill in the back. Emily glanced at her father, hunched over the steering wheel. He looked drained, gripping the wheel, gaze fixed in front, just getting home. Neither finding the energy to speak. Through the side window she saw dust rising as the wind strengthened;

banners flapped, shoppers angled themselves forward against the gusts, shielding their eyes. What if her mother had left? Would they have been happier? They would have been poor. No private school. Second-hand clothes. Images of the community centre in London flashed into her mind. Could that have been them, her mum lining up for help to get a job, like Margaret? She and Ben playing on a worn carpet? As soon as they braked in the driveway she was out of the car, the wind's sharp edges chilling her face in the seconds before she entered the house.

Checking herself in the mirror upstairs, she realised with surprise she still had her trench coat on. Still there from this morning. Her smart charcoal grey trench coat, tied tight around her waist. She took it off and laid it on her bed, wishing she could curl up beside it. How soon can I get a flight? She swallowed two painkillers and forced herself to go downstairs.

There hadn't been time to clear the boxes and dust out of the front room, so they squeezed into the back. George filling her father's armchair, Alice hidden in the other. Bill at the table, tapping his foot. Long and lean like Ben. Her dad stood at one end of the table, pouring beer and brandies. Television on, emitting a dull roar of speeding cars in a Grand Prix somewhere in the world. Emily unwrapped the sandwiches she had bought that morning, more sandwiches, feeling a little guilty that she hadn't made more effort. At least she'd thought to pick up a cheese platter, already assembled. She busied herself offering food, serviettes, avoiding Alice's eyes.

Conversation about how well-managed the funeral was, a fitting tribute, lovely flowers, George's business, the new house Bill had bought, distracted for a moment when a car spun off the race track. As Alice had said, not a family who knew how to talk about the harder things in life. The entrenched desire to always 'look right' buried feelings deep. Although Vivienne had been sick for a while, the two brothers did not expect their younger sister to go first. Difficult to comprehend. Even harder to know what to say. She was the talker. Emily would often come home from school to see her mother on the phone – to Alice, one of her brothers, a friend, tapping her cigarette into the ashtray by the phone as she talked, waving the smoke out of the window. She was the one who knew what was happening in the family, who passed the news around. Emily wondered what would happen now – she couldn't imagine anyone else taking up that role.

Everyone supplied with drinks and food, Emily sat on the chair against the wall, watching her father talking with George. Colour returning to his face, laughing even. Reminding her they were friends, had been for a long time, before marriage and families. She vaguely recalled her mother telling the story of meeting her father through her older brother, his handsome friend, who started noticing her as she grew out of girlhood. Emily listened to them retell old stories of driving around in old cars, getting stuck in out of the way places when a car broke down, waiting for days for a gear box to be trucked up in a hot dusty place where there was only a pub. More stories they wouldn't tell here. Bill and Alice talked around them, about their kids; about Bill's wife who had some blood clot condition so couldn't fly down today.

Emily waited for them to leave. It didn't take long. Bill had a plane to catch back to Sydney, George and Alice dropping him at the airport on their way home to Ballarat. Can't stay, have to catch my flight. Can't stay, have to give Bill a lift. Can't drink anymore, have to drive.

They stood on the porch. George clasped her hand, intent for a moment. 'You are still family. Don't be a stranger.'

She wondered what he meant. No contact for twenty years and little before that. She didn't expect that to change. They seemed remote, strangers. It was as though that was all that was needed, the act of saying the words would maintain the family.

George turned to her father. 'Come up to Ballarat Jack. Stay with us. We can go out. There's a good new pub.' He waved his large hand and hurried to his car, closely followed by Bill.

Alice warmer as she hugged her, quiet words when she was close. 'Take care.' As Emily raised her hand to the back of the car disappearing down the street, she thought it was likely that she would never see them again. Alice had used her one opportunity.

'That's done then', her father grunted. He turned back into the house, smaller, the effort gone out of him.

'I'm just going to sit here for a bit', he said, pouring another brandy. 'Can't face dinner.' He settled in the armchair in front of the blur of cars continuing to circuit the track.

Emily collected the plates and glasses and stacked the dishwasher. Tasks finished, she retreated to her room, closing the door. Still her space, even after twenty years. Only mid-afternoon, but she hung up her dress and lay on the bed, pulling the covers over her. Suddenly heavy. Shutting off the whirling of the day's events and conversations, just for a while.

Chapter Nine

In her child's single bed with Big Ted, home from school early with a dripping nose, cloudy head.

That familiar guttural voice penetrated the bed-clothes over her head. 'Useless boy … bloody waste of space.'

Louder, travelling up the stairs, filling the house. Ben's high voice interspersed with the shouts. Then hurried footsteps, breathing hard, closing his door tight. She strained her ears, hearing muffled sobs. Her father's face loomed large, harsh, reddening, spinning around her room; she buried her head under the covers again. Then her mother. Pleading. The words clearer now.

'You stupid woman, you'll turn him into a girl! Stop protecting him!'

'Jack, he's only little.'

'What do you think I'm paying that school for? Behind on his homework. All that fucking scribbling in his room and you encourage him!! He hasn't even started cleaning up the garden and how many times have I told him. When I was his age, I knew the meaning of work. Not him. Lazy shit. Are you blind? Stop mollycoddling him!!!'

Tears in her mother's voice. 'Please Jack. He's trying.'

'Not that I can bloody see! What kind of son have I got! Stupid bitch.'

Emily gripped Big Ted against her chest. Held onto his soft fur. The knots in her stomach tightening, increasing. She heard her father's heavy footsteps in the hall, she pulled up her knees, screwing herself into a tight ball around Big Ted.

'Jack, please, I'll talk to him.'

'Fat lot of good that will do.'

'Where are you going? Jack, don't.'

The front door slamming and the car starting up.

Mum?

The house suddenly quiet. Emily ran out to the landing in her nighty, looked over the bannisters, sniffing. Her mother sat below on the floor against the wall. Head down, shoulders drooped. She moved to run down the stairs, but thick glass rose around her, encasing her, trapping her. She banged on the glass with her fists,

'Mum! Are you all right? Are you all right? Are you all right?' Her mother didn't move. Her voice louder and louder, screams reverberating off the glass walls, filling her head. Overtaking her body.

Emily gasped. A big intake of air pushed her upright, adrenalin racing through her veins. In the double bed, her child's single bed gone. Her eyes cleared, scanning the room, her bookcase, her desk, her trench coat across the end of the bed, black dress hanging on the wardrobe door. She touched the pearls still around her neck. She stretched her arms wide. Her breath slowed.

A dream?

I've got to get out of here. Typed "flights Melbourne to London" into her laptop before remembering.

'Damn. It's 2012 and no fucking Internet! Damn! Damn! Damn!' She thumped her fist on the bed. 'Doesn't anything work here!!'

She slammed the lid down. The last glimmer of sun had retreated, leaving the room dull, a chill on her arms. Think Emily. Caroline. She sent her a text, please find me the next business class seat home.

Hours to go before she could allow herself to sleep again. Couldn't face downstairs. She picked up the crime novel she'd bought at the airport. Her eyes travelled down the page, seeing the words, but her mind was back in the funeral. She thought about the conversation with Christopher and Angus. Just like the rest of the family, she had downplayed her mother's achievements. She had dismissed her as weak, dependent on her husband, running around after Ben, cooking and cleaning, domestic duties, a middle-class housewife, art on the side. Emily determined to be different. A successful career woman managing her own life with her own money. Emily the executive, a regular presenter at breakfast seminars encouraging aspiring women, sought after as a mentor. But never considered supporting her mother.

She could see Alice's eyes boring into her. Hear Christopher's words. Her mother working hard to look right, even to her friends. She remembered talk of 'the housekeeping', sometimes her mother nervously asking for it, her father barking at her, forcing her to account for her purchases, his anger when something was misplaced, when dinner was late, the house untidy. She shut herself away from her father's demanding ways, his rages, ignored her mother's continual nervous chatter. Emily cringed as she saw herself shouting at her body in the coffin. Did nothing except run away.

Her head was thumping again. Still enough headache pills left in the packet beside the bed. Her phone beeped as she swallowed the second pill. She picked it up with relief; Caroline, God bless Caroline, booked on the evening flight tomorrow. Her last night in this house, one more day to get through.

The next morning, hungry for breakfast, she came into the kitchen and stopped, seeing her father already at the backroom table. Her automatic 'hello' stayed in her throat at the sight of him. Wrinkled hands wrapped around his forehead, wrists protruding from his dressing gown. His body sagged as though his strength and power was sucked out of him. A cup in front of him. She wondered how long he'd been there. At the sound of the kettle, he straightened and took a sip of his tea.

He cleared his throat. 'This is cold. Got another one there?'

'Sure.'

She carried the refilled teapot over to him, noticing the redness rimming his eyes as he glanced up at her.

'Did you sleep Dad?'

'Not so well. I tell my patients it takes time, they'll come through. I knew what was coming, but—'. He shook his head and sipped the tea.

Emily sat with him, surprised. 'Are you going to be all right?'

'I'll manage.'

'You know I have to go, I'm on tonight's flight.' Suddenly feeling guilty.

He nodded. 'Didn't think you'd stay long.'

Did he want her to stay? Was he relieved she was going?

'I'm needed back at work.' A straightforward explanation, easy to say.

'You work hard, don't you. Big job.' Looking at her, eyes connecting for a moment.

'I'm on the executive team.' Hoping to sound straightforward, pride seemed a vulnerability.

Did he know much about what she did? More than she realised? On the few occasions when he'd answered her phone call, he would say, 'You all right? I'll get Mum.' That was it for twenty years.

He nodded. 'You've done well.'

She looked down, uncertain how to respond to the unexpected praise.

'Well, if you're going, you'd better take your mother's jewellery with you. She wanted you to have it. Just look in her drawers.'

She waited until he went out, awkward about entering his bedroom. He seemed to go out in the morning, returning with a newspaper, a plastic supermarket bag. At the sound of the front door closing, she left her packing and headed downstairs. She had rarely come in here. A secret, alien place. She pushed the door into its enclosed silence and halted, peering inside. A dusty, musty kind of smell pervaded. The bed loomed high in the middle, unmade. Come on Emily, she marched in and drew back the heavy curtains and then the next layer, the light helping to normalise the room, making it more possible to be there.

Her mother had hidden the jewellery throughout her

drawers. Protected from thieves under lingerie. She felt like a thief herself. Intrusive to be rifling through underwear, stockings, bras. Emily wondered how her mum knew where she had put each little box or silk bag. In the top drawer, underneath linen handkerchiefs, was a pile of pillboxes, more pain relievers. They seemed to be everywhere. She turned her attention to the jewellery. She found a ring with small emeralds and diamonds, a pair of fiery opal earrings, elegant brooches, a jade necklace, another with freshwater pearls. Emily thought she remembered her mother talking about a ring for a significant wedding anniversary, showing her a birthday necklace before she left. Her father knew how to recognise an occasion, do the expected thing. An array of stylish quality pieces.

She sat back on her heels, the pile of bags and boxes on the dressing table. Adornments hiding an unhappy life. Wearing the right style with jewellery, clothes and shoes to admire was easy to manage. A doctor husband who bought her presents, children at private schools, a house in a sought-after suburb, a little of her own fame. Painting what she wanted the world to see, what she wanted to see. Emily gathered them up into a plastic bag and packed them in the inside pocket of her cabin bag, zipped shut.

Her father not yet home, she returned downstairs and wandered into her mum's studio. Papers spread across the work-table, books stacked on the floor, pencils, and brushes in holders, paints piled in boxes, notes, photos and colour strips pinned on a cork board together with bills. Chaos Emily could never work in. A contrast to her father's ordered desk. She wondered how long it had been since her mum had been here. Was she working on a book, unable to finish? She leaned across the table and picked up two small photo frames from the windowsill, her and Ben's childish faces looking out, Ben grinning, Emily more serious. Not sure how old. No surprise to find pills in a drawer, underneath envelopes and sticky note pads. More behind a shelf of drawing paper. She sat shuffling through quick sketches, detailed drawings, a few partly painted. Not sure if she was looking for something. She left at the sound of the key in the front door.

Ben was hard to reach. No answer. Multiple voice messages. He answered after lunch, sounding drowsy. 'I'm sick. Can't talk'.

Aftermath of the funeral? Hangover?

The day inched forward until the yellow taxi arrived on the slope of the driveway. She looked back at her father as she fastened her seatbelt, struck by his lonely figure, looking small in the doorway of the house he had dominated all her life. She turned away, heavy with the past that had crashed through her barriers.

Terrified of missing the plane, she was first to check in. She had been on edge as the taxi got caught in traffic, under the speed limit on the freeway, the driver wanting to chat. She nodded now and again, silently shouting 'hurry, hurry'. Only when she had received the nod from passport control releasing her to walk through the duty-free counters to the lounge did she ease. Each step taking her closer to London. London Emily. Executive Emily. She thought of when she would enter the door of her apartment, everything as she left it, calm, just her.

Coffee beside her, Emily flicked through shiny pictures of food, fashion, resorts, ears sharp for the call to board. A week between airport lounges. A week since that phone call. Her father's voice in her office before that. Two weeks that sucked her back into a life she had put firmly behind her. Thousands of miles and twenty years, yet those same tensions were waiting for her, grabbing at her, entangling her. Multiplying. How could she let that happen? She needed to slam that door shut again. Then there was Ben. He seemed to live on the edge of a cliff, about to fly or fall, never sure which. Maybe closer to the edge now. A baby could make or break him. She remembered her last conversation with her mum, that odd moment when she asked Emily to look after Ben if anything happened to her. He'd have to sort himself out. He had Natasha.

A wave of relief washed over her as the plane reversed out of its parking bay and made its way to the runway, a smiling attendant in the aisle putting on a life jacket. No engine failure, no delays, she was going. This could be the last time. She tensed with anticipation as they gathered speed, waiting for that moment when the wheels would lift, leaving everything behind on the ground.

Part Two

Unravelling

Chapter Ten

Emily twisted around in her seat, squaring her face to the window, eager for glimpses of small green fields visible between lumpy white clouds, villages with their church spires. She began a list in her head. Buy milk, yoghurt, fruit. A suitcase of dirty clothes waiting in the hold. One day to catch up on emails, write her weekly report, ready to walk in as though she had not been away. Back to her job, her flat and Phillip. Put a padlock on the last week.

She emerged from the bathroom to a grumpy queue. Fresh shirt, make-up, somewhat restored. Fastened her seatbelt as they descended along the Thames, sunshine brightening all those postcard sights. Home. Phillip was somewhere below, driving to the airport. She took a last glance at the flight path's lengthy line, thousands of miles behind them, almost as far away from Melbourne as she could go.

Off the plane, she headed towards immigration with practiced speed, manoeuvring around hundreds of other passengers filling the corridors and joined the fast-moving British queue. When she returned to the country of her birth officials treated her with suspicion, here there would be no awkward questions. Teetering between two lives.

Excited to be looking for a familiar face rather than the taxi sign. Someone for her in the crowds pressed against the barriers. She soon saw Phillip's tall figure, arms waving at her, pointing. Warmth spread inside, watching him hurry through families and suitcases, bumping into people as he turned his smile towards her. He looked keen to see her. Wrapped in his tight hug, she was horrified to find she was crying.

'Sorry, sorry', she choked out between tears, trying to hold them back.

'No problem at all. You cry as much as you like.'

He stroked her hair as she hid her face in the front of his shirt. She turned away, pulling out her hanky, swallowing.

'Sorry. It's jet lag. I never cry. How embarrassing.' She tried to smile. 'Too many hours on a plane.'

Phillip smiled and put his arm around her. 'I'm sure you've had a pretty tough time. It's so good to see you, I've missed you.' He kissed her forehead, his lips staying on her skin.

'Only a week.'

'A very long one, I'm guessing.'

'Like on another planet.' She shook her head. 'Let me go to the Ladies and then we can get out of here.'

She blew her nose several times in the cubicle. What brought that on? Why now? She hadn't cried since that awful time in the funeral parlour. Squeezing into a gap between women lining up in front of the mirror, she dabbed on more foundation and replenished her lipstick, attempting to recover the face she walked off the plane with.

She slid her free hand into Phillip's as they trudged through grey concrete to find his car. At last, her case was in his black Volkswagen boot and they were chugging down the ramps.

'Heathrow is madness. I could have caught a taxi.'

'Yes, but I wanted to come.' He kissed her, finding her mouth this time and touched her cheek. 'Your mother died, you've just flown half-way across the world. The least I could do. I wish I could have done more.'

A car beeped behind and he turned back to the steering wheel. Emily leant against him for a moment and rubbed his arm,

'It's so nice of you.'

She left her hand on his, not wanting to let go. Her eyes filled again when she pushed open the door to her flat. Her space. Overwhelming relief flooded through her as though somehow, she'd feared her treasured life might have disappeared, that returning to her family risked extinguishing all she held tight here. She opened the blinds, letting afternoon light pour into the living area, and turned to Phillip, tingling with elation.

'Home! You can't imagine how good it is to be here.'

'Tea? I'll make it. You relax.'

'That would be lovely.'

She rolled her case into the bedroom and stood for a moment, hearing Phillip open cupboard doors, the kettle heating. Every sound here is mine. They sat sipping from white china cups on the couch, a pot of green tea on the coffee table, watching a light shower create a faint rainbow over the houses, shops and apartments that surrounded her building. Thousands of people live in this square mile, no-one knows me, no demands on me, no obligations, my life is my own.

'So?' Phillip broke the quiet.

Jolted back to the week, give it a last thought, then shut that door.

'Difficult, horrible. What did I expect?'

He looked at her, head on one side, inviting more.

'Well not all bad. Good to see my brother, and Ashleigh,

my best friend of all time. You must meet her.' Surprised by her words. Did she mean that?

Phillip moved closer. 'I'd like to.'

Emily emptied her cup, avoiding Phillip's eyes. 'Being there reminded me why I left. It's like the walls were breathing the past. As though it was twenty years ago. My father is still difficult, aggressive, creates this kind of tension even if he's not saying anything. And all those people at the funeral. God!'

She stood and started clearing the tea crockery. 'You know, I don't want to talk about it. I'm so happy to be here in my flat, with you. One horrible week gone. I'm desperate to get back to my life.' If she let Phillip too far into that world, she wouldn't be able to escape it anywhere.

'Leave them.' He touched her arm. 'Come sit.' He rested his head against hers. She felt the rush of tension subside. 'I don't mean to pressure you to talk about things you don't want to. But I'm here if you do.'

'I know.'

He held her close. 'I'd love to stay but I guess you want to unpack, prepare for work.'

Emily looked up at him, grateful for how well he knew her. 'Yes, I really need a shower and tomorrow morning is not far away. I have to get organised.' She leant against him. 'Thank you,' she whispered, 'you seem to know exactly what I need'.

It had only been a week, she reminded herself as she stepped into the empty lift, arriving before the crowds. Some wouldn't even have noticed her absence or would have assumed she was at a conference. It felt much longer to her, swallowed up into her family, her past. A piece of time unconnected to anything else. She opened her office door, alive again, energised. In her Max Mara charcoal grey suit with chalky pin stripes, a find in the Selfridges sales, her mind buzzing with the day ahead. This is who I am. Up early for a spin class, back in routine. Emails up to date, executive meeting report done, the day's tasks prioritised. Ready.

The warmth from her team touched her as they welcomed her. Her pleasure grew as she walked among their desks, smiling at familiar Monday morning routines. William starting up his computer before he'd taken his coat off, Henrietta and Sharon laughing about the weekend, George carrying his coffee from the latest hot spot. Prepared with calm answers to their enquiries, moving the conversation into the work week she had missed. Caroline asked more in her office.

'How are you?'

She searched Emily's face as though to lift a veneer, peer underneath.

'Yes fine, absolutely. Glad to be back. Thank you so much for managing things here. Now can we go through my meetings before executive starts.' She and Caroline sitting across the desk, checking through her weekly commitments as they did every Monday.

She dropped by Alfred's office on her way to the board room, light-headed with relief to be here.

'Emily.' That familiar grin. 'Good to have you back. How was it all?'

'I'm glad someone noticed', she laughed. 'Yes, thank you. All's fine. Funerals are never fun, but it all went off all right. Shall we walk?'

I so love this, she thought, as they headed to the board room, at ease in her executive skin, smiling and nodding at people streaming in from the lifts, putting their lunch in fridges, making tea and coffee. More at home here in this office building with its daily buzz than she ever was in that house.

'Any dramas here?'

'We'll see. There were a few issues at the senior leader conference last week. We could have benefitted from your steady hand there. I'm sure it's nothing to worry about.'

'What do you mean? What happened?'. Suddenly unprepared.

Alfred lowered his voice. 'Oh, hopefully everyone has forgotten now, but there was an altercation. Anthony got involved. It was a bit heated.'

'Anything about HR?'

They'd reached the boardroom. 'No, no, you're fine.'

'Good morning all.' Emily smiled around the room.

It was mostly a pleasant group, better in Jeff's time, but they had still maintained a friendly atmosphere. When Anthony wasn't there, that is. She wished she could find out what happened last week, maybe she was lucky to miss it.

Anthony was punctual for once. Impatient as they went through their reports,

'Just fix it James. Quickly.'

Operations struggling with costs again. A nod on hers, no 'welcome back' from him.

'Right, now I want to talk about the senior leader conference.'

So not forgotten. Something was coming. She didn't even know the issue. 'Perceptions?' His questions always a test.

'Well organised', James got in first. 'It was worthwhile to get everyone together, an important opportunity for our senior team to understand our progress and issues we need to address.'

Good, her team had been behind the scenes making sure it ran smoothly. She must remember to thank William, in particular. She concentrated as others spoke, trying to glean what the issue was. Why didn't I call someone last week, unusual for her not to stay in touch, even on holiday. Contributions were general and careful, uncertain where Anthony was going with this. Suggestions for more time on the agenda for the finance report, better to be shorter or longer, praise for case study presentations. The nearest intimation of a heated discussion was comments about it being a useful forum to hear a range of views. Relieved to get broad support for holding the conference, they used to have them quarterly under Jeff. Anthony had cancelled two since he'd started.

'Well, none of you have mentioned the one obvious issue.'

Carefully managed faces around the table, expectant as he paused. Here we go, thought Emily.

'This was my first time with the senior leaders and frankly the standard of competency in that group shocked me. Far lower than a successful commercial company needs. I am not seeing a high-performing senior team there. You don't seem to realise what a competitive market we are in. I was astonished at their complacency.'

Emily kept her eyes on Anthony, with her concerned, interested look. James looked down and fiddled with his pen, Alfred bright and alert, David in his pressed navy suit over a creaseless white shirt, chimed in from his corner next to Anthony.

'I agree. Those are serious numbers I presented earlier, we are sliding in the wrong direction. It greatly concerned me that no one even asked a question when I showed them the trajectory last week.' Always keen to stay on side.

'Exactly! And what have we done about it? You don't seem to realise we have a problem. Do you think we'll meet our targets by sitting here? If your teams don't understand it makes me wonder about you. No more! This company has to make big changes. We can't rely on that group to pull us through. We need an objective expert view. So I have engaged PricewaterhouseCoopers to assess this business and come up with recommendations. I have instructed them to examine every aspect, and I expect each of you to give this review your full cooperation as a priority. Clear your diaries! Meeting over.'

He pushed his chair back and strode out of the room.

They all looked at each other.

'Good to get action at last', said David, straightening his suit jacket as he followed Anthony.

'Finance people love this stuff', Alfred sighed as he and Emily walked upstairs. 'We are in for a tough time I think.'

'So, what brought this on? What happened?'

'I don't even remember the issue. For many of them, it was their first direct contact with Anthony. They were used to having a debate with Jeff, some of them were trying to show how clever they were, but Anthony slapped down a couple of James's managers very smartly. People didn't say much after that. I suspect he's been planning these consultants for a while, last week gave him the opportunity'. He lowered his voice. 'Let's hope this isn't a smokescreen to investigate us'. He raised his eyebrows at her, his eyes serious for a moment, then lightened his tone again. 'Welcome back', as he swung down the sales corridor.

First day and we're into the fire, thought Emily. I know what I'm doing. One more challenge.

Office quiet, packing up for home, better call Ben, a quick one. Was it too early there? She'd give it a try.

'Ah Emily, all the way from London. Fuck, what time is it?'

'Sorry, got back yesterday. I wanted to see how you are.'

'Yeah, yeah, just wonderful, you didn't even say goodbye.'

'I tried; you weren't quite with it.'

'I'd been to my mother's funeral for chrissakes.'

My mother too, thought Emily. Change topic. 'Any luck on job hunting?'

'Give me a break, you woke me up. It's only been a few days.'

Can't say anything right in this conversation. She tried to make her voice sound relaxed. 'Only asking. Everything else ok?'

'Sure, for someone who's lost their mother.'

'It's hard, I know, we'll be sad for a long time. Best to get on with things.'

'Bloody hard Em! You have no idea. It's all right for you, far away.'

Emily halted a sigh before it became audible. 'I just find being busy helps.'

'Yeah, for you.'

'You have a baby to look forward to. That's something. How's Natasha?'

'She's ok.'

This is not going well. Perhaps too close to the funeral.

'Anyway, I'm on my way home, so I'll call you again in a few weeks. Take care.'

'Yeah. Sure.'

Emily picked up her briefcase and turned the light off. That duty done, not sure it was worth it. Ben wallowing, he needed to get his act together. Only a few months before the baby comes. Well, it was up to him. She had other things to worry about.

Chapter Eleven

Phillip sang in a choir. And at home. A rich tenor voice would float out of his kitchen together with cooking smells, fragments of arias interspersed with pots clashing on the stove. He liked to cook for her. She learned he preferred her relaxing in the cosy lounge room with a glass of wine, leaving him to measure spices, marinate meat, stirring and tasting.

At first she listened with surprise. Head up, ears attuned. Her mother's radio was the only singing in their kitchen. Never a singer, she had played violin at school. For her, a better alternative to standing at the back of the hockey field on Wednesday afternoons, hoping the ball wouldn't come near. She'd laughed, overhearing her mother on the phone talking as though she was a violinist in the Melbourne Symphony Orchestra. Rehearsals and lessons gave her a reason to delay coming home. She stopped in year 11, it had served its purpose.

Early in their relationship, she accepted Phillip's invitation to dinner at his place. A person's house told you a lot about them, she thought as she walked the few minutes from Clapham Common station. She stopped at the gate of a two-storey brown variegate- brick terrace, bay windows, upstairs and downstairs, a replica of every other house in the street. Disappointed that it said nothing about him apart from a slight worry he would be boring. The door opened to a flight of stairs, then he led her into a burst of colour. Moroccan and Turkish rugs in reds and blues, club couch and armchairs recovered in dark red fabric, cushions, shelves of books, spilling out to the coffee table, records, CDs, local art by young artists on the walls. A sharp contrast to the clean minimalist lines of her modern flat. But alive, inviting. She felt attracted to this man who explored life, who made his space his own, who surrounded himself with creativity. Some single men she had known lived alone in bare, functional flats. A place to sleep and store things, a stop along the way, as though they were waiting until they moved into an actual home with a wife who would create the ambience. Left to him by his mother, Phillip explained, eager to quell the notion he might be wealthy. He bought his sister out. A welcome change after his marriage was over. Later she heard a little more. His wife desperate for a baby, never got over a miscarriage, debilitating anxiety.

Soon after she returned, Phillip invited her to his choir's upcoming spring concert. Asked in a way that said, 'please come', rather than, 'if you're interested'. She noticed he had been careful not to miss rehearsals for the last couple of months. So she put it in her diary, telling Caroline it was a priority. Not something she'd done before. She'd noticed a lot of choirs in England. Those centuries of royal music or the prevalence of church going. There was a choir at work. Waste of time, growled Anthony, but it continued.

The Thursday night concert came in a small breathing space between interminable days of responding to the consultants' demands and waiting for their recommendations of inevitable changes and restructures. A reprieve from preparing data in multiple formats, endless meetings with accountants and so-called management experts in their sharp suits, firing questions, tapping on their laptops. Hard to get any actual work done, but it helped to push Melbourne back into the past.

'Bring something warm', he'd said. These old churches are always cold'.

She settled on narrow pants with a new green wool top, a full-length overcoat heavy over her arm on the brief walk from the tube to St James. Through the iron gates, down the steps into the vestibule where two elderly women in furs checked her ticket and smiled their welcome, ushering her into the main church where the pews were filling with overcoats, fur wraps, scarves and cushions. More prepared than her, she thought, as she settled on the hard wooden seat, her coat buttoned up against the chill of seventeenth century stone. She chose one end of a pew in the church's centre, with an unobstructed view down the aisle to magnificent stained-glass windows and the best chance of seeing Phillip. Not a St Paul's, but another Wren building steeped in history. She felt like a tourist peering towards the altar, bending her neck backwards to the ceiling, noting plaques for William Blake, James II and, predictably, Christopher Wren on the side walls.

Emily was surprised to see this many crowding in for a concert that wasn't in the Albert Hall or Festival Hall or even in one of the larger cathedrals. More than relatives and friends? She suspected Phillip downplayed the choir's standing. Her eyes flicked over the audience. Older people, dressed for a night out, jewellery contrasting silvery hair, couples closer to her own age, some on their own, perhaps a partner to someone performing, like her. She caught herself with a start, that word slipped out; Phillip, her partner.

Musicians gradually filled the area in front of the stage;

adjusting chairs, music stands, tuning up, she smiled to see the violinists, no regrets there. She joined the clapping for the conductor, then stillness as he raised his hands for a theatrical moment, and they were on their way. Impatient for the choir, though pleased to recognise the first orchestra piece from one of Phillip's Bach CDs.

Alert when the choir walked in, searching the men in their black tails and white shirts until the last row entered. A tug of warmth as Phillip turned to the audience, head well above the women in their long black dresses. Their voices soared in the acoustics. No wonder churches were a popular venue. She tried to identify Phillip amongst the strong melodic tenors, but he had warned her she wouldn't be able to. He had laughed—in fact if you can hear me I'm singing off tune. She watched his face, his focus and energy in the music. Reflected back to when they first met.

> She had liked him from the start, appreciating his professional style. An executive search consultant, new in a company she had used before. He placed her in her current role, 'you are ready for this promotion,' with the warm smile she had come to anticipate throughout their meetings. Unlike some search consultants, he seemed genuine, trustworthy, more interested in her than reaching his targets. He had that careful British respectfulness without being too formal. She realised she was looking forward to their next appointment; all about the job, she told herself. In the week between jobs, she ran into him at the theatre.
>
> She was waiting for Janice in the National Theatre foyer, a regular way they caught up over

the years from when they first met, both in junior HR roles. An extra meeting had delayed Janice, cancelling their usual dinner. Emily strolled along the river to Southbank, enjoying the luxury of not rushing from work, her anticipation increasing as the theatre lights came closer. Time to spare, she sat on one of the small stools in the foyer with a glass of champagne, sipping and watching the doors.

'Emily, hello.' A male voice beside her.

She looked up.

'Phillip', he said, that familiar smile.

She stood up, knocking the stool over, surprised by a shot of nerves. 'Sorry, out of context, how embarrassing.'

Grateful he didn't joke about her clumsiness as he picked up the stool.

'Are you celebrating? You start next week, don't you?' gesturing to the champagne.

'Yes, yes, Monday', regaining composure. 'I'm looking forward to it, thanks so much for all your support. I've given myself a few days' break.'

'What a good idea. Pity it's not longer.' His eyes warm on hers.

She remembered how she liked his voice. A voice of inner confidence, someone who knew his own mind, but interested in others, not full of ego. She looked more closely at him. Nice looking, though not outstandingly handsome. Tall, broad shoulders, sizeable frame. Older, perhaps by five years. He appeared relaxed, even in his tailored jacket and dark pants. She noted his quality white shirt, open at the neck. Well-cut brown hair, more likely from a hairdresser than a barber.

'Yes, I know, but they were keen to have me start and I'm excited. Lots to do. Are you looking forward to the play? Did you see the first in the trilogy?' Talking too fast, she knew.

'Yes, they're all long, but I like Stoppard.'

Emily laughed. 'He's still the Rosencrantz and Guildenstern man for me. Hangover from school I guess.'

'Are you waiting for someone?' he asked.

'My friend Janice, but she's running late from a meeting. How about you?' Flicked her eyes to his left hand, no wedding ring.

'My sister, we have a theatre subscription together, but she's often late too. Waits for her husband to get home for the children.'

Emily smiled, searching for something interesting to say in the space, liking that he didn't launch into a monologue. The first bells rang.

'Have we both been stood up, perhaps?' his eyes laughed.

For a moment Emily thought that mightn't be such a bad thing. Then Janice rushed through the doors towards her.

'Well ...' she turned away from Janice's curious face.

'Lovely to see you', said Phillip. 'I'll call you once you've settled in, see how you're going.' Shook her hand.

'I'd like that.' Emily found herself smiling into his eyes, alive eyes. And he was gone.

Janice caught her arm as they joined the queue at Door One, holding their tickets up.

'Very nice. Who was that?'

'Oh, just the search guy who got me the new job. Phillip.'

'Just the search guy. But nice.' Janice twisted her head to raise her eyebrows at Emily.

'Stop it. Come on, we are down here.'

'Anyway, congratulations. About time you got the big one. A celebratory champagne after?'

'I have time for anything this week. I'm a free woman', Emily whispered as the theatre darkened.

'Tell Mr Search Guy that.'

Emily elbowed her, feeling like a teenager.

She hadn't been looking for anyone. She'd finished with Andrew many months back and decided she was better off by herself. Relationships were complicated. Without distractions, she could focus all her energy on the new job. She didn't give Phillip much thought over the next few weeks as she settled in. Excited by the big changes she could make, revelling in the support and freedom Jeff, the CEO offered, she was in her element. Great role, more money, nice flat.

On the day when Phillip was making his follow-up visit, Emily knew that she was fussing over what to wear, putting on one shirt, taking it off to try another. Clothes collected on the bed. Don't be silly, it's only a meeting. She chose a light wool olive green suit with a short jacket that showed off her figure over a tapered skirt. The easy circular neckline of her white silk top softened the corporate look; a delicate jade and silver necklace set it off. Relaxed executive, that's the message, she told herself.

She saw him at reception scanning their company magazine as she walked towards him. Well dressed as always, he took care with his appearance. Again, struck by that warm voice when he greeted her. It makes you want to trust him, she thought. Goes with the territory, she reminded herself, good technique. She guided him into a glassed-in visitor room. Eastern London one way, busy corridor traffic the other. They quickly moved into the standard follow up meeting, a variety of questions which all asked, 'how's it going?'. Phillip making notes.

Notebook closed, he stood at the window. 'You have an impressive view here.' He half turned back to her. 'Ummm, are you ahh ... busy in the evenings?'

She took a second. 'Well, sometimes, not much.'

'I was wondering, perhaps dinner one night, or a drink?' shifting his eyes between her and the window. 'Sorry, this isn't particularly professional. It's fine to say no, absolutely fine. We can forget I said anything.'

Emily remembered him pushing his hair back from his forehead, adjusting his glasses. She smiled at the memory of his awkwardness, the first time she had seen him unsure of himself and then his relief when she smiled. 'That would be lovely.'

From that dinner in the Soho Italian restaurant, her interest grew. Her head assessing - intelligent, attractive, well-travelled, independent, successful in his career, liked books, films, art, theatre, tick, tick, tick. Underneath her buzzing analysis she felt drawn to his warmth, his ease, his thoughtfulness, his openness. She kept alert for signs of him trying to control her, trying to push into her life, waiting for the moment when she would want to pull away but as time went by, she realised her protective barriers were softening and she was moving closer to him.

A powerful chorus brought her back to the present, resounding throughout the church. Phillip looked alive with energy as the tenors took a momentary lead. She let the music engulf her, closing her eyes to the sounds of 'Gloria'. Pulled into an emotional space, away from analysis, judgement. Tense with emotion. If she had needed to speak, she knew she would struggle. Tears welled and subsided. And then it was over, bowing and clapping, some standing in their enthusiasm.

She kept her gaze on Phillip as he followed the others out, one behind the other. Unsure where he would come from, Emily stood against the wall near the vestibule, watching the orchestra pack up, talk replacing song. Flicked her eyes left and right until she saw his head above the crowd coming towards her. That rush of warmth again as she made her way to him. He was clearly happy.

She took his arm. 'That was wonderful.'

'Really? You liked it?'

He held her close beside him as they left the church,

nodding to other choir members as they bustled out with family and friends.

'Such great singing. So emotional, though', trying to sound casual. She found it hard to express how she felt, even to herself.

Phillip kissed her on the top of her head. 'Music can do that to you, take you out of yourself, to places you didn't know were there, open firmly shut doors—just a little.' He bent to meet her eyes and smiled. 'New for you?'

'You know me, not big on emotion.'

'That's why I love singing. It takes me away from the normal everyday, always has. Especially singing with others. There's something wonderful about the feeling of joining together in song.'

Emily nodded. 'I can think "I like that song or I don't". "A sad song" or "a cheerful song". But this overwhelming emotion—what's that about?'

'Does it matter? You've let a little more emotion in, allowed yourself to stop thinking. Music can soften the walls we build up, open us to experience some of our emotion. And you've been through a rather emotional time recently.'

'Okay mister psychologist. I'm emotionally repressed and if I only come to more of your concerts, I would become a better person', she laughed. 'Save me going to a therapist when I'm bitter and twisted.'

Phillip joined her laughter, then stopped as they were about to turn the corner. Putting both arms around her he kissed her and whispered, 'Or stay with me'.

She moved in closer, the warmth of his body seeped into her. Her eyes filled up.

'It was ... I was thinking about you in there.'

They stayed for a moment, people skirting around

them. She leaned against him in the curve of his arm as they took their time to walk the few blocks to Leicester Square. Oblivious to the crowds pouring into clubs and bars, leaving theatres and restaurants, streaming towards the underground, hailing cabs. Navigating the tube brought them back to their surroundings, tapping their Oyster cards at the gates, checking the trains on the northern line, down the steps.

Emily checked her watch and sighed. 'I'm sorry, I have an early start.'

'No, no that's fine. Me too. Not long before the weekend.'

As they rattled through the tunnels, their reflection in the window opposite caught Emily's attention. A close couple. Her stop first. She stayed on the platform until the train took him away.

Sunshine and pale blue skies accompanied their Sunday morning walk. Revelling in the tantalising prospect of summer, they walked for longer than usual, grabbing the last table for brunch in their favourite after-walk cafe, run by Australians.

'You're everywhere', laughed Phillip, the first time they ate there.

'At least we do excellent coffee.' A smell that took her back to Melbourne's Italian cafes. Avocado, poached eggs, smoked salmon, sourdough, their walk had made them hungry. After scraping up the last of the avocado, Phillip put his cutlery on his plate and looked at her.

'I was wondering', he hesitated, pushing his hair back, something was coming.

'I was wondering, if you'd thought anymore about possibly moving in together?' he fixed his gaze on her. 'Not straight away, a big decision I know. I'm not even sure if it's a good time to raise it, so soon after your mum. But well, I have now, after the other night.'

He looked down at his second coffee, stirring in the half teaspoon of sugar he allowed himself.

'It is a big one. I guess I'm still thinking about it.' Her heart beating faster, palms damp, Ashleigh's voice in her head, she should just say "yes".

Phillip interrupted. 'Don't worry, I shouldn't have mentioned it. Bad timing. Sorry, let's leave it for now.'

What would it mean? Would she have to give up her flat? Would he move in? What about her quiet space that she opened the door to every night?

'No, no, it's ok. I ... I don't know yet. Maybe?' She picked up her cup, tipped it to drink, already empty she put it back down. Saw the worry on his face, eyes anxious behind his glasses, she reached across the table and held his hand.

'I do want to be with you. It's just ... it would be such a significant step for me, I mean.' She could feel Phillip's intensity and looked aside for a moment. There was a quietness between them and around them, the noise of the busy café far away. Phillip always knew when she needed space. Thinking how to say this without harming him. Or them.

'This isn't about you. I've run a million miles from this question before, finished other relationships when I thought this was coming.' She saw his eyes widen. 'No, no that's not what I'm saying here. Really. I want us to be together, I do.' She tightened her hand on his. 'You know I've lived by myself for a long time, most of the years I've been in England. I'm not even sure that I would be good to live with, we might end up hating each other.' She inclined her head and softened her face. 'I like you too much to risk that happening. Can we give it time, talk about it some more?'

Worried he might think she was pushing him away. Surprised that she wasn't.

Phillip smiled, clasped his other hand around Emily's.

'Of course, yes, of course, we don't have to decide now. Let's see how we go. The most important thing for me is to know that you want to us to be together. The best thing. More coffee?'

Chapter Twelve

'Questions'. In large font, the last slide of the pack. Emily breathed an invisible sigh of relief. They had spent close to two hours viewing charts, graphs, spreadsheets and models followed by extensive lists of recommendations, each with sub points. Gavin Ayers the PWC managing partner had spoken to each slide in fulsome detail, proving he was worth his large invoice and now looked around the room for their response. You can always tell a man by his shoes, Emily thought. Gavin's were statement shoes in alligator skin that narrowed towards the front, appearing to elongate his foot. A modern professional, showing style and wealth. Gavin was personable, made you feel like he was on your side in the multiple interviews he had conducted with her, but she was in no doubt they were all under the microscope.

Anthony had leaned back in his chair throughout the presentation, revelling in the many complex slides with their arrows, boxes and circles, streams of statistics, nodding his approval at the recommendations. Probably wrote them, thought Emily. He would only allow things he agreed with to be presented. Emily didn't want to risk another barrage of criticism, so stayed quiet. Few comments, no challenges. A smart one from David displaying his financial expertise, James checking that they had included his regional people, Susan jumping ahead to a communication plan.

Anthony nodded at Gavin. The signal for him to leave.

Emily kept her eyes on Anthony, looking alert as he shook hands with Gavin and his support group of suited consultants. She wondered if there was a woman in his life, no photos on his heavy wooden desk. She imagined a small, timid woman who maintained order at home, picking up his dry cleaning. Or a 'lady who lunched', covered with gold jewellery. Or did he live by himself in some penthouse with a housekeeper to cook and clean? His expensive suits hung around his body rather than fitting well, as though he didn't need to care how he looked, sending a message that he was a man with urgent things to attend to. A large Rolex dominated his left wrist, emerging from his French shirt cuffs. 'Helicopter pad' Alfred had laughed over drinks one time as they debriefed from the latest diatribe. Anthony's face matched the rest of him but seemed to swell and redden even more when he was angry.

'So', his eyes roved around the group. 'You have the report. You know what we need to do. I want a plan from each of you, by the end of the week. Top priority.'

Emily decided to risk it. 'If I could suggest we spend a few minutes discussing it? Check whether we agree with all the recommendations, make sure we are all clear about what we are working on?'

Anthony reddened. Mistake, she thought. His eyes narrowed as he turned his body towards her.

'This report has come from an objective, expert analysis of the business, from one of the top consulting firms in the country, so which recommendation don't you agree with Emily?'

She resisted the urge to look away. 'Nothing in particular. I'm sure the consultants have done an excellent job. I thought a discussion could be useful before we work on our plans.

Check we all have the same understanding. There might be local knowledge we could add.'

'What's there to discuss? They've interviewed you all. Let me remind you it is the people in this room who have brought the business to the uncompetitive situation we are now in. Why would I listen to your advice?'

His aggression was building, clearly any comment was seen as a challenge.

'And since you ask Emily. I notice that there are several things here that you are responsible for—performance, leadership, competency levels, for a start! I don't think you are in a position to question!'

His face loomed large at the end of the table. Emily worked at keeping her expression bland, heart beating faster; she could feel her palms and forehead becoming damp. The responsibility of all of us, not just me, she thought, but stayed silent.

'That goes for all of you. Plans on my desk Thursday, close of business. No exception.' And he left.

'There we have it, boys and girls.' Alfred glanced around the table.

'I've already started mine.' David exited, head up.

'Watch him', Alfred murmured as he and Emily gathered their papers. 'There will be some political manoeuvres over the next few weeks I'm sure.'

Emily sat on the closed lid of the toilet, elbow on her knees, chin in her hands, cooling down. In this open-plan building where even offices were glass, toilet cubicles were the only place to hide. Anthony's belligerent ways were getting harder for her to deal with. I know what I'm doing, stay calm, work on the plan, get it done.

Anthony scheduled a special meeting for Friday morning to review the plans. Public whipping, Alfred called it. The night before, she sat eating pizza out of a cardboard box on the couch, going over her plan once more, she could recite it with her eyes closed. It had consumed the week, even cancelled Wednesday dinner with Phillip to work on it with her team. Must take them out to lunch when this was all over. Checked through the research she could call on. He would not catch her out.

When she fell asleep late that night she dreamt of falling down the stairs to the boardroom, walking down the first couple of steps then tripping, tumbling down, again and again. People watching, laughing. Landing at the bottom, looking up to Anthony as tall as the building, standing with his arms folded. Anthony turning into her father, back to Anthony, frowning, piercing her with cold eyes. She tried to escape up the stairs that became a downward moving escalator, sweating as it increased speed, falling backwards, crumpled, circled by a dozen giant Anthonys. Her father stepped forward and looked down at her. She woke before the alarm, heart racing, soaked with sweat and headed to the treadmill at the gym. She ran fast, willing herself not to fall, pushing out the fear.

'Good morning' she said, walking into the dark wooden room, determined to appear relaxed, confident in her charcoal suit.

'Good morning Emily.'

Alfred and James were already there. Whatever is happening we are invariably polite, she thought, half smiling to herself. She went to the bench and poured herself a cup of tea.

'Are we going to have fun today?' Humour might make this bearable.

The three grimaced at each other as she joined them with her cup and organised her papers.

'Don't we always?' James looked down at the spreadsheets in front of him, frowning. There had been a lot of focus on Operations, the biggest division, the consultants had recommended significant cost cutting, while delivering more. The familiar mantra. By ten minutes to nine everyone had arrived, waiting for Anthony, bent over their presentations. The days of easy chat and laughter in these meetings were long gone. Somehow Anthony didn't need to say much to make these mature, experienced executives feel fearful and incompetent.

She steeled herself for her turn, her attention inward, preparing her thoughts while James was in the spotlight. Anthony throwing another question before he even answered the first, James starting to fumble. This is what he thinks leadership is, Emily thought. In control, telling us what to do, pointing out where we are going wrong, the stick without the carrot. Is he like this at home? If there is a home.

'Emily, are we disturbing you?' Anthony's voice penetrated.

'Sorry, ready.'

Her slides up on the screen, she began. He broke in at slide three.

'HR fluff! I've read your plan. High-performing team, Emily. In every part of the business. We can't afford the dead wood taking up space here. This isn't anywhere near tough enough or fast enough. We don't have time to waste.'

Emily started an explanation of the labour laws. He

brushed her away with a sweep of his large hands, Rolex glinting.

'No excuses. Find a way around it, that's your job. I hold you responsible for every single staff member's performance in this business, and current performance is not up to standard. Not even close. Tell me this Emily. Why is it that salaries are high and we are still paying bonuses while profits are sliding? What do I have to do to get it into your head that this is not a cosy government agency anymore? We are a profit driven business in a highly competitive market.'

The veins on his face grew prominent, swelling on reddening skin, his voice a step away from shouting. Emily shifted her eyes and saw David nodding, pursing his lips. She hardened.

'Agreed. You will see my plan includes strategies both to retain our high performers and address poor performers, a holistic strategy. We need to ensure a motivating environment, or we risk losing our best people. The engagement survey told us which areas require work.' Looking straight at David.

'Soft HR rubbish', Anthony snorted. 'Top performers stay when we are successful. We need results.'

David nodded at Anthony, then looked back at Emily, lifting his chin. She opened her mouth, but Anthony hadn't finished.

'I've seen presentations like this at all the management conferences. I expect much more. I need people who can deliver. Is that you, Emily?'

He was shouting now, seeming to expand with every word. She was sure everyone in the corridor could hear him.

'You'd better decide if you are some kind of soft government HR officer or the business executive I pay you to be!'

Emily's chest tightened, hard to breathe, nausea rising. The pages of research in front of her blurred, her prepared arguments left her. She found herself retreating, her usual strength and assertiveness weakening, losing her voice, overcome by a growing fear. It took all her willpower to stay on her seat, to appear she was listening to the torrent of noise. Her internal thoughts drowned out other voices in the rest of the meeting. He doesn't trust me. Is he targeting me or is he the same with everyone? Is he trying to get rid of me? She worked at maintaining her professional face, masking the panic surge. By the time Anthony marched out of the room, she could stand and pick up her papers.

'That pay rise is fast disappearing', Alfred murmured as they walked towards the stairs.

'Keep your mind on the business rather than your pay rises', David's voice came from close behind. 'It's the numbers that count Alfred and you're not meeting yours.'

Emily turned around, 'Let's talk about your numbers David. Those engagement survey results are way below the norm. Have you looked at the feedback your people are giving you? You have problems in your own team.'

'We'll see what counts.' David swung off to the right, head up high.

'Thanks for the support but it may not have been a good idea' Alfred shook his head. 'He has the numbers and what does Anthony like? Numbers. I don't trust him, he's positioning himself.'

'I've had enough of being nice to arrogant people!' Emily's release of anger helped her to regain a sense of equilibrium. 'Another lovely day in paradise.' She forced a grin as they separated.

Way past lunchtime, she bit gratefully into the chicken

and salad sandwich Caroline had left on her desk. William tapped on the door and poked his head through. 'How did it go?'

'Not too bad, a little more to do, nothing we can't handle', she smiled. A flash of her mother's smile, a bright voice after one of those episodes. She used to find it annoying, a lie, shutting her out, now she was doing the same, a lie to protect, one thing she'd learnt from her mother.

He nodded and shut the door.

What to do.

Knowing Anthony was out for the rest of the day, she risked leaving early for the yoga class which had been part of her routine pre-Anthony. A peaceful studio, two floors up from the traffic noise below. When she passed the cross-legged Buddha and entered a room warmed by deep yellow late afternoon sun, she felt invited into a different mindset. The simplicity of the space with its wooden floor, red brick on either side, a single stylised purple flower decorating the white wall in front, helped her to breathe as she waited for the teacher to begin. Many miles from the boardroom.

She concentrated on the poses, pushing the meeting away. Lengthening her spine, gripping the muscles in her legs and arms, stretching up, flowing down, transitioning fluidly from one pose to the next, happy to follow instructions with no need to think. Inhale, exhale, the familiar rhythmic sequences focused her, calmed her emotions.

As the class slowed, Anthony's face loomed into her mind. Muscles, which had relaxed a little, tightened again with the effort of trying to shut out insistent visions of the morning's meeting. The final resting pose became a battle of tensing and releasing, tensing and releasing.

She kicked her apartment door closed behind her. Surveyed her calm, ordered space. One deep yoga breath. Here she was in control. She filled the kettle and drank green tea as she prepared fish and vegetables for dinner. Better to drink tea than wine tonight.

Empty plate on her lap, still in her stretchy black gear, bare feet on the ottoman. Thinking. He had criticised her before, criticised them all, nothing new there. This time she experienced the full force of his power, directed at her. Public whipping was right. Why did her self-confidence dissipate? She had a reputation for being able to deal with tough situations. She'd exited several executives, managed challenging staff reductions, even when it impacted friends. She recalled many times when a male colleague asked her to handle a conflict they were nervous about. Where was that person today? Mr HR! She was the expert. She should have fought back, angry that she didn't stand up for herself. Retreated. What was wrong with her? A little girl hiding in her bedroom. She got up and stretched tall towards the ceiling. I must be stronger tomorrow.

She struggled to sleep again, curled up on one side then the other, rolling over to look at the clock as it ticked through the night. She experimented using a technique she had read about, visualising each negative thought as a balloon that lifted away from her, going sky high, sending the stress far away. Her balloons stayed low, hovering clouds, dark and threatening. No sooner had she sent one balloon up another would crowd in. Balloons transformed into Anthony's face coming closer. Shouting, telling her she didn't know what she was doing, that her work was not up to standard, not ready for an executive role, that she wasn't achieving. A fraud. Images of standing alone by the board table, unable to speak, her colleagues' heads down. She gave in and took a sleeping pill.

Chapter Thirteen

Emily ran her hand over her collection of dresses, trying to decide what to wear the next day. Performance review with Anthony to look forward to. Pages of evidence proving her achievements ready in her briefcase. Now she needed to exude executive confidence in Anthony's office. Especially to herself, she grimaced. Dress or suit?

The phone rang.

'Hey Em,'

'Ben, how are you?'

She sat on the bed opposite four open wardrobe doors flicking her eyes along rows of suits, pants, jackets, dresses, shirts, skirts organised into work, casual, special occasion.

'Yeah ok. You know I'm going to be a dad soon.'

Of course she bloody knows. Why was he calling this time?

'Yes, exciting. When's the date? In a month or two? How's Natasha?' She pulled out a dark green dress and hung it on the doorknob. Maybe?

'Yes, yes, at her sister's.'

'Oh?' Emily's antenna up. 'Why?'

'Just a few days. For a little rest.' She must stop questioning Ben in her own mind, needing to believe in him. It was quite possible that Natasha wanted to spend some time with her sister.

'Ok. So, what are you doing?'

'Busy on a painting. Gotta find work though, when I find time. Bastards stopped my dole. Have to apply for hundreds of jobs to keep it. I'll hassle them to get it back.'

Still no job.

'Anything in the wind?' Was he even looking?

'A mate says he might have something soon. He's a gardener, picked up a council contract.'

'Ben, you're going to have a baby. You need money.' Emily could hear the parental edges in her voice. For heaven's sake, how old was he? Relying on government allowances and an odd sale at his age. Sometimes her father had a point.

'Yeah, we'll be all right. There'll be something. I've got stuff to do. Have to clear up the house for the baby. Don't know what her problem is, it was fine before, not like the baby will notice.'

So, there was more. She remembered the crowded chaos she had glimpsed.

'How's that going?'

'I'll get to it. She's onto me to apply for jobs, but the gardening'll come through soon and I've got to finish this painting.'

'You'll be busy.' Her sympathies were with Natasha. Time for Ben to work harder. She hung a black suit next to the dress.

'Don't suppose you've seen Dad?'

Emily had been putting off ringing him.

'What do you reckon! If only Mum was here.'

'Mmm.' Not another morose conversation. 'Ben, time's moving on. The baby won't wait for you to be ready.' He won't like that, but sympathy isn't going to help. 'Sorry, I need to go, I've got a busy day tomorrow. We'll talk again soon. I'll ring you.'

She'd better remember. Things didn't sound too good. He had been calling more often recently, what did he want from her? Some kind of support she supposed, hard to offer from ten thousand miles away. He probably used to call their mum; she would have been more sympathetic. She thought Natasha would keep him going, but was it getting a bit wobbly there? No, no, no, her plate was already too full, how could she take on Ben, surely Natasha and him were ok, just a few bumps, she imagined a baby on the horizon brought more stress, not that she'd know.

She decided on the green dress with a short black jacket. Elegant, professional. She kicked the wardrobe door closed. Bloody Ben. She was already struggling with pressure at work, he would have to sort himself out. The special one, her mother's favourite, the talented artist and where was he now, a house not fit for a baby, no regular income. God, she hoped Natasha would be back soon, she wasn't sure how Ben would cope without her. What an idiot!

She lay in bed, light on, frustration simmering, remembering the day when Ben got his offer letter.

> She walked in after uni, no work tonight, friends busy. Her mother was bustling around in their dining room, a pretty dress on, make-up. They rarely ate in here but today the table was laid with a white tablecloth, special occasion china and wine glasses shining with a recent wash, matching cutlery.
>
> 'What's happening? Is someone coming?'
>
> 'Oh, wonderful news. Her mother's face was alight. 'The National Art College has offered Ben

a place. So prestigious, they don't take many and Ben's in. So, a celebration.' She indicated the gleaming table, proud of her plan.

'Ok.' When did they ever have special dinners?

Upstairs, she threw her bag onto her bed and flopped down beside it. Where was a celebration for her top HSC score or when Melbourne University offered her a scholarship—not many of those available, but she got one. No special dinner for Emily. Ben only had to do one thing and there's champagne. Mean, she told herself, be generous. She knocked on his door.

'Yeah?' Ben was lying on his bed smoking.

'Ugh, don't let that smoke into my room.' She waved the air in front of her, making a space in the haze. 'Congrats, you're in.'

'Thanks. Can hardly believe it. Don't know what I would have done if I hadn't.'

Emily felt a twinge of guilt. It was good, she was pleased for him.

'Does Dad know?'

'Not yet, when he comes home. Not expecting any praise there.'

'Lucky Mum signed that preference form for you.'

'Yeah caused trouble though. The bastard wouldn't sign.'

There'd been a scene. At first her mum said Ben had to ask his father, head of the family. There had been shouting about the stupidity of art school, how it wasn't a career, what had he been paying fees for all these years and so on. He threw the form back at Ben, said he wouldn't sign until something sensible was on it. Ben pleaded with his mum over breakfast the next day until she signed it. Later, after her evening cafe shift, Emily noticed her mum was quieter than usual.

'You never had to go through any of that. Good girl Emily.' He stubbed out his cigarette in the ash tray beside his bed.

'I wasn't choosing art, was I. Anyway, it didn't matter to him. All that stuff about responsibility and providing. He expects that I'll marry some man who will provide, so he doesn't care what I do.'

Never cared, she thought. He couldn't say what I was doing if someone asked.

'Lucky you! Wish I was a girl!'

'You've got the hair for it! It's longer than mine. I could recommend a good hairdresser.' She flicked back her sleek-cut bob, patted Ben's mass, forced into a somewhat acceptable ponytail.

'Piss off.' Ben threw his pillow at her. They laughed. 'It doesn't matter anymore, I'm in and I'll be out of here as soon as I can. That's Mum calling.'

He swung his legs off the bed and opened his window wide. They heard the crunch of tyres on gravel. By the time their father turned his key they were sitting in their places at the table.

'Why are we eating in here? What's the champagne for?'

He peered into the dining room, the bottle standing tall in its cooler.

'Hello, come and join us. Ben has a place in the

National Art College. His first choice. Isn't that wonderful!'

Their mum speaking brightly, as she always did when she expected a problem.

He snorted, 'Christ!' Shook his head and went into his study, the thump of his briefcase thrown against the wall audible in the dining room.

Emily watched her father at the edge of her sideways vision, hunched over his food, into red wine after downing his champagne, no toast. Aware of her mother's stream of chatter in the background, replacing television; filling the space to protect the celebration against splinters widening into chasms, engulfing them all.

'Everyone finished? Lovely. Give me your plates. I'll just fetch the dessert, I won't be a minute.' Her voice trailed into the kitchen, leaving them with a sudden silence.

'Well Ben, you're on your own now.' Her father raised his head, turned to him, eyes small and hard. 'I'm not wasting any more of my money on you. You can go off to art school, play around with this self-indulgent shit and see where that gets you. You'll find out when you have to pay rent, put food on the table.' He drained his glass. 'I've spent years trying to instil sense into you. Thousands of dollars that I worked for, so you could have a decent education, and this is what you do. No more. Bloody fool. Don't come running to me, I'm finished with you.' Distaste screwing his face.

'Don't you worry, I won't be anywhere near you. I'll be out of here real soon.' Success and champagne cheering him on, lowered his voice, 'You fucking bastard'. Just loud enough for them to hear.

Their father jumped up, face turning purple, his chair falling hard on the floor. His fist coming for Ben's head, across the corner of the table. Ben ducked, banging into Emily's arm, then stood. They faced each other, adrenalin pumping, Ben taller and stronger. His father swore under his breath, picked up the bottle of red and left, knocking into her mother as she came in with dessert.

'This is your fault, stupid woman!'

The door of his study slammed, resounding through the house.

'Mum, you alright?'

Ben ran to her as she staggered against the sideboard and covered her mouth with her free hand, keeping her grip on the plate with the other.

'Yes, yes, it's nothing, I tripped.' She straightened, waving him away 'I'm fine. Let's have dessert … lovely tart … from that special shop.'

She sat breathing heavily and cut three pieces. Their heads bowed over the table. No chatter left.

She had to admit it – that aggressive, bullying man was right. Ground Ben into the dirt, treated her mum poorly, filled their house with fear, but he was right. Ben was proudly on the dole. He had talent, won awards at the best art school in Australia, had exhibitions that her mother talked about in every phone call. And here he is, grumbling about having to work. She imagined him sitting in that living area surrounded by mess, perhaps painting, unlikely to be cleaning, probably drinking. While she, Emily, had worked hard to have a successful career, supported herself. She grew up determined to be strong, to shape her life the way she wanted it, never to depend on a man. She was proud of herself, even if no-one else was. It was time for Ben to grow up, stand on his own two feet.

Lunchtime. Ordeal over. Fifteen minutes to walk around the Gherkin and back, clear her head. She texted Phillip in the lift.

'Dinner tonight?'

His reply came before she reached her office. 'Curry at mine?'

'Hello, this is nice', Phillip smiling at his front door. A long kiss. 'I've missed you.'

'Yes, I'm sorry, work has overwhelmed me. A bottle of wine to apologise for cancelling Wednesday night at such short notice, I tried to hang onto it but no chance. I picked up these naans from around the corner. They'll need reheating.'

'Great, thanks. We'll have a feast. I had time so we have two curries, a raita, I'll do saffron rice soon. But come and sit down first. Let's have a glass.'

Emily sat back in the rich reds of the couch, relaxing with the sound of gentle jazz piano. There were already wine glasses and a small bowl of nuts on the recycled wood coffee table, he was making an effort. He poured a French Chablis and joined her, angling himself towards her.

'Cheers.' They clinked, quiet for a moment.

'So, work's busy?'

'God yes! I'm glad to see the back of those consultants.

They seem to forget we've got an actual job to do.' She took another sip and reached for the nuts.

'How's Anthony been?'

'Oh, you know, he's always challenging, seems to think he's there to drag us all out of the dark ages. Save us from ourselves. Loved the consultants', she rolled her eyes and leant back into the couch.

'Is he being reasonable about it?' Phillip asked.

Her mind went back to this morning's performance review.

His Rolex arm sweeping aside her pages of achievements. Interrupting her prepared speech, 'Meeting your objectives is only the basics. Are you an executive or some mid-level manager? That's the question I'm asking.'

'We'll get there'. Another handful of nuts, her glass finished. Phillip got up to refill the nuts from a jar in the kitchen, bringing the wine with him.

'You can manage him though?'

Her heart-rate increasing as he paced in a circle around her. Her neck rigid as he came close enough for her to smell his after shave, looking straight ahead, away from the buttons straining on his shirt. A fog of fear growing in her brain, struggling to concentrate, willing herself to stay in the room. A pathetic silence as he delivered his message—on notice for another month while he reconsidered her performance.

'He's such a contrast to Jeff.'

'It's always hard to make a big change.'

'Yes, but there are ways. He's so controlling. Can you believe he's demanding to sign off the performance ratings and pay increases this year? My job, I would have thought.'

'Why's that?'

'Doesn't trust me, that's obvious. We suffer frequent rants that we're not performing, that we're too soft. He wants to drive down ratings, not pay the bonuses. Bet he'll still be expecting his bonus.'

'Mmm ... I guess he's new. Let him find his feet. It's often a bit rocky at the start.'

Phillip took a long drink and refilled their glasses.

'He's not that new! From day one he acted as though he'd absolutely found his feet!' She realised her voice was rising and steadied herself. 'I'm thinking about starting to look around. I've been there a while. Put your search hat on. Is it a good time?'

'Well, whatever's right for you. Perceptions could be a problem, you know how suspicious us recruiters are.' He stood. 'I should finish preparing dinner.'

'I wondered that.'

'Better to not look like you're running away. I'm sure it will all calm down.'

'I can try toughing it out a little longer'. What if she didn't make it?

'Good plan. You're strong.' If only he knew.

Another session hiding in the toilet cubicle, one step back from vomiting, her phone beeping a reminder of a meeting she should be at as she sat on the lid, breathing her way through panic.

Phillip edged to the kitchen. 'I should put the rice on or we'll finish this bottle without food. It won't take long. Choose some more music if you like'.

She hadn't noticed the jazz ending, her head full of this morning's review. She flicked through his CD collection, looking for dinner music, chose a low-key Miles Davis. Don't let Anthony spoil this evening.

Emily smiled to herself in the lift to her apartment. Enjoyable time over Phillip's curries. A release from the churning anxiety eating at her stomach. Better when they had moved away from work talk. Phillip seemed a little dismissive tonight, not as supportive as usual, perhaps she was looking for too much, letting Anthony get to her.

She dropped the envelopes she had picked up from the letter-box downstairs on the table. Bills, advertising disguised as letters. Then she saw a handwritten one. She turned it over to read "S. Griffiths". Not a familiar name. Opening the envelope, she skipped to the end first—Susan Griffiths, nee Green. Frowned for a moment and then her eyes widened in surprise—cousin Susan, daughter of her father's brother. Their families had not seen each other for decades. When she was young, they had regular holidays together up on the north coast. She could vaguely remember throwing herself around in shore breaks, building sandcastles decorated with shells and seaweed, sitting in enormous holes dug out near the tide, occasional boat trips. Susan was a few years older. There was a brother, Emily remembered being nervous of him. Often tasked with looking after the younger ones on the beach, he sat high on the sand dunes shouting instructions. What was his name? Frank. She didn't know what had happened with him either. She was pretty sure that her dad and his brother were no longer in contact, that there had been a falling out. No-one had expected their presence at the funeral.

Dear Emily

It has been a very long time since we have seen each other, you may not even remember me, your cousin, daughter of your father's brother Bill, and Laura.

I was sorry to hear about your loss, I hope she did not suffer too much. My Mum found out from the obituaries. I gather no-one from our side came to the funeral; our families have not been in contact for a long time although our mothers did occasionally talk on the phone. While I have not seen your mother for many years, I have fond memories of her being kind to me as a girl.

You may not know that I moved to England in my early twenties to study and have made a life for myself here. I teach at Cambridge now, I am married and have a daughter.

Mum told me you were also living here. Your mother must have said. Anyway, I hope you don't mind, I tracked you down and hope this letter has come to the right address.

I wondered if you would like to have lunch? The train from Cambridge is only an hour to London, so I would be happy to meet you in town. Would a weekend suit you?

Emily took her coat off. Thinking. Well, she didn't know what to think. Somewhat pleased that Susan had attempted to find her. But here was more of her past inserting itself into her life when she was striving to push it back to where it belonged. They'd both been living here for years, had her mother mentioned it? Why now? Curiosity, politeness, whatever it was, overcame her trepidation, she would call.

Emily made herself a cup of tea and sat down to finish tomorrow's presentation. She stared at the PowerPoint slides, trying to remember when those holidays had stopped, and why. Too young to know. Things just happened, or they didn't. She couldn't recall any discussion about their relatives on her father's side, normal in their family where everything seemed to happen behind closed doors, rather than talked about around a meal table. Dinner at her house was heavy with the tension of the unsaid, the seven o'clock news protecting them from silence, from the risk of saying the wrong thing. Emily slapped down the laptop lid and put it back in her briefcase, she'd do it in the morning.

Chapter Fourteen

Emily chose a seat where she could see the door. Early, giving her time to prepare herself. How would she recognise Susan? She didn't have family photos. The dim memory of a young girl playing on the beach wouldn't help. What did Cambridge academics look like? Their brief phone conversation was polite, a little nervous, concentrating on finding a date. No clues there. After offering to book, she realised she hadn't asked what Susan liked to eat. Was she vegetarian, vegan even? What price range? She must be on a reasonable salary. This restaurant, five minutes' walk from King's Cross train station, should cover all bases. She opened the menu to check, relieved to see vegetarian options, just in case. She sighed, readying herself for the inevitable family conversation.

A burst of street noise alerted Emily to the door opening. Each time bringing a shot of nerves to her stomach, subsiding as she looked away from a couple, a small group of women, a family. A longer glance at a woman by herself in a Burberry trench coat, until she sat at a table for one. Probably not Burberry. Emily imagined an academic from Cambridge in shabby British tweed. Then a sizeable woman filled the doorway, pausing a moment, scanning the tables and came towards her smiling with a question in her face. 'Emily?'

A look of comfortable chaos surrounded Susan. Long hair, streaks of brown and grey, most of it captured in a bun, the rest spilling over her purple woollen wrap. A painted enamel brooch fastened the wrap over a loose embroidered dress. Overweight, not to the point of obesity, but far beyond what Emily would allow herself to approach. Her bag floated behind her, unfastened, displaying the many things stuffed in there. If she saw her in the street Emily might have dismissed her in that quick, judgmental way she was prone to. When Susan sat opposite her though, her intelligent eyes caught Emily. Eyes that looked straight into hers, warm as they greeted each other again after a fleeting handshake.

'Emily, after so long.'

'We were children the last time.' My cousin, thought Emily, as she took in the person opposite.

'How strange,' said Susan, 'we both ended up here'.

'The pull of the Motherland,' Emily laughed, 'or that magic British passport our fathers gave us'.

Catch up introductory conversation, what each was doing, where they were living, Susan's husband and daughter, Phillip. Entrée and wine arrived. Thankfully Susan was keen for a bottle and wasn't vegetarian.

Susan said, 'I don't know about you, but for me it was escape.'

Right into it, Emily thought. She filled up their glasses with the pinot grigio.

'Yes?'

Not ready to respond. Susan far less hesitant.

'Not sure if you heard anything,' Emily shook her head 'but life was tough for me, getting worse in my teens, I had to get out. Dad was a drinker and Frank; do you remember my older brother? He was a nasty piece of work. I can see that now'. She took a mouthful of the pale green wine.

'That sounds difficult.'

Emily sipped from her soupspoon, looking at Susan, uncertain how much to ask, but Susan didn't need questions.

'Well, I guess I came to talk about family. Start with Frank. He couldn't put a foot wrong in my father's eyes. He was preparing Frank to be the successful one. They poured money into his education. My father regularly took him off for weekends out bush, and as he got older, longer trips to exotic places like Thailand. God knows what they did there. Me, I was a nobody. Mind you, it was a relief for Mum and me when they were away. She was a scared little person when he was there, terrified of him. He dominated the house, dominated her, lots of verbal abuse, even physical when he was especially drunk. No broken bones, bruises though. Even when drunk, he was clever enough to keep it low level. We never called the police. A message to remind her who was boss. He was such a bastard. And there were other women. He finally left Mum years ago for one of them, younger of course. Best thing for her, though by then, he and Frank had worn her down so much she never regained her energy or confidence. She lives a small life now, but at least she is safe.

Susan drank from her water glass before continuing.

'I felt very alone. I'm sure Mum loved me in her own way, but Dad and Frank demanded her attention. I was finding adolescence hard. Frank would make comments about my breasts, would grab them, rub up against me, taunt me with what boys wanted to do to me. Mum would try to stop him, but Dad just laughed. He didn't go further than that, but it was all pretty awful. So, I became the problem child. I wagged school, even had a spate of lighting fires, probably looking for attention. I got in with a bad crowd in my early teens, drinking, some drug taking—nothing too serious, some weed. And I was a bit wild, lost my virginity too young, all that.'

She took a breath and finished the cooling tortellini on her plate, scraping her fork around the edge, the table quiet for a moment in this busy restaurant. Emily looked at her intently, taken aback by Susan's openness, she'd only just met her.

'So now a Cambridge lecturer? Something must have changed?'

'The funny thing was that I was bright, brighter than Frank, despite what my father thought. That still sounds bitter, I guess. Anyway, after a few awful years, at the beginning of year eleven, I pulled myself together. I realised that doing really, really well at school was a way out. My friends only talked about boring jobs in offices and shops. That felt like a trap and I knew I was better than that. So, I put my head down, moved away from that social group and made sure I got top marks. And it worked. We were living in Brisbane but Sydney University offered me a scholarship, so I could leave, then after a year there I applied for an exchange to LSE here and stayed.'

'You have done so well.' She's impressive, Emily thought. 'And Frank?' Aware she was hoping Susan was the family success story, not Frank.

'Frank scraped through school and uni, a good time boy, only average ability. Maybe he thought it was all beneath him. He relied on dad who called in a few favours with mates and got him a start in an accounting firm. I haven't seen him for years but if I read between the lines, he networked his way up the ladder. Married his blonde secretary, I met her once. When I last saw him, he looked like that successful corporate person who drinks with important people a lot. Anyway, let's not waste our time on Frank. How about you?'

Emily resisted an urge to wriggle away from Susan's deep look into her eyes. No avoiding after that.

'Ok, some similarities, actually,'

Emily took another sip of wine, readying herself. A second bottle might be needed.

'Sorry, only talk if you want to. I do this, blurt out my story. Probably years of talking to counsellors.'

'No, no its fine. Umm, so like yours, my father dominated our house, very controlling. He wasn't interested in me, but all of us were always on egg shells, nervous of the moment when he would explode. He raged at Ben, putting him down at every opportunity. Ben didn't seem to match up to any of his expectations, especially with his focus on Art, not something my father considered appropriate for his son. He went to a top art college but Dad continued to tell him he was wasting his life, a failure, and he struggles to hold it together. He's going through a particularly difficult time with Mum dying. He has a lovely partner, baby on the way, but even that's getting a bit rocky. Sorry, that's more about Ben, I guess.'

'Awful. So unfair. He was tiny when we had those holidays. So what about you, you look like you have come through pretty well', scanning Emily's carefully made-up face, quality linen shirt, brand name jeans, French handbag on the chair beside her.

Emily allowed herself a smile. 'I worked out early that I was not the target, and I just needed to stay out of sight, keep to myself. At the same time, I felt neglected, irrelevant. Mum was extremely focused on Ben, she was proud of his art and she tried to protect him from Dad, to her detriment. He was always criticising her, demeaning her. Like your mum. Though I have to say I do think Dad was loyal, technically anyway, I've never heard a whisper of affairs and they stayed together until the end, whether that's good or not is a question. For me, as soon as I walked in the door I felt suffocated by the tension, like I had claustrophobia. Dad was so aggressive, and everything had to be his way. I never invited friends around because something could happen. But like you I was smart, did well at school and uni but planned to leave at some point. Then I came travelling with a friend and realised I wasn't going back. I wanted to be far away from my family, cut the ties. It wasn't quite like that, but the first time I returned was this year when Mum died—twenty years later.'

Emily took a gulp of wine, oblivious to the taste as it slid down her throat. Embarrassed to admit how long it had been. She surprised herself, telling the story, putting it together, hearing it as she spoke. Susan was listening with an intense focus that she rarely experienced from anyone.

'Half your life spent here ... Well, both of us. The right thing for you though.'

'In London I could leave that first period far behind, create something new. I feel safer here. Sounds silly. I mean, nothing happened to me.'

Emily concentrated on cutting chicken, a little discomforted by how much she'd revealed.

'No, no, I understand that completely. What was it like when you returned?'

'I didn't want to go, was almost frightened of going. Ridiculous. I had spent twenty years keeping them all far away, resisting any thought of returning and then there I was.

As though nothing had changed. Except for Mum, she had already gone. I missed her.'

Another gulp of wine, back in that phone call in the airport lounge, in the house with her father, her mother in the coffin, Alice at the funeral.

'Ok. Was that hard?'

Emily blinked and refocused, relieved Susan asked rather than assumed, not pouring out the usual sympathies.

'Kind of. Perhaps it would have been more difficult for me to see her after twenty years and her so sick, I don't know. Though I *am* worried she died unhappy, thinking her daughter didn't care. It was pretty awful, in that house again, the funeral and discovering that Mum had suffered much more with him than I realised. Maybe I'd blanked it out. Since then, it's as though a little crack opened and memories are flooding through. I can't close it. And to be honest, I'm feeling guilty, I should have acted, said something. All I did was avoid and then leave. And I did it again—I left the day after the funeral.'

Emily looked down at her plate and ate another mouthful of the grilled chicken salad. How was it she could talk like this to someone she had only known as a child, in reality a stranger?

'Definitely don't blame yourself. Us women are good at that. You were young. Growing up. You did the best you could.'

Emily laughed. 'You should meet Phillip. That's what he says.'

'Well he's right. Good man, he sounds supportive. You are not responsible for your father's actions.' Susan looked a little fierce, eyes flashing. 'One thing I learnt from counselling.'

'I didn't before, kept myself apart, their problem. But after going back, it's been difficult.'

'God, your father was so much like mine. Though yours a touch better? More responsible, perhaps.'

'Responsibility is his middle name.' Funny, Emily thought, how a quality like responsibility could be admired or used as a weapon.

'Did you meet our grandfather? Apparently, he was a drunk.'

'No, we didn't see family, except yours.' She felt embarrassed to sound so ignorant.

'Mum said he died of alcoholism. And I bet he gave those sons of his a hard time. He worked down at the Chatham dockyards before they migrated. Tough environment down there. When I think about my father and now yours, I wonder what it was like for them. Nothing excuses them, but there was history.'

'Do you know why they broke off contact?'

'Mum said there was some kind of argument over our grandfather's Will which never got resolved. And also.... hmm, I'm wondering if this was the actual reason.'

'What's that?'

'Well, Mum let something slip one time and I think my father tried to or did have sex with your mother on the last holiday. Maybe rape, maybe not, I doubt it was consensual.'

Emily's eyes widened. She'd heard nothing like this. Susan had such a blunt way of talking.

'I could be adding one and one to make three or four, but I do remember you all left early, in a hurry, my mum crying, me confused about what was happening. I can't ask her now, she is not so well these days and it would upset her too much.

I don't talk to my father anymore. So, I guess we won't know, unless you ...?' Susan looked up at Emily.

As Susan talked, a foggy memory took shape. Her father running between the rented holiday house and the car, throwing bags in the boot, shouting at her and Ben to grab their things, Emily complaining, wanting to go to the beach, her mother stiff in the front seat, saying little on the long drive home. Only Susan waving as they reversed out of the driveway. That was the last time.

Emily shook her head. 'I remember leaving, but that's all, nothing gets talked about in our house. I never understood why those holidays stopped. God, my poor mum.' Was her father protecting his wife? Breaking off contact with his abusive brother? Or did he blame his wife, angry with her betraying him? An anger that continued through their marriage. She would never ask him.

Second cup of coffee finished, Emily realised the restaurant had gradually emptied without them noticing, waiters laying dinner tables around them, serving an occasional tea and cake in that late afternoon lull before pre-theatre crowds began.

Susan looked in her bag, finding the brooch to do up her wrap,

'I should catch this next train.'

Emily stretched her shoulders back. 'That was quite a marathon.'

'Yes, it was time to meet. For me, anyway. I'd been wanting to meet you for many years, not sure what stopped me. Now with your mum, something galvanised me. To be honest, I wanted to see if your experiences were anything like mine. We both have our scars. In a way, that makes me feel better, not that I would have wished any of this on you.'

Emily stood, staying still for a moment, before speaking. 'But we have come through it, we should be proud of ourselves. You and I are survivors.'

Yes, she had survived, so much stronger than Ben. Twenty years away helped that. Did her mum see herself as a survivor?

When they opened the door, Emily was startled by Saturday afternoon activity of people, cars, buses, blasting her senses. Stepping into the street, they emerged from a bubble that had captured them for the last few hours, breaking the tight skin stretched around memories and intense conversation. They stood against the wall of the restaurant, eyes blinking against the sun's low rays, surrounded by pedestrians.

Susan took both her arms. 'Thank you so much, this has been amazing for me,' again that warm gaze.

'Perhaps we could see each other now and again?' Emily didn't want this heavy session to be their only contact.

'Definitely. You and Phillip could come up to our place. I promise I can be more fun than today', Susan laughed. 'Let's do that. I'll call you.'

'We'd love to', said Emily, hoping she sounded more than polite.

A strong hug and then her flowing dress moved through the crowds towards the station, a splash of purple crossing the road, then gone.

Chapter Fifteen

Emily meandered along the shopping street, filling in time before meeting Phillip at the cinema. An opportunity to find that skirt she had been looking for to go with her new green and white silk shirt. She wandered in and out of shops; too long, too short, wrong colour, too narrow. Hands and eyes on the clothes, head somewhere else. So much streaming into her brain. It was getting harder to leave it all behind.

Ben. She hadn't heard from him in a while. What time was it there now? Who knows what times he kept, anyway. She turned into a small park and scanned the seats, none empty on this sunny afternoon, so she took one end of a bench, an older woman eating a sandwich at the other, pigeons pecking fallen crumbs.

'Hel ... lo,'

'Hi Ben, it's Emily. Sorry, did I wake you?'

'Em ... good. Good ... in bed ... not very .... well'. She immediately regretted ringing.

'What's wrong?'

'Sick, feel bad', struggling to form the words. She could guess what kind of self-inflicted sick. Again.

'That's no good. How's Natasha?'

'A little ... break ... with her sister. I'm going to be a ... dad, Em.'

'Yes, that will be great. Not long now. Is she coming home soon?' Like her mother, how easily she slipped into that determinedly bright response. When did Natasha go to her sister's?

'Yeah, yeah. Just have to ... clear up the ... house, get some ... work.'

Emily closed her eyes. How many times had she heard this?

'Mum's gone Em.'

'Remember, I was at the funeral.' It was like talking to a child.

'Silly me ... yes ... you came. Well, I have to go ... need to sleep. I'm not feeling ... well ... sick. Ring me again ... Goodbye.'

'Shit! What is he fucking doing? What's going on?'

She realised she'd spoken aloud when the older woman changed seats, startling the pigeons who rose in a squawking flurry. Embarrassed, she left the park, jaw clenched, and hurried to meet Phillip.

He was standing outside the Odeon, looking up and down the street. Emily released her frown, swallowing the frustration.

'I've got tickets', he said smiling. 'Reasonable seats. How are you? How was Susan?'

Emily kissed his warm face. 'Yes, she's lovely. A lot of family talk.'

Phillip raised his eyebrows, but she shook her head. 'Later. Feel like ice-cream?'

'Not a wine?' He tapped his watch. 'It's late enough.'

'You can. I'm still recovering from our lunch-time bottle.'

They were seeing *Man on Wire*, an extraordinary story of a Frenchman who walked on a high wire between the twin towers in New York, towers that weren't there anymore. Not something Emily aspired to. As a child she would sit at the top of a slide looking down at the steep shining metal until those waiting on the steps behind threatened to push her. She avoided fairground rides, had never skied, happier with two feet on the ground.

She sat in red upholstery eating vanilla ice cream out of a cardboard tub with its little wooden paddle that passed for a spoon. Apparently, choc-tops were an Australian thing. Before the first trailer had finished her mind drifted back to lunch. That intense conversation. One family member she was pleased to have met but talking with Susan added yet another layer of pressure, swelling into her brain, taking over. Her dysfunctional family trapped in a bigger tangle. How much more could she manage? Thank God she had Ben rather than Frank! But horrible Frank seemed to be doing ok and Ben … And then Susan's father, a wilder, more dangerous version of hers. Her father was not a drunk, he had his moments but you wouldn't call him a drunk, and there wasn't the physical violence in their house that Susan had experienced. That story of their last holiday. She wished she knew whether that was a caring moment from her father.

Ads, trailers and ice cream finished, she tried to focus on the film. Phillippe, filling the screen, stepping out with confidence on that thin wire. She thought about Ben, teetering on his own wire, barely standing, trying to hang onto something. Although a lot more confident than her brother, she stayed on solid ground, not for her the uncertainties that artists lived with. Ground that wasn't as firm as it used to be, spider cracks appearing, her resilience fraying at the edges. That black cloud which she had kept at bay for so long was moving in closer. She looked sideways at Phillip, leaning forward tense with concentration at Phillippe, so high, nothing beneath him. He continued to be a lovely thing in her life, he stood apart from her work and family difficulties, offering support, enjoyment, warmth, affection, she would even say love. But not entirely easy, the 'what next' question hovered. She knew he was waiting for her.

Emily stretched her memory back to those long-ago holidays. She remembered games of beach cricket, unaware of any undercurrents. Was Susan's father playing with them? She recalled her father teaching her to body surf, cheering as she sped down a wave for the first time. How did he become the sour, aggressive, angry man that she learnt to avoid? What did Janet say at the funeral – a fine man, such a wonderful match, envious of her friend's fortune. Hard to believe she was talking about her father. Sounded like his upbringing played a role.

He married later than most, probably enjoyed being single. Was he in love with her mother or was he caught by the pregnancy – me, she reminded herself, that was me. Susan's words echoed – "whatever the reason, there's no excuse for either of the brothers". And her mother, struggling with her own husband and then his brother, did he attack her, what the hell happened? Waves of anger rose in her as she sat in the dark, these two men who had caused so much pain and fear in their families. How dare they! Her fists clenched, muscles tightening. With a start she realised the credits were rolling.

'Wasn't that amazing?' Phillip turned towards her.

'Yes, incredible', finding her bag under the seat.

'Where to now? There's a great new wine bar around the corner.'

'Yes let's.' She tried to match Phillip's enthusiasm.

She gazed out at the street from her stool at the window bench, still light with British summertime.

'Are you ok?' Phillips voice penetrated.

'Um yes, sorry.' She had no idea what he had been saying.

'You haven't touched your wine.'

'You know, you're right, I don't think I'm great company tonight. Would you mind awfully if I went home?'

'Are you sick?' He swivelled around towards her.

'Just a headache', she gave a brief laugh. 'Drank too much at lunch.'

'Let's go, I'll come with you.' He felt in his pocket for his wallet.

'No, no, it's ok. I'll call you. I've just got to go.'

Emily kissed him and left the bar. She glanced back at him through the window, standing by their stools, rubbing his forehead, frowning, her full wine glass on the bench. Poor Phillip, she'd ring him tomorrow. Right now, she didn't want to talk to anyone.

She gripped a hand-strap in the train, a confusion of memories whirling faster and faster through her brain as they rattled through tunnels. Overwhelmed with cycles of her mother, her father, Susan's family, Ben, on repeat. Hard to breathe, trapped in this small cylinder, so far underground. At last released to her station she ran up the narrow stone steps, gasping mouthfuls of fresh air as she strode towards her apartment, zig-zagging between couples and groups starting their Saturday night. Grateful for an empty lift, she leaned against the mirror that formed the back wall, fixing her eyes on the floor numbers, counting until it reached hers, keys ready in her hand. Here, in her space, door closed, the waves of anxiety subsided.

She remembered coming home one evening after a shift at the café. The lights were on, but the house was quiet. No television, no radio, no sounds of activity. Strange, her mum's car was in the driveway. Her father's missing but that wasn't unusual, late surgery or a meeting or something. She looked in the back room, surprised to see dinner dishes still on the table, dirty saucepans on the bench. Two places set.

'Mum?' She called up the hallway.

Glanced tentatively in the open door of their bedroom, no-one there. She climbed the stairs frowning and opened Ben's door, empty, no smoke, he hadn't been there for a while. Puzzled, she turned into her room and switched the light on to see her mum lying on the bed.

'Mum??'

Her mother sat up with a jerk, 'Oh, ummm, oh, Emily, sorry, I must have fallen asleep. What time is it?'

'It's about nine. Why are you here? Are you all right?'

'Yes, yes, of course.' She smoothed her hair. 'I, err, I just came up to clean the bathroom and thought I'd lie down for a few minutes. Silly me, I was tired, yes, busy day.'

She got up and turned away, concentrating on the bedclothes, straightening, tucking, folding, smoothing. Emily didn't move. Her mother hurried out of the room, a sideways glance at Emily.

'I must clear up the kitchen'.

Emily heard her quick footsteps on the stairs, a door close, soon followed by the clash of dishes. Weird. She washed her face in the bathroom, collecting the cleaning bottles and unused cloth.

Later, returning them downstairs to the laundry, she found her mother in front of the bookcase, re-shelving a pile of books. She turned with a big smile.

'Hello, these books are such a mess. Can never find what I want, time to tidy it up,'

'Now?'

'Why not, best to keep busy.'

Emily's sense of unease remained, despite her mother's light tone and smiles. Something wasn't right.

'Where's Dad?'

Her mum turned back to the books, straightening them. 'Oh, he had an emergency. He'll be home later. How was work?'

She hadn't thought about that odd evening for many years. It seemed clearer now than it did then. One of those memories finding its way into her consciousness, travelling from a deep hiding place. She never knew exactly what happened that night, another in a continuing series of incidents. Whether those events happened in full view or were secreted behind smiles, whether they occurred when she was there or when she was absent, their tentacles clawed her. Tightened the tension, thickened the silence, increased her mother's jitteriness around her father, alerting her to greater wariness, reinforcing her long-made decision to leave.

Emily switched on the kettle and left it to boil, wandering into her bedroom. She stood for a moment, then opened her wardrobe to a set of drawers and pulled out the bottom one. Her hand searched underneath a layer of scarves and gloves to find her mother's jewellery where it had lain since she returned. Still in the double plastic bags it had travelled in from her mother's drawers to hers. She emptied the jumble of pieces onto her bed and gently disentangled them, ignoring the kettle's piercing whistle.

Amongst the array of silver and jade, emeralds, opals, amethyst she recognised one or two that her mother had worn frequently. She wondered how many were gifts from her father. She imagined her mother's happiness as she unwrapped the small parcels, signs that he did love her after all. Were any an apology after a brutal interaction? A piece she found hard to wear?

Emily stood on a chair in front of her wardrobe to reach a collection of pretty boxes she hadn't wanted to throw away. Choosing a wide flattish box, with a lid of red and gold, she took the red velvety cloth that had once protected its initial inhabitant, a bottle of perfume, and spread it across the bottom of the box. Up on the chair again, stretching her arm up until her hand closed on tissue paper. Emily wrapped each piece of jewellery in its own sheet of soft white tissue and placed it on the cloth. Not sure that she would wear them, but she could take care of these precious things. She couldn't change the past but, in some way, felt she was now reaching out to her mother. She replaced the lid and gently kissed it, sliding the box into its own space on the shelf.

Chapter Sixteen

'That's done, what's next?' Caroline's hands hovered over Emily's keyboard.

Emily peered over her shoulder. 'No, sorry let's change that second column, give me a minute, got to get this right.' She leant over the documents spread across her desk, frowning.

'How long until Anthony?'

'Another five minutes.'

'Think Emily, think, where is it?'

Shuffled through papers, pulling one out. Her phone rang, an external call. She circled the number and handed it to Caroline, as she answered.

'Hello Em.'

'Hi Ben. I'm in the middle of something.' Damn, she wished she hadn't picked up.

'I'm a dad. A baby girl. Annie.'

At last some good news, she swallowed her annoyance.

'Congratulations, that's wonderful. Everyone all right? Were you there at the birth?'

'I was there. Downstairs. The fucking hospital wouldn't let me go up.'

She nodded at the question on Caroline's face. 'Yes, go ahead', she mouthed.

'Was there a problem?' She could guess.

'They're the fucking problem. I'm the dad!'

'What happened?'

'Bunch of liars. I'd only had a couple.'

God. Emily imagined the hospital foyer, scenes of staff restraining her drunken brother, dragging him away as he tried to stagger upstairs to his baby.

'For heaven's sake Ben!' She breathed out, not the time to be angry. 'How's Natasha? Have you seen the baby yet?'

'What do you think! I'm her dad. So tiny. She looks like me. I'm going to be such a wonderful dad.' His pride flowed through the phone. He could be, she thought, all those lovely warm qualities. She could imagine him being devoted to Annie.

'And Natasha?'

'Yeah she's fine. Tired. Her sister will look after her for a bit. I need to get things sorted, make it right for my daughter.'

He'd known what he needed to do for months, and still he wasn't prepared. She didn't know anything about babies, but wouldn't seeing her, holding her, galvanise him, with that rush of love that parents seemed to experience. She wondered what Natasha was saying. This could be his last chance.

'You'd love them both at home with you. Will you tell Dad?'

'Why would I do that? Poor Mum, she'd love my little Annie, her first grandchild.'

'I'll call him if you like, he should know.'

Caroline came back into the room waving the printed document, pointing at her watch.

'Ben, I have to go. Congratulations. Say it to Natasha, too. Enjoy your baby.' She hesitated, trying to come across as a friend rather than a parent. 'Ben, please, stay off the drink, hey. Think of Annie.'

'Yes yes, bossy boots.'

'Bye, I'll call you soon. Wonderful news, bye.'

She chewed her lip as she put the phone down. She wished she could feel more confidence in Ben. This should be a time for celebration, popping champagne, rushing out to the nearest baby clothes shop, but worry clouded her thoughts. Ben, Ben, she thought, this could be the best time in your life, don't throw it away. Did he realise his chances were dwindling?

'Emily.' Caroline at the door. Late for Anthony. She replenished her lipstick in two strokes and made her legs go as fast as possible without running, sliding her hand on the handrail of the stairs as she went down, catching her breath outside his office.

Later that evening, dishwasher humming, she reached for her laptop and remembered she promised to call her father. Better get it over with.

'Baby, huh? There you go. Let's see how he manages that.'

Didn't even ask her name.

'Are you ok?'

'You have to keep going.' An emptiness in his voice.

'Are you getting out?'

'Sometimes. Still on a couple of committees.'

Well, she thought, here is an opportunity if he wants to take it. 'I can't talk for long, just wanted to give you the news that you are a grandfather.'

'Very good then.'

Would he ever meet his granddaughter? She caught a picture of him sitting alone in the backroom. What did he do all day? What were those committees? Had her mum mentioned Rotary? Was there a medical board? Likely to only be once a month. Television, newspaper, books. There were those model cars. She remembered seeing them polished on the shelves above his desk a few months ago. Remembered the nausea.

Her and Ben, how old were they? Still in primary school. Maybe she was late primary.

Emily was enjoying her after school ritual, cordial, biscuit and television when her mum leaned over the kitchen bench,

'We've run out of milk. I'll only be a minute. Look after Ben.'

Scurried down the hall, back to pick up her keys, down the hall again. Where was Ben? She left the ABC and found him at her father's desk, standing on his father's leather chair, picking up the model cars, one by one, turning them over in his hands.

'Ben, you're not allowed.'

'I'm being careful.' He brought two of the cars down to the floor, knelt beside them, moving them in circles. 'Dad isn't home.'

He pushed them harder as the car wheels caught on the fibres of the carpet.

Every two or three weeks, their dad would go out on a Saturday morning and return with a sizeable box, taking it to his shed. Sometimes Emily stood underneath the tree where her father wouldn't see her and watch him through the shed window, his dust-coat on, frowning over the bench as he glued tiny pieces together, painting individual parts from pots of special paint. Vintage cars, not the matchbox kind. Now she realised they were collector's items, could be worth a lot of money. Back then they were toys they weren't allowed to play with.

'They'll go faster on the lino. Come on, let's have a race. Just one. I'll put them back after. Promise. Here, this one's yours.'

Emily took the blue car Ben pressed into her hand, following him into the kitchen. She knew she should have made Ben stop straight away but hard to make him. She thought they might be safer on the shiny lino, protect those fragile wheels.

Ben revving the engines, 'Vroom, vroom. Come on, here's the start. Vroom. Mine's gonna win.'

'Ok. Only one minute, then we must put them back.'

The cars zoomed along the short stretch of lino beside the kitchen bench. Gaining their own momentum on the slippery surface, Ben clapping. Which one went off course? Veering and wobbling as they sped, and before she could catch them,

'Whoa', shouted Ben. 'Smash!'

He jumped up in excitement. Emily's bare legs pressed on the cold lino, frozen as she saw three little wheels spinning around the floor, a dent in the door of the green car as it lay on its roof, a thin silvery bumper bar hanging off the blue car, attached on only one corner.

'Ben', she whispered. 'We've got to fix this.'

Ben's excitement at the smash changed to horror. He squatted down, tried to force a wheel into position on the green car.

'He won't notice if we put them back really carefully.'

The bumper bar fell to the floor as Emily picked up the blue car. They needed the special glue.

'Of course, he will, you idiot. Look at them, what are we going to do?'

She rushed out to the shed and pulled at the padlock, shaking it, willing it to spring open. Tried to push the sliding window but it wouldn't move. Ran back in the house to Ben, crouched on the floor trying to press out a dent. Startled by the sound of the key in the front door.

'I'm back.'

Quick steps down the hall. They looked up at her as she appeared in the doorway,

'What have you done?' Her eyes big, mouth open.

'I'm fixing it '

Ben was pushing his thumbs hard at the dent, frowning in concentration.

'Stop it, Ben. Leave it, you'll make it worse. What can we do, Mum?'

'I was only away for 5 minutes. How did you let this happen? You know how much he loves those cars.'

Milk and keys still in her hand.

'The wind, we opened the window, and the wind came in and blew them off, or you were cleaning and knocked them.' Anything other than what happened. Ben nodded furiously, head down over the car. Her mum ran her free hand through her hair.

'He cleans them himself.' Shook her head. 'It would have to be a powerful wind.'

Emily glanced through the back window to the sunny skies and graceful trees moving in the light breeze.

'Or we could throw them in the bin and say someone stole them.'

'He would find out anyway.' Her mum sat on the stool, elbow on the bench and rubbed her forehead, her face creased with lines.

'Why on earth did you touch them? Emily, I left you in charge.'

Emily stood with her back against the wall, Ben flung himself on his mum.

'I'm sorry, I'm sorry, I was being careful, I was.'

She patted his head. 'I know Ben, I know. But we've got a problem here.'

Emily found a box at the bottom of the pantry and fitted the two damaged cars in, positioning the wheels in their correct places. She placed the box on her father's desk, a tissue over the cars. Nothing else they could do. She came back into the kitchen and crouched, smoothing her hand over the floor, checking she had all the pieces. Her mother stood up, put the milk in the fridge.

'Go up to your rooms until it's time for dinner.'

They ran up the stairs, Emily elbowing Ben in the ribs as she pushed past him, rushing to her bed. She lay curled up, her stomach knotted, eyes on the clock. Let him be late today. Sounds of Ben vomiting in the toilet. Right on six o'clock the sound of car tyres on the gravel, key turning in the lock, his tread into the house. She crept to her door to listen, willing him not to go to his desk, not yet.

Please, this once, please put your briefcase in the hall.

'What's this?!!'

She folded her arms tight around her stomach, heard her mother's footsteps.

'An accident, Jack. We can fix it. Go easy on them. Please. I've spoken to them already. They are very sorry. They're only young. Accidents happen.'

Heavier steps into the hall, his voice travelling up the stairs. 'Emily! Ben! Here. Now.'

'Ben', Emily whispered into his room. 'Come on, we have to go down.'

He looked at her, appealing. She nodded. They walked down slowly, side by side, their eyes on the box in his hand, his figure looming at the bottom step. They stopped two steps up.

'What were you doing?' his face rigid, eyes hard, mouth tight. No shouting yet.

Emily started, Ben shrinking into her side. 'We are very sorry Dad. We didn't mean to, they are so nice, we were just looking and we dropped them. We're sorry. Aren't we Ben?'

'Yes, very, very sorry', muffled voice.

'Dropped them! Looks like something else happened here.'

He turned over the two broken cars in the box, taking in the damage, and then full volume.

'What were you doing? You are never, ever, allowed to touch them. What were you doing?'.

The three jerked. Emily felt nausea rising in waves. She struggled to speak clearly.

'Sorry Dad. Just an accident. We're sorry. We'll fix them.'

'And how do you think you're going to do that? How?' Scornful.

Emily knew she would cry if she opened her mouth.

'Answer my question! Ben! What were you doing?'

'Nothing Dad, an accident', mumbling.

'What. Were. You. Doing? Come down here, you little coward.'

Ben stepped down, one foot at a time, his head lowering from level with his father's chin to his chest to the belt of his trousers.

Hands on his hips, his father towered above him.

'You stupid boy, you were playing weren't you.'

Ben nodded and started to cry.

'Little weakling! Own up! Let me hear you!' Volume up again.

'Yes', a small voice.

'Yes what! Louder!!!'

'Yes Dad', between sobs.

Emily's eyes widened in horror as he undid his belt buckle, breathing faster, panic rising.

'Jack, no. They know what they've done. They won't ever do it again, will you?' voice wavering.

'No Dad, we'll never touch them again.' She nudged Ben.

'No Dad, we won't, never.'

'I'll make sure of that. Emily, go to your room. I don't want to see you until the morning. You hear me?'

Emily made her shaking legs run up the stairs, gasping for breath at the top. She stood holding her door.

'Bend over! And stop crying. What are you, a girl?'

Ben trying to stifle his sobs.

Whack as the belt came down. And Again. Emily flinched.

'So next time you decide to touch things which aren't yours, remember what will happen. This and more. If I have to beat it into you, I will. Upstairs. Now, before I change my mind.'

Emily closed her door and ran to her bed, putting the pillow over her head, pushing her face into the smooth cold bottom sheet. Her body shivering, crying now. Stupid Ben. Why didn't she stop him? The front door slammed, the sound penetrating the pillow, shaking the house with its force. She stayed hidden, gripping each side of the pillow; her muscles tightened further when her door opened, then released hearing her mother's voice.

'Emily? Are you all right? I brought you a little something to eat.'

She peered out. 'Thanks Mum.' She felt her mum's hand on her back.

'You know your dad. He boils over sometimes. Those cars, they're special. He'll get over it. He does love you both. But you're fine, Emily, you're a strong girl. We have to help Ben though. You're ok?'

Emily nodded. From under the pillow she could

see her mum's lap as she sat beside her on the bed.
Felt her kiss on her shoulder.

'I'm going to Ben now.'

Left to herself again, she pushed the pillow aside
and sat up, red-eyed, eating the biscuits, crunching
the apple, chewing each mouthful, hearing her
mother's soothing tone over Ben's sobs, through
the closed door.

Chapter Seventeen

Emily screwed up the paper tight in her fist and threw it at the three other balls on her table. Fresh sheet.

'This year has been difficult for me, with my mother dying.'

Cross out. Couldn't look weak, didn't want sympathy.

'I've decided to take a break ...'

She'd have to explain why.

'I'm exploring other possibilities ...'

She would be now. She could outright lie and say she already had another job, confidential at this stage. Could she sound believable? They'd find out.

'Fuck!'

How could this happen to her? Tears pushed through, shock, anger, shame.

It started that morning with Caroline at the door. 'Excuse me Emily, Anthony's asked for the pay rises. Didn't I see them go through a couple of days ago?'

Oh no. She had signed them off. What was wrong with her? She knew Anthony wanted final approval. Emily who never made a mistake, but there had been one or two recently, recovered before anyone noticed, she hoped. She'd had to fight to concentrate in the last few weeks, her sleep broken with Ben's calls, distracted by Anthony's daily demands, her head whirling.

'Ah yes, can we retrieve them? Could William help?'

Voice steady, face calm, belying rising panic, her heart beating faster; no hope of asking David for a favour, he would delight in this. Caroline or William might manage it through their colleagues. Fifteen minutes later they were both standing in front of her desk, solemn. William not meeting her eyes, Caroline twisting her rings.

'Sorry Emily, we tried. Finance has processed them, to meet pay cut off.'

'Ok, thanks, I'll deal with it.'

She resisted the urge to put her head in her hands, to cry, throw something. She'd better go down there before someone else told him.

He already knew. David, he wouldn't have wasted a second. He leaned back in his chair, eyes watching her try to explain her way out of it. She ran out of words.

'This is the last straw, Emily. Since the day I arrived you have let me down. They told me you were a top HR executive, but you don't reach my expectations. You are already under review and now with this massive error, you, one', he held up a finger, 'reinforced low performance standards'. A second finger. 'Two, wasted company money and three, disobeyed my specific instructions.' he hinged his fingers to point them at her. 'Three major consequences'. Even tone today.

Her mouth felt dry, hard to swallow. Hold

yourself together Emily. He opened a drawer and brought out an envelope. David would have done it.

'I've given you every opportunity. I delayed your rating to give you a chance to prove yourself, but your performance has declined further. You are not up to it. This is a big job.'

He was waiting for this and she had made it easy for him. She hardened inside. No more satisfaction for him. She would go with dignity. No tears, no anger. Perhaps their most civil conversation. Agreed on exit terms, checked the numbers, what would and wouldn't be said.

'Leave tomorrow.'

The last words she would hear from that fat face. At least she wasn't being marched out of the building. She closed his door, nodded at his assistant, and turned to the stairs. No more descents to Anthony, nerves rising into her stomach. Hand on rail, one step at a time, careful not to fall. Jaw gripped. Reaching the top, she headed straight for her office, averting her eyes from people going to meetings, getting coffee, filling their water bottles.

Relieved to see Caroline's empty chair, she picked up her bag, laptop and coat and walked out again, willing herself not to rush. She took the fire escape. No smiles and chats to avoid down the grey stone flights. Through the exit door to a side street. The pavement dirty wet from a downpour. Damn, left her umbrella in the office. Avoiding the front of her tower, she walked fast to escape the continuing rain. She forced herself to slow on the tube's upper steps, shiny wet, then increased speed along the tunnels, humidity rising to greet her as she neared the platform. Only three hours ago she was one of hundreds of city workers, pressed against each other, briefcases between their legs, laptops bumping into shoulders. Now she had a choice of seats, a woman with shopping bags next to her, a tourist family opposite, a scattering of suits. No-one looked. She breathed in the fresh air as she exited the station into the high street, a few minutes to home. She felt her hair sticking to her head as she hurried towards her building. Lift empty, she stared at the doors as it shot up to her apartment, rain drips sliding off her coat into mini puddles. She rifled through her bag for keys, praying they weren't still on her desk. In. Door closed. She threw her coat on the floor, and fell back on the couch, eyes wide open, rigid.

Sacked. Not that the announcement would describe it in that way, they had agreed carefully constructed words to accompany the cheque. But sacked. So stupid, she had let things slip when she knew she was in danger. Why hadn't she looked for another role, what made her stay? Now he had won. Taken away the opportunity to leave with a triumphant smile as she moved to a new role. Emily landing an enviable job. Covered in glory. Lucky Emily escaping. Emily with options. A slap in the face for Anthony, exposed as the poor leader he was. Instead she could hear his casual comments, protecting his victory, 'wasn't up to the challenge,' 'couldn't meet my expectations,' 'difficult to work with.'

Emily snapped her attention to the present. What was

she doing here? She would allow no one to say she ran away. Not her. A senior executive leaves with her head up, poised, dignified. He would not have the pleasure of seeing her slink off cowed. Right, get in first, take control of the messaging before the communication juggernaut started. They must hear it from her, not Anthony. Texted Caroline, 'Sorry had to rush out, be back soon'.

She swept the little balls of paper into the bin. She'd think of something. Into the bathroom to replenish her make-up, the hairdryer restoring her smooth bob and removing the damp from her clothes; changing them would arouse suspicions. She stood tall in front of the full-length mirror for a moment. An executive.

Her resolve carried her through to the end of the next day, telling people a story of family pressures, needing time off, ready for a change.

Alfred knew. He shut his office door. 'What!! The dog! You?? You're better than any of us!'

'I guess he would always go for someone. I'm an easy target. He's never liked me. I'm sure he's already chosen my successor, probably interviewed them. It'll be a relief to get out of here. Won't have to deal with this shit anymore.'

'Are you all right? Emily. What am I going to do without you?' He put his hand on her arm. 'Better not hug in here, the gossip'll be around the building in five minutes.'

Emily laughed. She would miss Alfred. 'I'm fine. I was planning to leave anyway. This just brings it forward a little.'

'Dinner. A top restaurant. I'll pull a few strings for a booking. Unless Anthony ...?'

'Wouldn't have crossed his mind.' Not that she wanted it to. A farewell dinner with Anthony? She imagined the group sitting around the restaurant table on their best behaviour, waiting for her to arrive, his embarrassment when she didn't turn up.

'No, of course not. Tomorrow. No Anthony, no David, only the ones you want, my company card, he owes you.'

Finished. Late the next night she turned the key in the door of her apartment, farewells and thank yous behind her. Expensive team lunch while her credit card was still active, maintaining a smile, sounding positive, happy even. Surprised by a lovely gift, working hard to hold back tears at that moment. A hilarious meal with colleagues buoyed by good French burgundy, James showing an amazing ability to imitate Anthony. Then it was over. Done. Her dignity intact. Rich food and many glasses of wine sent her to an exhausted sleep.

Woken in a fog by her phone. What was the time? She knew who it would be. Why hadn't she turned it off?

'Ben.'

'Em. I feel like shit.'

'Ben, it's the middle of the night.'

Last thing she needed right now. How many hours had she slept? Some weeks he called every night. Her sleep was shallow in those weeks, closing her eyes wondering how many hours before his call. Resisted the temptation to put her phone on silent. Always sick, well, drunk, rarely a reasonable conversation. No wonder she made mistakes.

'Tash ... not here ... where's 'Tash ... Annie ...'

She leaned over and switched her bedside lamp on, forcing her eyes open.

'Ben, you know where she is.' Still a little drunk herself, hard to think.

'No ... no ... gone. And ... and ... I worked last week. She says I've gotta work … then I do, just like she wants … she still won't come back.'

'What did you do?'

'I worked … did you listen to me … I fuckin' worked … but I hurt my back.'

'The gardening work?'

'Yeah, gardening … hard work.'

'Ok.' How many times had she heard about this one job?

'But I've gotta get my baby back. Reckon I'll go to court.'

'Is that a good idea?'

'Course. I'm her dad. Bitch didn't let me see her. I'll force her'.

Her head was clearing. Court? Easy to predict who would win there. She doubted Ben could even organise a hearing.

'Better to sort it out with Natasha, talk it through, make sure you're sober first.'

'She shut the fucking door', he shouted down the phone. 'My baby. Why won't she let me see her?'

Not hard to guess why. Had he lost all his chances? She wondered if she should call Natasha herself? No, what would she say? None of her business.

'Ben. I'm exhausted. Stop drinking. Find a job. Think about what you're losing here.' She was on repeat, with little hope of getting through.

'Yes, yes. I worked, hurt my back. I'm sick. Can't work when I'm sick'.

'Ben, I need to sleep. I'll talk to you another time.'

She saw so clearly what he needed to do. She switched her phone off and slammed it on the bed. How much longer could this go on? How far would he fall before he realised? She dreaded the thought of Ben by himself, without Natasha, without his mum, his sister thousands of miles away. Who else was there? Hard to see a happy ending.

She fell back asleep. Black balloons filled her unconscious. A child running, gigantic balloons following, overtaking her, pushing her to the ground. She was rolling, fighting, as they surrounded her, pressed down on her, no space left to breathe.

She woke with a gasp, her heart racing, groaned to see 6.00 am on the clock. Too early. Her body deciding it was time to wake up, her mind shouting no. She turned over, curled under the sheet, but recent events knotted her head. Insistent, as though they had been waiting for her, hovering at the edge of her sleep, ready to pounce the second she opened her eyes. There was her cycle class, then what? Best to stay in routine or she'd turn into some unemployed layabout.

She jumped up, threw on her gym clothes and was soon cycling up hills, down hills. More resistance, less resistance, fast, faster. 'Come on, you can do it, remember why you came.' The instructor keeping them motivated until sweat dripped off her face and arms, her top soaked. Two days ago, she was hurrying through the stretches, lining up with other workers to shower, use the hair dryer, joining the faces at the mirror, dabbing foundation, applying lipstick. There would be one less today.

Morning radio on, she took her time over tea, muesli and newspaper, telling herself what a luxury this was. No bulging inbox, no meetings, no papers to write, no voice mail messages to deal with. She could do whatever she wanted. The corridor sounds of footsteps, doors closing, lift pinging, they all faded as people left for work. She sat in the silence, staring at the paper, not reading. What was she going to do?

Tired, she was so tired, her brain a muddle, remnants of a

hangover hovering. She lay on her bed and fell into a restless doze, her head rewinding conversations with Anthony, with Ben, again and again. And then a deeper sleep, falling down endless flights of stairs, tumbling out of control, Anthony at the bottom, watching her fall, looming over her when she came to a stop, unable to move. Ben appeared beside her, a small crouched shape, curved over his knees, face hidden. Anthony laughing, his voice resounding, his mouth opening wider until it was bigger than him, then bang, she splintered into hundreds of pieces. Shards of glass flying through the building. Startling her awake. I must get up.

A second shower, the running water clearing her head, waking her senses. Time to organise; write lists, people to contact, food to buy. She was not falling apart. Number one priority, new job, first item, make times with head-hunters. She relied on lists to help her manage work overload, looking for the sense of control they provided when her head was crowded. Ticking off tasks at the end of a day sent her home calm. Today her list would offer a semblance of structure to the hours stretching ahead, remind her she had things to do. No one outside work knew yet, not Phillip, not Janice, not Ashleigh. She picked up her phone, put it down again, circled her kitchen, began boiling the kettle, switched it off. What was she going to do first?

It was much later in the day when she rang Phillip. He was there within the hour.

'Emily, I'm so sorry. Poor you.'

As he hugged her she began crying, waves of choking tears overcoming her efforts to breathe and speak. She pulled away from him and ran into the bathroom, leaning against the closed door, sliding down to sit on the cold tiles. Her job, Ben, her father, mother, Anthony, pounded her head, hammering. What was left? A failure, after all.

Embarrassed that Phillip was sitting at her table, witnessing her collapse. Emily not coping. What will he think of me? She soaked a flannel and held it against her face. Still a disaster. Make-up covered up the worst.

Phillip turned around from his seat, a hesitant smile as though he wasn't sure whether he should. A teapot and two cups in front of him.

'Sorry about that. Don't know what came over me. I'm ok now. Tea, how lovely, thank you'. Heavy inside. Was she her mother?

'Come and sit. Let me pour you a cup.'

She breathed in the warm aromas.

'So, how are you? When did all this happen? Why didn't you call me earlier?' He looked strained.

She sat across the table from him and sipped the tea.

'I don't know. Just had to survive the last couple of days. Fucking Anthony! Worst leader ever. Did you meet him?'

Phillip shifted in his seat. 'Oh, not sure. Anyway, forget him. He doesn't matter anymore.'

'So what do I do? How do I minimise the damage? I have to move on. I can't let that man win.'

The last time she remembered being desperate for a job was at the beginning of her career. That moment of conscious decision, or admission, she was staying in London. No longer a back packer in hostels, getting by with waitressing jobs. Time to find a professional job, a flat, create a life. After the first one, it was a series of promotions and head-hunter calls. Now she had to call them. Call them sounding confident, calm, manage their questions. How could she say what happened?

'That won't be a problem. Your resumé is strong. You just need a credible story. I can help you with that. I'll put you in touch with some people, make sure you are talking to reputable recruiters, conflict of interest for me to do the work.'

She nodded. 'Thank you. I need all the help I can get.'

Phillip took both her hands. 'You'll be fine, but Emily, think about giving yourself a break. I'm sure your payout will last you for a while. It's been a such a difficult few months, what with work, Ben, your mother, so much pressure across your life. I know you're strong, if it was just one problem, you'd be fine, but this year ... many people would have given up by now. Why not look after yourself, take a holiday?'

Emily looked at him in horror. 'Oh no, what would I do? I have to work. This is my career we're talking about.' She pulled her hands away. 'What if it takes months? What if there are no jobs? What if the money runs out? I'll be forgotten. I've got to start now.'

And what if this has damaged my reputation, she thought? What if this is the end of my career?

Chapter Eighteen

Emily brushed a strand of hair off the jacket of her favourite charcoal suit and fastened one button, a nod of approval to the executive woman in the mirror. These were the best days, resurrecting professional Emily to meet with search consultants, projecting success, credibility and confidence. The real Emily, the one she liked, calm and controlled. She entered their office buildings in her black Italian court shoes, reminding herself who she was. She had her story ready.

'Time for a change', she would say or 'I'm looking for my next challenge.' 'Perhaps a different industry.' Always smiling.

After the second discussion she was no longer worried about how they regarded her departure. It seemed Anthony's reputation was well known.

At other times explosions of rage rose into her chest, overtaking her brain, spilling out. She shouted at a call centre operator about a billing problem, marched out of a shop with a derisive comment at the assistant when they didn't have her size; refused to pay for a cup of weak coffee, stomping out of the cafe, trying to ignore the sideways looks from other customers. She had to stop herself from elbowing slow walkers on the street, wanting to yell at them to look up from their phones. Embarrassed when she realised she had said, 'hurry up can't you,' to a sixteen-year-old supermarket cashier fumbling with the card reader, loud enough for the rest of the queue to hear. Surprised to see the streets busy during the day. What do all these people do? They're not all sick or on holidays. Housewives? Unemployed? Part timers? Retired? She wanted to hold up a sign saying 'I am a successful executive.'

Wednesday of the third week. Too many items on her list already ticked. The cutlery drawer was sparkling, three bags of clothes had gone to the charity shop, the linen cupboard was in perfect order, organised according to type, colour and size, every towel and sheet washed, she'd reorganised her crockery shelves, twice. Everyone she knew worked.

At least today there was her regular mid-week dinner with Phillip to look forward to. Soon after breakfast she set about the task of choosing what to wear. Stood staring into her wardrobe. Rejected suits, they had been neglected recently, meetings with consultants in a lull, but to wear one she would have to invent a reason, lie to Phillip. Pulled out her best brand jeans, then replaced them. Even expensive ones communicated not working. How to fit in with after-work diners when she wasn't working.

At lunchtime Phillip texted that he would be half an hour late.

'Sure, no problem', she responded, slamming her phone on the table.

After reading every article in *The Guardian* in her quiet flat and changing outfits three times, she left, hoping she'd managed a business casual look. Walking there would fill the time. Blended into the streams of people leaving their offices, many delaying their crowded commute to make the most of extended daylight hours, meeting up with friends at bars and restaurants. At least that was one thing she was still doing.

She arrived early, despite the shop windows. Emily waited in the restaurant, retreating from the fumes of buses, cabs and cars stopping and starting in the narrow streets. She was always the late one, rushing in, apologising, tearing herself away from a long meeting or an urgent presentation. Now she was first at their usual table, trying to appear like she was enjoying time to herself at the end of a busy day.

A skip of pleasure as Phillip's pale brown hair passed above the stylised black letters of the restaurant name on the window. And then his head through the door, glasses perched below a frown, his thinking frown she often joked. She jumped out of her seat and kissed him, lightly touching his face,

'You're sweating.'

'Hello', a smile replacing the lines in his forehead. Squeezing her arm, 'Yes, I rushed, sorry I'm late, an extra meeting, my last client didn't stop talking. Have you been here long?'

'Just got here. Busy day?'

'Tell me about it! Still more to do', pointing at his laptop, as he placed it on the chair beside him. 'Have you chosen?'

Emily chattered, trying to find interesting things to say, the news, her coming appointments with search consultants. Her first conversation today. Phillip munched bread, nodding. As they started their main meals, his frown returned.

'Sorry, this is boring, it's been a quiet day. You're thinking again. Are you back at work?' laughed Emily.

'Actually, there is something.'

'Am I going to like it?' playfully covering a little uncertainty with his change of tone.

Uncertainty increasing to nervousness as he put his knife and fork down and took a breath.

'You know we have the account for your company, your past company I should say.'

'You placed me, remember, that's how we met', smiling at the memory. What was he on about?

'Yes', his smile cleared almost as soon as it came. 'And you're aware I work on executive roles, like yours.'

Emily nodded, trying to follow.

'Well, you may not, um ... that ... well ...'

'Oh my God, Anthony. You put Anthony in there!' Her eyes wide, her fork in mid-air, a mushroom spiked halfway down the prongs.

'Mmm, yes. It wouldn't have been right to say anything while you were still there.'

'Anthony. You chose Anthony! How could you?'

'Well, your board wanted someone tough. He had solid experience turning around older businesses.'

'Tough. That's one word for it. You must have known what he was like.'

'There were rumours. I suspected his style might be a little challenging, but I judged it a minor risk.'

He looked at a point at the back of the restaurant to the left of Emily and swallowed, betraying his confident professional tone.

'Minor! You knew!' Rage entered the bottom of her stomach, her voice shook. 'Everyone knows what he's like. Everyone. So you put him in there, chose him, knowing that your decision would give me a terrible time! What the hell were you thinking!'

'It wasn't only me. This was high profile; my boss had a

big say and the board Chair was keen. They were previous colleagues. This was an important account for us.'

He looked down and moved the pasta around with his fork.

'Bet that was a nice fat commission! And you couldn't even warn me?'

'Conflict of interest, not ethical.'

He sat straighter, trying to return the conversation to a professional level. Emily's mind a twisted tangle, adrenalin high.

'Don't you back away from this. You placed someone who you knew would cause me massive amounts of stress. Your decision. Your choice. And what's happened to me? Jobless! Destroyed! Where was any concern for me!'

Emily tried to slow her thinking, control the chaos inside her head.

'To be fair, that was Anthony', he changed tack. 'Emily, look I'm sorry.' She pulled her hand away sharply as he reached across the table. 'Honestly, I didn't think it would be this bad. Maybe it was more than he could manage. He did sound stressed. I was sure you'd come through it. I am truly sorry.' A film of sweat had returned to his forehead.

'Don't make fucking excuses for Anthony. He still has his job last time I looked!' Another thought occurred to her. 'So now I see why you were encouraging me to stay. It wouldn't have done you any good, would it, your "placement" leaving too soon, talking about the poor behaviour of the CEO who you had also placed, raising questions about your judgement. If I had resigned, I would be in a much stronger position, and happier, by the way, but oh no, stay Emily, better for your career. Better for whose fucking career?'

'It wasn't like that.'

'So what was it like, Phillip? And tell me, how did you manage that follow up meeting you do. Secret planning so I wouldn't see you? Was that your ethics too?' She felt wave after wave of anger surging through her body.

'No, no we always meet CEOs in our offices, with the chair. Normal process.' Professional voice, examining his wine glass, picking it up then returning it to the table without drinking.

'Champagne all round, I bet.' Her eyes like stones.

'Emily, surely you know I would never, ever, do anything to hurt you. I just thought it was time to say, to be honest with you', his words tumbling, panicking,

'Because you were worried I'd find out, now I'm talking to your colleagues. All this caring for me, all this being oh so supportive, what was that? Guilt? A pretence? You even lied to me when I asked you if you'd met him.'

She heard her voice resounding around the restaurant, but she didn't care.

'No, no. Emily, please, please believe me.'

They looked at each other across the table, food cooling, wine glasses full. The couple alongside them had their heads down, concentrating on their meal, cutlery clinking against their plates in the silence.

'And you've kept it a secret all this time. I trusted you! You're not the person I thought you were. What else is going on?'

'Nothing, no nothing. I wanted to say something, I truly did, but I couldn't work out how.' Phillip pulled at his hair, his fists dragging at both sides of his head. 'Things were going so well between us, we'd begun talking about moving in together and it had taken so long for us to even have that conversation and then, when things were getting worse at work for you I didn't know what to do. I was scared, I guess, afraid of spoiling everything. You're so important to me, Emily. Please can we get through this?'

'Get through this? As though it doesn't matter? The worst experience of my life. How can I ever trust you again?'

Emily felt her jaw would crack if she moved it. Ice cold inside, muscles rigid. She suddenly disliked his large face looking up at her, noticed his hair thinning at the front, grey strands emerging at his temples, the lines on his forehead, his mouth twisted, the small childhood scar on his cheek looked ugly now, his arms fleshy instead of strong.

'Fuck this.'

She pushed her chair back and picked up her bag.

'Emily, don't go, please, we can sort this out.'

'What? Pretend it didn't happen? My life is gone. I've lost my job, probably my career, all because of you. And you couldn't even warn me. What kind of relationship is possible anymore?'

The waiters were moving around the small restaurant refilling glasses, murmuring to diners, avoiding their table. Emily felt she was on a stage, dominating the room, an audience listening with their eyes averted.

'I'm going. You can pay. I didn't eat, anyway. The least you can fucking do.'

She took a big gulp out of her wine glass and turned out of reach as she walked past his chair.

'No, let me come.'

Phillip fumbling for his wallet in his bag, clumsy, slow in his haste as Emily strode out of the restaurant, ahead of the waiter rushing to open the door.

She increased her pace along the footpath, stepping on and off the curb, oblivious to honking horns, turned corners in rapid succession, preventing Phillip from following her. She stopped in a laneway and leaned against a wall, breathing heavily, her chest hurting with effort, the wall's rough stone digging into her shoulders. A sharp-edged breeze whipped her arms, the warm summer evening cooling. Damn, her jacket was still in the restaurant. Goodbye to that jacket. She wasn't going back, probably ever. She glanced at her surroundings, no bars or restaurants, the closed door of a cafe beside her, a trio of shuttered shops beyond. God, where am I?

She followed the sound of traffic and hailed a cab. Sank into the anonymous safety of the back seat. Switched off her phone when Phillip's name lit up the screen. Impatient as they edged forward. Suddenly panicked that Phillip would head to her flat, with the excuse of her jacket, at this pace he'd be there before her. She'd be faster on the tube. Stuffing a note in the driver's hand she ran across the road, skipping in front of a bus, bag banging against her side.

No Phillip in the foyer. Her hands shook outside her door as she tossed through wallet, phone, make-up, oyster card, at last the keys and then she was in, deadlocking behind her. She threw her bag on the table and stomped around, wiped the clean sink, straightened the toaster, opened the dishwasher, picking up a plate realised it was still dirty and slammed it down on the bench, watching a crack spread until it broke apart in two pieces. Fuck fuck fuck! How could he do that to her? And if he kept that secret for so long, what else wasn't he telling her!

Chapter Nineteen

Five am. Emily stared at the ceiling, wondering if she had slept at all. She switched her phone on, four missed calls from Phillip. One person she would not ring. Thank God she'd never given him a key. No calls from Ben for once. Lucky for him, she thought, no patience for him today. She turned it off and put it in her bedside drawer. No appointments in her calendar, forget the gym, no need to go out, her fridge had enough food. She would survive on biscuits if she had to.

A day on the couch bingeing gritty crime serials. The grittier the better to absorb her full attention. Curtains drawn, curled up under a wrap, in pyjamas, getting up only for food, drinks, bathroom. Bridget Jones without the ice cream. Or the singing. When she took a break between episodes of Swedish murders, snippets of last night's conversation would slide into her brain. Phillip's face. Fury at his betrayal kept her hard, a barrier against loss creeping in.

By late afternoon there were plates and bowls surrounding the couch, used cups on the coffee table. Her back was protesting against being in the same position all day. Eyes sore from television and not enough sleep. Too early for alcohol? Was the tonic cold? Other people were at work, shopping, seeing friends. In another life at four o'clock on a Thursday afternoon she would have been deep in meetings. Now she was pouring a gin and tonic. She wandered around her flat, stretching the stiffness from her body, glass in hand, stepping between the crockery. Perhaps enough television. She pulled out a novel from the bookshelf, flicked its pages, returned it, rested her hand on her mother's book for a moment then turned away from the bookshelves, draining her drink. What was she going to do? She took a second gin back to the couch and the next episode.

The following morning, she stood under the hot shower, long after soaping and rinsing, trying to clear her head. A longer sleep helped along by sleeping tablets. She had to pull herself together. Put on clothes, eat breakfast. Opening the curtains allowed light to enter a room of dirty crockery and glasses. Oh God. Energy returned, she cleared dishes into the dishwasher, rubbed at cup and glass circles on the coffee table, vacuumed crumbs, plumped cushions, until she had restored order. Now she could eat.

It might be early enough to try Ashleigh. She left her half-eaten toast to retrieve her phone. Deleted the missed calls, voice mails and texts before messaging to see if Ashleigh was free for a Skype.

'Hello, this is nice. Hey - are you sick? You look awful'

Maybe the video was a mistake.

'Yeah, sorry.'

Ashleigh's face filled the screen, head tilted. 'What's going on?'

'God, where to start? Ash … it's … it's … everything … Life's a shit, basically.'

'What happened? Is it Phillip?'

She felt Ashleigh reaching out to her as strongly as if she was with her on the couch. Hold it together, Emily. She nodded, 'Mmm, Phillip, my job … all gone'.

'What? Oh no.' Ashleigh's eyes intensified.

One moment of warm sympathy and then tears leaked onto her face, flowed, dissipating any attempt to sound like she was managing. She choked words out between sobs.

'What's happening to me ... my evil boss sacked me, power-hungry, controlling bastard, never liked me ... took the first opportunity which I stupidly gave him ... and Phillip, Phillip was the one who put him there ... lied to me ... never told me ... never warned me. It's been so stressful with Anthony, worst time in my entire career ... and now this ... I can't sleep ... can't think. And Ben keeps ringing, not coping, drinking himself into a mess ... everything was going so well, then Mum died, and my life starts falling apart ... I can't do this ...'

'Oh Emily. Poor you, this sounds unbelievably tough. I wish I could give you a hug.'

Emily blew her nose. 'Me too.'

'God, I'm crying now.' Ashleigh rubbed her eyes. 'I'm sure it will work out with Phillip.'

'How can it? How can I ever trust him again? And who knows what else he's lying about.'

'Perhaps he just made a mistake, got caught up in something and didn't know what to do. He sounds too good to let go.'

'Don't let him off the hook! I trusted him. I felt like he cared about me, he was really there for me, or so I thought. And now I find out he's a total shit. Thank God I didn't move in with him. Hang on.' Emily returned with a box of tissues. 'I was so happy to be back in London, away from all that family stuff but so many memories keep coming ... dreams, I can't shut them down ... everything good in my life ... there's nothing left.'

Used tissues scattered around her.

'Emily', Ashleigh spoke firmly, slowly. 'Right now, it all looks terrible. But you will get through. You're a strong person. You will feel better. Give it some time, let things rest for a while. Then you'll find another job and, when you're ready, you can talk to Phillip.'

Emily shook her head, looking down, trying to stop the tears re-surging.

'You just need time. Your mother dying was huge. You returned to your family after twenty years, that's big enough by itself. It's like that was the start, everything else followed. Everything connects even if we can't see it. Look. Why not come over for a few weeks? Take a break from London. Stay with us, it's chaotic here, but we'd love to have you. I'll take some leave. Things can look different when you're away, give you space to recover.'

'God, twice in one year. I mean, thank you, but it's the one place in the world I've been avoiding.'

'Not the same as last time though. You and me. You don't even have to tell your father you're here unless you want to.'

'I just need to pull myself together.'

'Think about it. We're thousands of miles away, that might feel a whole better. I'll call you tomorrow. Do something you like doing, take care of yourself.'

Emily shut the lid of the laptop and stared out of the window at the nearby apartment buildings. Melbourne again? She was desperate to leave last time. She'd tried hard to put her family behind her on her return. Where they were before her mother died. Close the door again. But they wouldn't stay there. Ben especially, kept pushing into her life, a demanding child making sure she was paying attention. Her first twenty years rising, alive again. Wouldn't it be worse if she was there?

Phillip would be at work. Everyone was at work. She could risk going for a run. Into the bathroom for a touch of makeup, hide her patchy stressed skin.

'Fuck!' Beside the sunscreen in her bathroom cabinet was a bottle of Clinique for Men deodorant, Homme after shave, and his razor. Her stomach contracted. She gathered them up and threw them into the bin. No, they couldn't be here, jumping out at her every time she lifted the lid. She picked them out of the rubbish and ran into the kitchen for a bag. Tempted to throw them out of the window, imagined watching them hurtle to a satisfying smash on the ground below. Too many unintended consequences. She opened her door a slither and put the bag in the corridor. She would take it with her downstairs into the shared rubbish skips. Her flat was clear of him.

Lycra pants on, runners laced, but she stayed sitting on the bed remembering when she'd offered that he could leave some essentials, here in her flat. It had taken her a while. He was the only one she had invited, had guarded against suggesting that kind of permanence to anyone else, didn't want them to think they were settled in her life. Phillip didn't ask. His wash bag sat on the shelf while he was here and then accompanied him home. She had tried to sound practical, casual.

> 'If it would make it easier for you, I can clear a space.'
>
> 'Ok, thanks, that'd be good', responding as though it was nothing. His eyes meeting hers. They both knew it was a turning point.

She gave herself a shake, shook out the memory of his

face. Don't think about him. No more tears. Luckily she hadn't gone as far as clothes in her wardrobe – he would have lost them to the rubbish skip too.

She ran hard along the Thames Path, pounding her chest, pushing her stress out, her body working again after the couch day.

Post-run coffee in hand, Emily strolled between the tourists, conscious of sweat dampening her hair and skin. She drank half before throwing the cup in a bin. Should have asked for three shots. What if she did go to Melbourne? Out of London. No risk of Phillip knocking on her door, on holiday rather than being unemployed. With Ashleigh, the one person in the world she completely trusted, felt supported by, she had known her longer than anyone. Only two weeks, she wouldn't miss out on a job in that time. She could avoid going to the house.

Three days later Emily was pulling shirts, t-shirts, jeans off their hangers and into her suitcase, jumpers and underwear from her drawer, banging them flat into her case with her palm. Threw in running gear. Paused. Southern hemisphere. Replaced the thick woollens with spring cardigans. Sleeping pills for those long hours in the air.

A tired older looking face stared back at her from the mirror, lines prominent at the corners of her mouth. Bands of dark under her eyes. Time to put Emily together again. Foundation, concealer, plenty of concealer, stretching her lips to apply lipstick. Drops to brighten her eyes. Fridge empty, rubbish outside. Done. Another hour before she needed to leave. She strode in and out of rooms, checking, rechecking.

She rolled her case down the platform to the Heathrow Express, walking with poise and confidence, in charge of herself. Emily was back. She glanced at the suits and holidaymakers in the lounge, crowding around the food, filling their glasses with free alcohol and made her way to the quieter end, looking for a cubicle. Hid her head between the partitions and rang Phillip.

'Emily.'

She steeled herself against his voice, first time she'd heard it since that night. The sound of his relief. As though it would be all right.

'I'm so glad you called, I've been so worried.'

'I'm going to Melbourne.'

'Oh? When?'

'Now. I'm at the airport.'

'Ok.' She could hear him gathering his thoughts. 'Has something happened?'

'No, no', her voice too high. 'Thought I'd visit Ashleigh.'

'Well ... err ... that sounds like a good idea, um, how long for?'

'A few weeks.'

'Oh Emily, we have to talk. You haven't answered my calls, I didn't know what to do. I so want to see you. When can we talk?'

'I can't deal with this right now. Please don't contact me.'

She ended the call and sat staring at the nicks in the white plaster wall, elbows on the desk, still holding her phone. Why did she call him? Fighting a pang of loss. It's over. It's over. Then swung around on the swivel chair, out of the cubicle, to the bar. Enough time for a gin and tonic.

Was this a good idea? She looked across the fields as they queued for take-off, too late to change her mind. Only a few months ago she was almost running to Melbourne airport to board her flight home, determined never to return. And four months later, returning in a mess. Shouldn't she have stayed, faced her problems, sorted them out? She peered through the window, only one plane in front now. Definitely going. Time with Ashleigh would help her out of this state, find her strength again. Restart life. And see Ben. His pleasure that she was coming surprised her. Maybe there was something she could do there, help him get back on his feet. It might just take a little encouragement. Do something positive for a change.

Part Three

Returning

Chapter Twenty

Three hours to go. Recent stresses ten thousand miles behind her. Emily slid her blind up half-way, allowing a sharp splinter of early morning sun. She pressed her nose against the glass looking for those magnificent swathes of purples and reds, but today a lid of flat cloud stretched out to the horizon. White thickening to grey as they neared their destination. One grey day exchanged for another.

'Emily.'

Ashleigh's smile at the barrier right in front of the door. Then curls bouncing as she ran to the end of the barriers. Phillip was the last person to meet her. Put that thought away. Ashleigh enveloped her in a tight hug,

'I am so soooo glad you came.'

Emily gulped back threatening tears. Can't make a habit of crying at airports. 'It's so wonderful to see you.' The words sounded plain, inadequate, compared to the deep release she experienced with Ashleigh's' warm welcome. Here was someone who genuinely cared for her.

'You got through fast. I thought I'd have to wait for ages.'

'I have to confess I was walking fast enough to be trotting. Beating the hordes to immigration.'

Ashleigh laughed, 'I can so imagine you doing that'.

The familiar silvery laugh, a musical laugh intensifying the warmth in her eyes. The glow in Ashleigh's face attracted others to a possibility of being part of such enjoyment.

Attracted Emily. While she worried and analysed, Ashleigh sparkled and lightened but had a depth of insight that she, Emily, struggled to reach by herself.

Her doubts about coming here disappeared. This was the best place for her right now. Trust Ashleigh to know.

'Come on, let's get out of here. Simon's sorting out the girls and I have the day off. Yay!'

'Sorry about this, peak hour.' Ashleigh dismissed the lines of cars chugging along the freeway with a wave of her hand. Usually the impatient one, today Emily sat back without irritation, London was so far away, she had nowhere she needed to be, no-one to avoid.

They were driving to East Melbourne where Ashleigh had found a flat, one block from the Fitzroy Gardens, an easy walk to the CBD. Emily had eventually refused Ashleigh's offer to stay with them. Visions of negotiating the bathroom with four others, the twins running around, never being by herself, all a bit overwhelming for someone who lived alone.

Up two flights of concrete steps to a dark red door, Ashleigh flung it open.

'Here we are, welcome home.'

Pink and white buds of early blossom greeted her as she entered, filling the floor-length window opposite. Inside, large bright red and orange poppies competed for attention on the curtains, covering the quilt cover on the bed alongside the window, and scattered across the two-seater couch, matching the orange chairs either side of the table. Emily blinked. A long way from the elegant quiet of her London flat.

'What a great little studio, Ashleigh. Thanks so much for organising it. It was lovely of you to invite me. I hope you don't mind, but you're so busy and I think I need my own space.'

'Not a problem. Looks ok doesn't it? Decoration a bit over the top perhaps', she laughed. 'Not quite your style. But it seems to have everything.' Opening and shutting cupboard doors and drawers in the narrow kitchen along the wall.

'Breakfast? I brought goodies.'

'Please. Last one was hours ago.'

Muesli, fruit, eggs, toast and take-away coffee that Ashleigh collected from a nearby café.

'Almost human again,' Emily grimaced, 'apart from needing a shower, that is'. She picked up a remaining piece of mandarin from the bowl.

'So how are you going?' Ashleigh pushed her plate aside. 'You scared me on that Skype. Not the person I know.'

'Sorry, that was an awful moment. Thank God it was you and not anyone else.'

'So?'

'Well, better than then. I'm trying. It already feels good to be away from London. I might have never left my bed.'

'That I would not believe.'

'Except for coffee', grinning, then she paused. 'I don't know that I've ever been that low before. I scared myself. You're the only one I talk to Ash.' She held her gaze for a moment.

Ashleigh smiled. 'We have plenty of time now you're here'.

'Think about it though. I spend half my life making sure I am not here and where do I come when I'm down? Sounds a bit crazy.'

Ashleigh put her hand on her arm. 'A holiday. Give

you some space. Reenergise. You can forget about all that depressing stuff, nothing here to remind you.'

'Bloody hope so. At least here I'm not sitting in my flat wondering what to do with myself, thinking about how everyone is working except me, worried that Phillip will knock on the door any minute or rehearsing what I'd say if I bump into him.'

'None of that matters here. Just enjoy yourself.'

'I want to catch up with Ben. He knows I'm here. He actually sounded excited when I rang. My father doesn't, I guess I'd better see him at some stage.'

'Only if you choose to. You and I are going to have some fun. Simon's on duty. I've scattered days off through the couple of weeks. You and I will go to films, drive somewhere, have dinner, drink too much, dance to late night music like we used to do', Ashleigh laughed. 'If I can stay awake, that is.'

'We'll be the oldest ones in the pub, looking for a seat, snoozing against the wall', Emily shook her head, grinning. 'So long since I've done that kind of thing. I feel old thinking about it.'

Later, empty case under the bed, clothes on the hangers, wash bag emptied into the bathroom drawers. Home for a while. Even with the onslaught of the poppies.

Ashleigh gone to collect the twins and prepare dinner, 'Simon will pick you up.' Rare to have others looking after her. Normally she resisted it, she could manage on her own, but now she welcomed Ashleigh's care, her hard edges softening, no need to protect herself. Time for some sun, trick her body into daytime. Rain slashed the window as she laced up her runners. Damn. She peered up through the tight blossom buds, maybe it won't last long.

Ok, call Ben.

'This number is no longer active. Please check the number and try again.'

What? Must have made a mistake. She concentrated on pressing each number. 'This number is …' He had answered only a few days ago. Sounded clear, the closest to happy she had heard for a while. She threw the phone on the couch beside her and stared out at the rain drooping the blossom. Couldn't he even pay his bills? She'd have to go there.

Emily picked up her phone again, looked in her contact list for her farher, then cancelled. Not today.

Sun replaced the rain, so she ran down the concrete steps, turning into the gardens, breathing in the damp green. Wrong time of day to run, too many strollers, children playing, but enough space for brisk walking, get her blood moving, stretch her limbs. After several circuits she leaned back on a bench seat, drawing the sun into her body, seeping through the layers of her skin, warming, slowing.

Voices close by penetrated. She opened her eyes to see a woman spreading out a picnic blanket on the damp grass, two girls in school uniform, maybe late primary age, each holding a corner. Her eyes flicked towards them, away and back again. It was an upmarket area, a Nanny? No, the one closest to her was a younger version of her mother; oval-shaped face, cream coloured skin with a sprinkle of freckles. The trio were chatting, the mother handing out biscuits from her basket, the girls on their stomachs, eating. The dark-haired one held up an exercise book showing her mother her school-work. A perfect picture for those housewife magazines, 'After School Family Activities,' or 'Quality Time with Your Children'.

Emily's stomach tightened, screwing into a hard ball. When did her mother do anything with her after school?

When did either of her parents show any interest in her schoolwork, ever ask more than, 'done your homework'? Picnics! Couldn't imagine that. Emily hated that family on the rug, wanted to shout at the girl to stop her laughing, imagined a dog eating their biscuits, baring its teeth at them. This must be a pretence, putting on a show, denying some dark secret. She looked away, arguing with herself, not fair to be angry with her mother, she had a lot to manage, she did what she could. What about me? A persistent small voice piercing her logic, her efforts to be reasonable.

She left the gardens, back to her flat, the sky lowering until a few spots of rain splattered the steps up to the door of her building. The end of that happy little picnic.

'I feel such a failure.'

Emily and Ashleigh were in the kitchen, leaning against the bench with a glass of wine, Simon putting the twins to bed. The rain was heavy now, pouring down the window behind the sink, spilling out of the gutters in a stream. Somehow, she didn't resent Ashleigh's warm, lively family. She surprised herself, dishing up pasta, pushing the girls' chairs into the table, talking to them as they spread tomato sauce over their faces, laughing up at her. Dinner with them reminded her of the days when she went home with Ashleigh after uni, joining her chaotic loud family for a meal. There was always room for someone else, lots of fierce arguments ending in laughter. No silences. One of those shock moments when she realised other families were not like hers.

'Look at all this you've got.' Emily spread her arms wide, straightening her glass as the wine lurched towards the rim. 'Me? Lost my job, lost my partner. I can't manage anything. Everything was going so well. Now this.'

Ashleigh turned to her. 'None of that was you. Stuff happens. A little too much this year, for sure. But you,' she clinked her glass against Emily's, 'you're strong, you'll be ok'.

'You always say that. The strong one! Yeah sure, me, who ran away, who ignored what was happening around her, let my father rule the roost. Procrastinated so much that I was too late to see my mother. More to the point, let her die without seeing me. Still haven't found a man, at my age, a trustworthy one anyway! And now, sacked from my job, the thing I was most proud of'. She emptied her glass.

'Stop it. You'll be fine. Just give yourself some time. In a few months you'll have forgotten all this. Now', she picked up the bottle. 'More red wine and let me find the box of truffles I hid from the twins.'

Chapter Twenty-One

Emily tried Ben's number again, hearing the same message, before heading across the gardens to the train station. Not too hard to travel to Footscray. No possibility of checking if he was home, but thought he was unlikely to be out early in the day. Past rail yards and expanses of coloured shipping containers, crossing the Maribyrnong river into streets of houses squashed against each other. Far from the spacious, manicured suburb she'd grown up in.

More familiarity this time, recognising the stretch of Vietnamese shops and restaurants leading away from the station. Alert to sharp-sour aromas coming from narrow doorways. Peering in grocery stores with boxes of vegetables piled into every space around their small frontages, lengthening back into aisles of dark crowded shelves. Surprised by tall Africans in bright-coloured clothes, graceful in their long strides, towering above other shoppers. She passed the blue-painted restaurant where she had eaten with Ben. Maybe they would go there today.

The gate was already open. Jammed on the concrete. She stopped on the path where weeds crept in from the sides, pushing through cracks. Closed blinds. Uncertainty nudged at the edges of her plan. He sounded good before she left London. But then, no phone. What if he wasn't home? How would she contact him? She realised she was assuming he was still there by himself. Were Natasha and Annie back?

Would there be nappies on the washing line? No, she was sure he would have called her fast if they'd come back. There was no sound when she pressed the doorbell, so she opened the torn fly wire screen and knocked on the door with her knuckles. Again, harder. Glanced along the veranda for any indication of human presence, the same broken couch and box of bottles, piled high. After knocking for a third time, she heard a noise inside.

'Ben', she called through the heavy wood of the old door, hoping it was him. What if he'd moved out. 'Ben, it's Emily.' Relieved to hear footsteps.

Ben's tall figure appeared in the slither of an open doorway.

'Hey, good to see you.'

'Em', Ben gave a slight smile. 'You're here. I didn't know you were coming.'

Emily took a tentative step towards him, meeting a barrier of urine, sweat and alcohol odour against a hug. She stepped back again as he opened the door wider, blinking his eyes against the northerly sun pushing its way into the house. He stood exposed in that harsh light, his unwashed face a greyish yellow, a thick vertical streak of blood congealed on his forehead. His jeans hung low, sliding down his too-thin hips. Blood spots splattered the front of his t-shirt.

Stay calm, Emily, stay calm. Fixing her smile, she brought warmth into her voice.

'I rang but your phone wasn't working.'

'Oh yeah, bastards turned it off.'

'Did you …?' she stopped herself from being the parent. 'So, are you going to let me in?'

She kept a light tone, camouflaging her shock at the sight of him. Ben didn't move.

'Come on, it's fine. I can't stay here.' Emily gave a brief laugh. 'I thought we'd have some lunch down the street.'

'Run out of money.'

'Don't worry I'll pay.'

She put one foot on the step, surreptitiously holding her breath as she stepped into the smell. Ben moved aside.

'Perhaps have a shower before we go', trying to sound relaxed. 'Do something about that cut?'

He fingered his forehead. 'Yeah, I fell over.'

She followed him down a corridor, skirting around three bulging black garbage bags. A stack of frames leant against the wall, rolls of canvases on the floor beside them.

'Is this your work?'

'Yeah, from the studio. I need to sort it out.'

'You're not there anymore?'

'Naah, had enough.'

He hesitated in front of the door that ended the hall. 'Can you wait here, I haven't cleaned up, been busy.'

'That's ok', brightly. 'I'll be fine, you shower.'

He retraced his steps and disappeared into a room they'd passed. Emily let her smile go, tense as she pushed the door into the combined kitchen-sitting area. It took a minute to adjust her eyes to the darkness, relieved only by a strip of light between curtains that didn't quite meet. The narrow band of light continued down the centre of a couch, its cushions barely visible beneath clothes, newspapers, blankets. An armchair, the only possible seat. Dark patches stained its bluish cloth. She stayed standing. Plates with the remains of food lay in front of the armchair, some lumps unrecognisable under a layer of hairy mould. Cigarette ash flowed over the edges of a china bowl into thick grey heaps on the coffee table. Empty bottles filled much of the rest of the floor-space, leaving narrow passageways of brown and yellow patterned carpet. Brown beer bottles, clear glass that once held spirits, wine flagons, some standing, others lying on their sides dripping, a few broken scattering shards of glass. She retreated from a potent smell coming from under a newspaper in a corner. Didn't want to see what that might be.

She turned her head to the tiny kitchen. Little evidence of cooking. Tins and packets littered the bench—some opened with dregs of beans or dry noodles remaining, others unopened. The rubbish bin dominated the square of lino, contents pushing the lid open. More bottles, drink cans. Used cups filled the sink. Emily fixed her feet onto an available patch of carpet, the stench filling her nostrils. Rigid. Was it only a few months ago that she was here, thinking it was a messy artist's home? Pristine compared to this. No wonder Natasha left.

She could hear the shower, like inside rain. Fragments of voices penetrated from outside, the thump of heavy boxes landing on concrete. Other lives continued.

She pulled the door hard as she escaped back into the hall. Shut tight. She stood in the centre of the narrow corridor, holding her bag, only the soles of her shoes touching any part of this place. Tried to slow her breathing. Waiting to leave. Could she wait on the porch?

Relieved when Ben reappeared. Glanced up, knowing she was checking. Wet hair, face still an odd colour but at least washed, a shadow of a bruise remaining, blood reduced to a thin cut. Cleaner clothes, presentable enough. A belt gathered his jeans above angular hips that jutted through the material, his stomach shrunken, ribs visible under his t-shirt. He had always been long and lean, the artist with his inky hair hanging around an angular pale face, but this was not the man-of-mystery image he had previously cultivated.

'Let's go, come on', walking past him. 'You could do with a feed.'

Ben looked down at himself. 'Yeah, lost a bit of weight.'

Emily increased speed as she neared the front door. Light and air. Not stopping until she reached the gate. Her back to the house, she breathed in several deep gulps, expelling the odours out of her nose and lungs, clearing the shock out of her system.

'I think we sat at this table last time. Is it yours?' Relieved to be in the bright clean restaurant.

Ben laughed, awake with hot shower, fresh air and sunlight. 'I wish. I don't have the money to eat out.'

'Let's stick with tea, hey.'

No response, but he turned the drinks page over to a lengthy list of food items. Emily poured from the thermos already on the table into the small cups that arrived with the plastic covered menu. Lunchtime was as busy as dinner, tables filled, fed, emptied, refilled. Young Vietnamese were back and forth from the kitchen that was behind a curtain, carrying platters and large bowls of soup. Emily welcomed the pungent smells filling her nostrils, pushing out the sick feeling in her stomach, returning her appetite. They ordered spring rolls, noodles, lemongrass chicken.

'So how come you're here?'

Ben sipped tea, both hands clasped around the cup, covering the blue Chinese writing. Dark eyes above the rim.

'Well. Ashleigh invited me, a holiday to catch up, I wasn't here long enough when I came before.'

'Don't you work all the time?'

'Just taking a break.' No, she was not like him. 'Anyway, how's Annie going?'

A smile brought colour to his face. 'My baby girl, she's so gorgeous. She knows who I am, she smiles at me.'

'Do you see her much?'

'Of course, I'm her dad.'

'Perhaps I could come too when you go next?'

'Mmm, when I'm better.'

Platters of chicken and spring rolls arrived with a bowl of noodles. Ben piled chicken onto his plate, topping it with lettuce, mint and bean sprouts.

'This looks good. I think I missed dinner last night.'

Emily dipped a spring roll into a saucer of thick reddish sauce.

'So how about you and Natasha?'

'Yeah, yeah, they'll come home soon. When I'm well. She's just at her sister's for a little while.' Ben kept his eyes on his food.

'The place is a bit of a mess.'

'Yeah, yeah, gonna start tomorrow, then they'll come home.'

Was that ever going to happen? Emily edged closer. 'You've been saying that for a while.'

'I'm sick! I can't clear up while I'm sick.' He jabbed his chopsticks into the plate.

'Ben', she hesitated. He looked up at her. She had to say something. 'Ben it's the drinking. If you don't stop, you might lose them.'

'Yeah. I'm stopping. I am. I'll be better soon. It's been a hard few months. With Mum going and everything.'

Emily wanted to shout at him, "Can't you see what you're doing," but she made her voice gentle. 'I know.'

Ben shrank down in his chair, looking into his half-eaten bowl, tapping his chopsticks on its side.

'You've had a tough time, it can be hard to get well by yourself.' Careful not to criticise.

'What do you mean? I'll be ok.'

Take it easy Emily told herself, don't scare him off. 'There are places you can go, stay for a while, they help you to recover, faster.'

'What places?'

She smiled. 'You know, rehab, they can help.'

'Not going there! A mate went. Nearly killed him. He left. Escaped from the Nazis in there.'

'I could find a good one. It'd be free accommodation.'

'No. I'll be fine. A few more days.'

'Well, how about I investigate, just to see? I can pay.'

Ben jumped up and bolted out the back of the restaurant. Emily sighed and finished the rest of the chicken. She had started on the untouched noodles when he returned.

'Sorry', sitting down, paler. 'A bit sick. Ate too fast. I'll just have tea.'

He pushed away his plate and sat sipping.

'Are you painting?'

'Yep, I'll get back to it. Got a bit busy after Annie came.'

'Have you anything you can sell to tide you over?'. Thinking of the stack in the hall.

'Might be something. Gotta find another gallery.' She raised her eyebrows. 'The owner had a go at me, he was ripping me off.' Mumbling. 'When I'm better I'll look.'

Ben's energy seemed to have gone. He slumped in his chair, lifting his head to nod occasionally as Emily tried to chat.

'I'm tired, I need to go home', he said after a while.

'Can you lend me some money? Just until the next payment comes.'

'I'll come with you to buy food if you like?' Not going to fall into that trap.

She got up and paid at the counter. Luckily she'd brought cash, the only option here. Ben was already outside, she could see his back against the glass, a cigarette lit. Emily joined him on the pavement, making space for people continuing to enter and leave the restaurant.

'Ok, where will we go? Is that a market over there?'

Ben held his cigarette away from her. 'I'll do it. Just give me fifty. You'll get it back.'

'It's ok. I don't mind.'

'I've got food. Run out of beer.'

'Ben, you know that's not a good idea.'

'I need a drink. Just one drink, come on Em. Please', looking somewhere in her direction, near her but not at her.

'Come on. The market's just across the street. We could buy a few things there.'

'Bye bye then. You go home. Go on. Go home.'

'Ben.'

She watched him trudge down the street, almost a stumble. He looked like an old man, hunched over. What was he doing? She stood on her toes. Who was he talking to? People were shaking their heads and moving past. She realised he was begging. Her brother. She took a few steps in his direction, stopped, stretching her neck to keep watch until she couldn't see him anymore.

Emily was finding it harder to breathe as she neared the train station, she made herself focus to find the right platform, her breath coming in short sharp jabs against her chest. Was this what a panic attack felt like? Somehow, she got herself into the carriage and onto a seat, concentrating hard to slow her breath. Her head rattled with the train as it headed towards the city. Images of Ben when he opened his front door, begging on the streets, the rubbish tip he was living in, exploding in her brain.

Chapter Twenty-Two

Emily's fingers found the snooze button to stop her "go for a run" alarm beeping and fell into a heavy doze. An hour later, eyes open with a start, she pushed the bed- clothes aside before her eyelids closed again. How long was it going to take before she was in the time zone? Not too late to run. Soon she was jogging to the gardens, warming her muscles, ready to increase speed and heart rate. She hesitated at the edge of the park, the paths busy with office workers. Some striding along, laptop bags swinging, things to do. Others making the most of their last moments before surrendering to air-conditioning and work demands. She knew which one she would be.

Despite having to dodge the commuters, Emily was soon jogging in an easy rhythm. Thinking. If only she had paid more attention in those irritating phone calls, asked more, listened to those cries for help beneath Ben's complaining, supported him. She realised her regular messages of 'just get a job' were way off the mark. He could hardly get out of bed. How did this happen? She understood he was struggling with their mum's death, but how did he lose himself to this extent? After yesterday, she could see there was little chance of him being able to pull himself out of this hole. She had thought Natasha would keep him stable but managing a new baby would demand all her energy. She suspected that relationship was over. Ben needed professional help, she had the funds, the problem was getting him to agree. How to help him see he was destroying himself and to believe a change was possible.

'Look where you're going', a man in a suit shouted, rubbing his navy clad arm. 'Sorry', she called as he stomped past. It wouldn't have hurt that much. What was he like to work with?

She stepped off the path to stretch her hamstrings, surprised to feel sun warming her skin, early spring flowers close by. Her head had been too full to notice. A slow jog across the grass, allowing herself to enjoy the emerging day. Give Ben some time. He might feel too pressured if she tried again so soon. She needed him to listen. And, if she was honest, she couldn't face that house for a second day.

After breakfast she turned her mind to her father. Better call.

'You're here?'

'Yes. Just a quick visit.'

'Didn't think we'd see you. Come for a cup of tea?'

'Err, ok', taken by surprise. She hadn't thought beyond the need to ring him.

'Today then?'

Not much in his day, well her day was empty too, her only plan was theatre with Ashleigh tonight. Might as well, then she wouldn't have to think about it again.

How many times had she walked this route home from the station. In university years, often at night, after a work shift at the café or listening to bands in Fitzroy pubs with friends, racing to catch the last train. Cars chugged in long lines beside her, previously a residential street, now used as a major arterial. People around here seemed to use their cars to go anywhere. She had no need for a car in London. The traffic noise dimmed as she turned into their street. As a student she remembered being nervous in the quiet dark, houses asleep, trying to hurry without running, alert for sounds behind her, holding keys in her hand at the ready. Today in daylight, walking past people weeding their gardens, sweeping their paths, she was nervous about what was ahead, not behind.

On the cold doorstep, out of the sun, she steeled herself as his footsteps came closer towards the door.

'Back again. Come in then.'

She followed him down the hall, trying to quell the familiar rising agitation. Just a visitor. Just a cup of tea. There were already two cups on the bench, a tea bag in each, the kettle close to boiling. They sat at the table. The room looked unchanged from her last visit.

'How are you Dad?'

'I'm all right', looking at her from under those bushy eyebrows.

'What do you do with yourself?'

'Usual things.' What were they?

'How's the job?' Had he ever asked before?

'It's fine, thanks.' No-one here needed to know.

She glanced around. Her mother's books in the bookcase, her ornaments on the windowsill, her DVDs piled up on the floor beside the television. Her studio door was closed.

'How did you go with mum's things?'

'The front room's empty. Christopher came and took what he wanted.'

'How about her clothes?'

'Not yet.' He looked down at his tea, turned the cup around.

Feeling guilty for running home to London so soon after the funeral, she offered,

'Would you like me to sort them out? I'm here. I could do it now?'

'All right then. You might as well. You know where to go. Garbage bags in the laundry. Keep anything you want.'

His bedroom was easier to be in this time, the curtains already open, the bed made. She wrinkled her nose at the old-person smell that pervaded, but this was easy compared to yesterday. She turned her back to the bed and opened the wardrobe. Her mother's clothes, bags, shoes. Doubted he had touched these doors. A dress covered with yellow and orange spring flowers caught her eye. She imagined her mum in it, with matching heels. This was the dress her mother would have chosen to wear in the coffin rather than the plain navy she ended up in, a funeral dress, the dress of a doctor's wife. She took a breath, don't think Emily. Do. Just a task, empty the wardrobe into the bags. Fast. Dresses, blouses, skirts off hangers, pull jumpers and cardigans out of shelves and into bags. Until the final hanger holding a tan and blue blouse. Emily touched the sleeve, remembering a couple of days before she left, rolling jeans and t-shirts into her new backpack when her mother came upstairs.

'See what I bought today', unwrapping the tissue. 'Lovely colours, so vibrant, a little pick-me-up to get through Friday.'

The first time she wore it was the last time Emily saw her alive. She pressed her cheek against the thinned silk, the faded colours. Her mother had kept it long past its use-by date. Had she looked at it sometimes with the same memory of its first wear? Snapping back to task, she folded the blouse, pressed it on top of a jam-packed bag and turned her attention to shoes, handbags, underwear. Cupboards and drawers emptied of their style and colour. Emily stared into the hollow space, no longer her mum's, before closing the wardrobe doors. No-one in their family was likely to open them again. She turned away and sighed at the bags crowding the floor space. She couldn't leave them there.

'I've finished, can I borrow your car to take it all to the op-shop?'

He was back in his usual chair, hunched over, head protruding forward as he watched the television. Did he look older than a few months ago, or hadn't she noticed?

'Keys in the hall', keeping his eyes on the screen.

No offers of help so she picked up a bag, keys in the other hand. She had arrived with the weather changing from its sunny start to increasing grey. Now she opened the front door to rain. She peered out from under the porch, not too heavy, she didn't want to wait around. She began piling bags into the car. No longer just a shower. She stuffed them in the boot, in the back seat, in the passenger seat, blocking the side windows, running between car and house, getting the job done. Rain streaked down her face like silent crying.

She sat for a moment in the car with the heater on, her face drying to damp. Remembered a large charity shop in Camberwell and backed out of the driveway. Always busy in Bourke road, the parking spaces near the shop taken. She gripped the steering wheel tighter, what the fuck am I going to do with all this? She circled the block, finding a car-park stretching behind the endless line of shops, a vacant space next to an overflowing charity bin. Tempted to throw the contents of her car on top of the wet bags already spilling around the bin, but the clothes were too good. Her mother's. She would not leave parts of her mother in a supermarket car park.

She ran through the rain to the charity shop's back door. Assistants fluffed around looking for a trolley, finding an umbrella, worrying about the rain. Everything seemed difficult. Can you come another time? She fixed a smile, not going away until this was done. She wanted to shout, can't you be helpful!! This is my mother. A smaller inside voice begging it to be over. Reminded herself, these are volunteers. A man older than her mother by at least a decade appeared with a trolley and a surprising smile. The rain over for now, her frustration gradually eased as they worked in rhythm together, filling the trolley, guiding it to the shop, emptying, returning, refilling, small talk. He shook her hand after the last trip, 'take care my dear.'

She sat with the engine running. Moments ago, her mother's things surrounded her. An unexpected sense of loss washed over her, feeling alone in the car's emptiness. Recurring goodbyes. Images of crying beside the open coffin, frozen at the funeral as she heard the coffin slide away behind the curtains. The strangeness of grief for someone who she hadn't seen for most of her adult life.

'Are you going or what?' Suddenly aware of a car in front, horn beeping, a man's head out of the window, shouting.

'Sorry.' She let the handbrake off and drove out, avoiding eye contact.

No thanks when she returned, as expected. Looked like her father hadn't moved, but then surprised her by standing and offering lunch.

'There's soup, bread, cheese.'

She hesitated, then accepted, it wouldn't take long. Canned tomato soup appeared on the table, steaming in their bowls, bag of bread between them.

'You like it in England?'

Another question. 'Yes, I do.'

'You know I grew up there. Probably different now.'

'In Kent, wasn't it?'

'Yes, near the Chatham dockyards. You been there?'

'No'. It had never occurred to her.

'It was tough back then. We didn't have much. I always worked, newspaper rounds, odd jobs at the dockyards that father got me, anything to bring some money in. Mum was sick a lot, she had to stop work, so it was up to Dad and me.'

'What about your brother?'

'Hmmph, if Dad forced him.'

Emily nodded, sipping soup. He'd learnt responsibility at a young age.

'I knew the meaning of work, not like your brother.' She stiffened, then released as he continued. 'Up early before school, again after school. Home jobs as well. Mum often in bed. Nothing came easy. My father was a hard man.'

'What was wrong with your mum?'

He shrugged. 'I never knew. I think about it sometimes now with my training, but I was young, she died before we migrated to Australia.'

Both his mother and wife dying too early. Emily had heard little about his parents, she hadn't met his father, maybe father and son fell out. She recalled Susan's description of an alcoholic.

'That sounds hard.'

'The way it was, you don't know how lucky you are,'

She never thought of herself as lucky but compared with her dad's experience; good school, uni, she didn't have to work while she was at school, had the things she needed. He wouldn't have had breathing space to think about whether he was happy. She wondered how he felt when his mother died. Suspected he bottled it up, kept going.

'So how did you become a doctor?'

He sat up straighter and looked at her over his glasses.

'Same. Studied hard, worked hard. Worked nights and weekends to support myself through Uni. My father had a better job here after we migrated, there was enough for the basics until I finished school, then I was on my own.' He swallowed the last of his soup.

'Sounds like quite an effort.' Impressive, she had to admit. Remembered the framed certificates prominent on his study walls, monogrammed pens displayed on his desk.

'It was what you did. To make anything of myself, not end up like my father. I wanted you both to have a better chance than that. You kids have no idea. Private schools, university. Much good that did Ben! All on a plate for him', he snorted. 'Some things don't change.' He tapped the side of his hand on the table, firmer with each word. 'You have to work to find your way in life, take responsibility for yourself.' He relaxed his hand, leant back. 'At least you understood that, your career, got some money behind you. Didn't rely on me.'

Close to a compliment. For a job she had lost. Would not let him see that failure. No chink of weakness in front of him, she would never ask him for help.

'You look like her you know.'

'Who? Mum?' startled.

He nodded. 'When she was young. You've got her eyes.' He glanced across the table at her and then away, cleared his throat. 'All done?'

Emily washed the dishes in the sink, didn't look like he was using the dishwasher. Her mum would have done this a thousand times. What was life like here after her and Ben left? They only had a few months together before she was born, not enough time to learn to live together. Perhaps things became calmer, a little happier? She hoped her mother's last years were better than Emily's memories. And now a house for one with too many rooms, empty wardrobes in the bedroom. She noticed the sound of the television had returned, realising her father had turned it off for lunch. Time to go. She dried her hands on the tea towel and picked up her bag.

'You going?' Shifted his gaze from the television.

'Yes, thanks for lunch.'

'All right then. Are you coming again?' Was there a flicker of "please come?"

'Ok. I'll call you?'

'Very good then.'

She strolled to the train station. It was the first time in her forty-odd years she could remember him talking about his past. A conversation with her.

Her phone rang halfway up the steps to her flat. Ben's number on the screen surprised her, she'd been expecting Ashleigh.

'Ben?'

'Hi Em.'

'You've got your phone back?' she sat on the top step.

'Yeah, Centrelink came through.' He sounded brighter, coherent. 'Yep, cleaning myself up. Bought food at the market this morning.'

'Hey that's great Ben.' She could hear her older sister voice.

'You coming over?'

'How about tomorrow? I'm catching up with Ashleigh tonight.'

'Yes, yes, tomorrow.'

'What about lunch again at your Vietnamese? I could meet you there?' No need to go to the house.

The call finished, she stayed for a moment in the afternoon sun. Perhaps he had listened to her?

Chapter Twenty-Three

Emily sat by the window drinking tea, their usual table taken, watching a continuous stream of people with diverse nationalities walk past. Then Ben. Stubbed a cigarette under his foot on the path before pushing the door. Clean clothes, hair shower-damp. She had to stop this constant checking. A smoky smell as he hugged her.

'Looking better today, Ben', noticing the greyness of his skin, his once bright eyes far back in his face.

'Yep. Had breakfast. No drinks. Pulling myself together.'

Emily smiled. 'So good to hear.' Could her visit have motivated him so quickly? Embarrassed that his sister saw him in that terrible state? Made him realise what he was doing? She desperately wanted to believe it.

The waiter arrived at their table. Rice paper rolls, spicy vegetables, not too much this time.

'I went to Dad's yesterday.'

Ben's snort sounded like her father's. 'Bet that was fun.'

'I guess you haven't seen him?'

Ben raised his eyebrows.

'We had a chat.'

'That's a change.'

'I think he's lonely.'

'I don't give a stuff. No-one wants to be with that bastard. No sympathy from me.'

Ben was working his way through the food this time. They might need to order more.

'Mmm. He invited me for lunch, talked about his past. You know he had a tough life early on.'

Ben shrugged.

'Hey, I was wondering what it was like for Mum when it was just them, before she got sick I mean. Less for him to be angry about without us there.' Meaning Ben.

'Hard to say. You know Mum, she never let on, always tried to make everything sound wonderful. I didn't go there much, I'd meet her for lunch or something. You could tell, though. She was still trying to please him, keep him happy, stop him getting angry.'

He gave an abrupt laugh, not a humorous one. 'Do you remember that time when I got a bike?'

She nodded. Yes, the sight of Ben riding around the front garden on a brand-new shiny bike when she came home from school. It wasn't his birthday. They never bought her one.

'Dad had come home at lunchtime and left it for me. "See", she said, over and over, beaming, "your dad loves you, look what he bought you." I was so excited that I finally had a bike, like the other kids. I wanted to believe her, hoped and hoped that he did love me and it was all just a horrible mistake and things would change. Stupid me. I ran up to Dad when he came home to say thank you, he just said something like, "make sure you look after it or it goes back to the shop." He bought it the day after one of those awful tirades, I don't think you were there, he got a bit out of control with that belt. Kinda like a sorry, but things didn't change. The bike became yet another thing for him to get stuck into me about, if I left it in the driveway or didn't oil the chain or pump up the tires. For months Mum kept telling me how he loved me, trying to sound believable, saying it was just his way. "He bought you a bike, remember." She so wanted to make it right.'

'Perhaps it was a split second of "sorry." His family were too poor for him to have a bike. I mostly remember being annoyed that you got one, and I didn't.' No reward for the hard-working dutiful girl.

'I told you about those pills I found, didn't I?'

'Yeah.'

'Certain they were Mum's. Piles of them hidden behind jars in the pantry, in her bedroom drawers, pain killers, tension relievers, anxiety, stress. I guess some of them helped with the cancer, but I wonder how long she'd been taking them.'

'Poor Mum. Doesn't surprise me though. The thing is,' he swallowed and frowned, 'the thing is, I know, that most of the shit she copped from him was because of me. What if I wasn't there or if I was the shiny hard-working Doctor like he wanted me to be? Reckon life would have been better for her. That's my demon'.

He fumbled in his pockets until he found a cigarette, put it on the table, picked it up, rolled it around in his fingers.

'Ben, you can't think like that. She loved you, she was proud of you. You can't blame yourself for what Dad did, he was who he was, you were not responsible for him.' Remembered Susan's strong words.

'Well I fucking do. I should have done something, protected her. He'd shout at me then her, I was too scared, hid behind her, she always looked after me. Who looked after her? Why didn't I stand up to him?' He pushed his chair back. 'Gotta piss.'

Emily was upstairs in her room, sitting at her

desk, radio on, loud enough to drown out the words downstairs, quiet enough to keep alert. Raised voices that continued after Ben burst out of the back-room, ran up the stairs and slammed his bedroom door. Her father's voice loud, her mother's faint. Her mother crying. Was this one occasion she was remembering or some kind of mix of many? She remembered the feel of her heart rate getting faster, turning up the music. Her mother's red face later, concentrating hard on the dishes after her father had stormed out of the house.

'I need to smoke that', Ben's voice broke in. 'Let's go.' He lit the cigarette before he'd reached the door.

Emily left too much money on the table and followed him. 'Do you want to walk for a bit? Can we go down to the river from here?'

They walked in silence past new expensive looking apartments on the banks of the Maribyrnong. Ben drawing hard on his cigarette. Hope they have double glazing, Emily thought, the drone of trucks on nearby roads contrasting the peaceful river scene that fronted the real estate brochures. They jumped out of the way of a rowing coach riding towards them, wobbling on his bike, shouting through a megaphone to the scull crew on the water. The traffic faded into a background hum as they followed the path into a parkland of regrown young gums, red bottle brush emerging.

'I'm going to see Annie tomorrow.'

'You'll love that. Could I come too?' She really ought to at least see her new niece, take a present. Natasha might help her understand what was going on with Ben.

'Maybe. Gotta call 'Tash first. She doesn't like me just turning up.'

She quelled her frustration, another of Ben's vague intentions.

'You could see Annie more often if you stay clean.'

'Yeah, and they'll come home.'

'Ben …', hesitating.

'What?'

She chose her words, how to keep him hopeful enough to act, but realistic. 'I'm sure they will come back. It's just, it might take a while.'

She stepped behind him to swap sides, avoiding the smoke of his second cigarette blowing towards the river.

'Actually, Em I have a little problem.' Always something.

'What's that?'

'The landlord came around. He's kicking me out.'

'When?'

'Soon.'

'They can't evict you immediately, can they? Don't they have to give you notice?'

'He said he'd sent letters, I didn't get them.'

Emily remembered a mess of unopened mail flattened against the wall behind the door.

'So, what will you do? Do you have somewhere else to go?'

'A mate's got a bungalow. I might stay there for a while.'

'What about that idea of rehab?' she laughed. 'Free accommodation.'

'Don't need it.'

One day and he's over it. Today was an improvement, but she had no confidence it would last. The best she could hope for was that this respite would give him a chance to think, listen to her.

'They'd feed you', she smiled, trying to keep the push out of her voice.

'I'd go crazy. Those places are like prisons. And what about my baby girl?'

'Not for long, just to help you over the hump. Easier when you've got support. It's an idea. Another option. You'll have to do something about the house though, or they'll charge you.' Please don't ask me to help, recoiling from the memory of that fetid chaos.

'Yeah yeah, course.'

Ben went home, tired of the walk or the conversation. Emily on the train. As they crossed the bridge over the river she looked down to the path they'd walked on. Please God help him. Bring back my brother. Can you pray if you've never gone to church, not even sure if God is there? Annie could be the incentive he needed. Natasha would be clear about him needing to be in a good state to visit. He seemed reluctant for her to go with him. What was that about?

She thought over their restaurant conversation. How could she explain to anyone else why they were so scared of their father? There were no black eyes, no-one knocked unconscious, no emergency phone calls. But they knew, all of them. Knew to be on high alert whenever he was there. Just as bad as when they were expecting him, running around, making sure there was nothing that might annoy him. It was like there was this heavy weight bearing down on them making it hard to move, hard to breathe. It lightened momentarily when Emily was out, returning as she neared home, fear increasing as she opened the front door. A fear they shared. Of what?

Chapter Twenty-Four

Last time her dad rang, her mother was dying.

'Your brother's here.' His voice was flat, matter of fact, a barrier to contain his emotion.

'What? When?'

'This morning. He's upstairs. You coming?' A little breathless, unusual for him. Was he anxious? Angry? He wasn't giving anything away. 'Can you come?'

'Is later ok?'

'Dinner then.' Not a question.

'What's going on?' Ashleigh dipped a piece of crusty bread into her minestrone. A quick lunch on the footpath in Lygon Street, before a movie.

'Ben. He's turned up at Dad's.'

'You mean, just to visit?'

'Unlikely. He must be desperate to go there. I thought things were improving with Ben. Oh God, those two together. This is not good at all.'

'Do you need to head over there now?'

'No, no. They're adults. Let's see the film, I'll go after.'

Adults, if only, Emily thought as they walked across the road to the cinema. My bloody family. Why do I have to sort it out? Is this what her mother used to do? Well, she'd be back in London soon. Then it's up to them.

Afternoon peak hour. Emily held onto the hand strap, pressed in either side, as the tram lurched down to Flinders

Street, more people pushing in at every stop. What the hell is he doing? She hadn't heard from him for a few days, a positive sign she had thought. Hoped he had seen Annie, stayed off the drink. The train station platform reminded her of London. She stepped back from the crowds squeezing into the carriages, wait for the next one rather than flatten herself against the door. She stood on the yellow line, commuters crowding around her, no polite queues in Melbourne. Annoyed she was even here.

What did her father expect her to do? She knew she'd agreed to call, been putting it off. The thought had lain heavy on her, as she inched forward to a conversation about the way he had treated them all. A speech. Trying out words in her head. Could she do it? Over and over in her mind. It had occurred to her it was unlikely that anyone ever had. Her mum and Ben wouldn't have. There was Alice, but she had talked to her, not her father. If she didn't he would live the rest of his life never having to face it. It was just wrong. She couldn't let him get away with it.

The talk around Ashleigh's dinner table two nights ago was Julia Gillard's misogyny speech. Simon had found it on You Tube for her. The first female prime minister berating the opposition leader for his months of misogynistic comments. She had ignored it, sidestepped the fight, determinedly doing her job, and then she cracked. Had enough. It was wonderful to see her berate him with such strength and power, and even better it went viral with women everywhere cheering her on. And men, Simon reminded them.

None of them had challenged her father, each finding their own ways of managing, escaping, hiding, creeping around him, placating, trying not to cause an outburst. It was time to find her courage. When she lived there she was too young, too scared, just shut her eyes and ran away. Too late to change anything, but she had to speak. Before she returned home. What could he do to her?

She navigated her way between the other passengers to step onto the Camberwell platform, looked for a moment across the tracks at the city-bound train, then turned to walk up the hill.

Her father's heavy tread came up the hall seconds after she pressed the doorbell.

'Come in.'

She glanced up the stairs as she followed him to the kitchen. He thrust a wrinkled brochure into her hands,

'Here you are. We'll have Chinese, whatever you want. The number's at the bottom. They deliver.' Noticed he seemed agitated. She wondered what their conversation had been.

She peered at the faded marks on the menu, checking what he liked, ticks against sweet and sour chicken, black bean beef, oriental vegetables, steamed rice.

'For Ben too? Is he still here?'

Her father had gone back to the television and his bottle of beer, an empty on the coffee table. He shrugged,

'Upstairs.'

She ordered, most likely too much, but they might need leftovers if Ben was staying. She'd better go up. His door was closed.

'Ben?'

She took the sound inside for permission to open the door, put her hand in front of her nose against the smoke filling the room.

'Em. You're here.'

He was lounging on his bed, leaning back against the

pillows, an ashtray balanced on the mattress. A bottle on the bedside table without its cap, some kind of spirits, two beer bottles on the floor. She coughed and waved the smoke away.

'More to the point, what are you doing here? Not a social visit, I assume', pointing to the bags beside the bed. He turned away from the hard edge in her voice,

'A couple of days', he mumbled. 'The landlord's after me.'

'After you. What do you mean?'

'Rent. Not much. He's kicked me out. He can wait.'

'For heaven's sake, Ben!'

She walked over to the window, banged it several times to open it wide and turned back to him.

'Here! What are you doing here! Is this ok with Dad?'

'It's my room, he doesn't use it.' Belligerent.

'What about the mate with the bungalow?'

'Couldn't get onto him.'

More likely wouldn't have him.

'Ben. You can't keep going like this.' She picked up the spirits bottle. 'And what happened to staying off the drink?'

He looked up at her. 'Hey that's mine. Just having one or two.'

She moved closer to the window, breathed in the fresh air, dispersing the smoke. She tried to sound more supportive. Getting annoyed at him wouldn't solve anything.

'Look Ben, you know it won't work, you with Dad, here. No good for either of you. Let's try to think of an alternative. Come and eat, I've ordered Chinese. We can talk after. Ok?'

Ben nodded, stretched out his hand. 'My bottle.'

She screwed the cap on and put it on the desk. 'How about we leave it here.'

Ben followed her down the stairs, holding onto the bannister, staying behind her as they entered the back room.

He stood by the door, leaning against the wall, his eyes half closed.

'Money's on the bench.' Her father stayed fixed on the television as he spoke, not even a slight acknowledgment of Ben. He'd handed the problem to her. China and cutlery clinked as Emily set three places, adding to the voice of the ABC newsreader. Noticed a third bottle on the coffee table.

The doorbell. Dinner might help. A sweet meaty smell rose out of the plastic containers as she removed the lids.

'Food's here.'

Emily chewed the bland beef in its thick dark sauce that passed for black bean, wondering what to do. The other two eating as if it was the first meal of the day. The only voices a blurry background of the news. When his plate was clear her father lifted his head.

'What are you doing here Ben?'

'Yeah, just a couple of nights, upstairs, you won't see me.' Eyes down on his food.

'Have you been kicked out?' Ben ate another mouthful.

'I said, have you been kicked out?' Louder this time.

Emily tightened inside, watched the colour rise in her father's face.

'No, yeah.'

'Which is it?'

'Just need to stay one or two nights until I sort things out.'

Emily tossed around in her head whether she should offer for him to stay with her in the flat, but there was no spare room. Unlikely to only be a day or two, she'd be stuck with him. Smoky drunk Ben lying on the couch across from her bed.

'He won't be here long Dad. We'll work something out.'

She had to find an alternative, fast. Somehow.

'Hmmmphh.'

Ben took his plate to the kitchen bench. 'I'm going upstairs.'

'Stop right there!' Her father leant back in his seat, chin up. Ben halted, shifting his feet, glancing at the door.

'I know why you're here. Nothing changes with you.' He drank from his glass, keeping his eyes on Ben. 'They've kicked you out. You have nowhere to live. Looks like your girlfriend won't have you and so you crawl back here.'

Oh no, here we go, aggression filled the room.

'Dad, maybe another time', Emily murmured. Pathetic, she thought.

'Keep out of this.' He stood up, moving past her towards Ben. 'You're supposed to be a father. You don't have a job. And now you don't have a place to live. How can you support your child? What the bloody hell are you doing!'

'Dad, Dad, just stop. This isn't the way.' Stronger this time.

He looked at her in surprise. She took a deep breath. Ready or not this was the moment. Find that courage Emily.

She tried to keep her voice calm, like they had taught her in conflict resolution training. 'What I mean is, this is what you've been doing all our lives. This house, this family has been full of tension, aggression, anger, you at Ben, and even at Mum.'

She felt her insides shaking, but she'd started now. She stood to strengthen herself, not have him intimidate her by looking down at her, his face dark, eyes piercing.

'Yeah Dad.'

'Let me finish.' She wished Ben wasn't here.

'What good has all that shouting done? Why did you need to control us? Did you notice or even care what it was like for us? You terrorised Ben, right from when he was small, made him feel worthless, how do you think that helped him? When did you recognise anything he'd done? Even once? You just kept telling him he wasn't good enough.'

'Yeah, you bastard.'

'Ben!' She should have thought more carefully about saying all this with Ben here. The moment seemed to be there. If she had a fleeting thought, it was that Ben might feel supported, and calm down. Instead, he was getting more excited, like this was encouragement for him to join in. Gone too far to stop now. She couldn't imagine being able to do this again.

'And it wasn't just Ben. Do you know how unhappy Mum was? Always anxious to meet your expectations, trying to protect Ben from you, never able to have the life she wanted. Because of you.'

'Don't bring your mother into this. None of your business', he growled. 'Actually, none of this is anything to do with you. You know nothing. Running off to London, never coming back. What do you think that did to your mum? How happy did that make her huh?' He lifted his head, jaw out, challenging.

Ok. Hit me where it hurts. He's good at that. Don't let it stop you, Emily. Think Julia Gillard.

'Don't forget I grew up here, twenty years. Long enough to see the damage you did, to live it. Somehow, I escaped your anger, but it was a terrible twenty years. Why do you think I left?' Her voice was going higher, losing its reasonable tone. 'We were always terrified of you, never knew when you would explode. Mum was afraid of you; couldn't you see that? What if you'd supported Ben, encouraged him instead of demeaning him at every opportunity. It never stopped!'

'That's enough! What do you know about parenting, about marriage? Two things you've avoided. How dare you lecture me.'

She took a step back, experiencing his anger directed at her for the first time. He turned to Ben.

'And you. You come running here when you can't manage your life. Nothing to do with me, Ben, your life and what a mess you've made of it. Is it my fault that you have no job, nowhere to live, lost your girlfriend and your child? My fault, is it?'

'It's none of your fucking business what I do. I'll be out of here real soon. You think I want to be here, with you? You've been a bastard to Mum and me my whole life. Just leave me alone.'

Emily looked up at their reddening, tightly screwed faces as they stood facing each other.

'Come on stop this.' She could hear her voice weaker now. No more speeches from her.

'The honest truth is that your mother was no help to you.' Her father ignored her, moved closer to Ben, jabbing his finger in the air in front of his face. 'I gave you every opportunity to make something of yourself. Wasted my money in school fees. Tried to make you see sense. But no, you knew better. Your mother was stupid enough to support you. Look what good that did you.'

'Fuck you!!' Ben stood tall over his father. 'Don't you talk about Mum like that. She was the only one who cared about me. You never gave a fuck about her or me. That fucking awful school. You only sent me there so you could show off to your rich mates.'

Emily wanted to melt into the wall, disappear, be

anywhere but here. No hope of stopping this. Both buoyed with alcohol.

'I can't believe a son of mine would turn out like you. A complete failure. What have you done? An alcoholic wreck with nothing to be proud of. Your mother would be ashamed of you! Ashamed!'

Head tilted up, bulging eyes boring into Ben. Older, frailer, but still the father of their childhood.

'Face the truth for once in your life. She ran around after you for years. God knows I told her not to. I knew it would make you soft but she didn't listen, and this is the way you repay her. Christ I'm glad she isn't here to see the mess you're in', his whole face a sneer.

'Don't talk about Mum. You bastard, you made her life a misery, you're a bully! A fucking bully!'

Emily saw Ben's rage overtaking him, billowing, propelling him towards his father. No Ben. Stop. Don't, please don't. She pleaded inside her head.

'And look at you! Useless! A failure! A waste of space!'

Ben shouted, 'Stop it! Stop it! Just shut the fuck up!!'

For once he was powerful. For once he wasn't running away. He gripped his father's shoulders, shaking them back and forth, harder, harder. His father tried to manoeuvre out, duck under Ben's arms, scared now, but Ben hung on, his hands glued.

Emily jumped up. 'Ben. Ben. Stop it. No!' she dragged at his shirt. Adrenalin powering through him, he didn't notice.

'Why don't you die, you old bastard. I wish it was you that died instead of Mum.'

His father's scarlet face faded to white, awash with sweat, he gasped for breath, a choking sound coming out of his mouth. He clasped the left side of his chest and Emily watched in horror as he staggered and fell out of Ben's grip, crashing on the floor. Then nothing. He didn't move, didn't speak. Blood began to drip out of his head where he had knocked into a corner of the table.

'Ben.'

Emily stood frozen. A thick fog of silence descended around her, television chatter somewhere far away. Ben took a step back, eyes large. They looked down at their father, landed on his hip, torso twisted forward, face crushed onto the floor, one leg buckled up, blood drops forming on the carpet.

'Ambulance.' Emily moved into action, 000, how did she remember that?

'Yes, he's breathing. Ok don't move him, don't move him. Aspirin. I'll look, please be quick.'

'Mum's pills.' She ran to the pantry, relieved to see the piles of boxes still at the back of the shelves. Pulled them out, discarding to the floor as she searched. 'Not aspirin, not aspirin, we have to find the aspirin. No aspirin here. What'll we do? How can we give him anything, anyway? Can't see his face, he's unconscious. God, come on ambulance.'

Ben was leaning on the bench, moaning. 'He's dead, I killed him, I killed him. What's going to happen?'

'Ben pull yourself together. He's not dead, you have not killed him. More likely a heart attack, he's knocked his head.'

Ben staggered out of the room. The bathroom door slammed. He was still there when the siren came blaring into the street, red lights flashing through the windows.

'Where is he?'

Two paramedics ran in carrying equipment. She somehow answered their questions, then pressed against the wall as they walked past with her father on the stretcher, a bruise developing on his chalk-white face. She followed, watching from the porch as they slid him into the ambulance, putting a mask over his nose and mouth. One stayed with him, the other came back to Emily.

'He's ok, we're giving him oxygen, but we need to take him to hospital. We're taking him to the Epworth in Richmond so call there in about an hour and they'll be able to give you an update.'

Emily nodded and stood shivering until they turned into the main road. She could still hear the siren as she shut the front door against the neighbours.

'Ben.'

She knocked on the bathroom door, not waiting for a reply to open it. Ben was sitting on the tiles, vomit in the bath, his head on his knees, arms tight around his chest.

'I've done a terrible thing. What will happen to me?'

'Don't be so bloody stupid! He had a heart attack and fell. That's it. You two were shouting at each other and then he had a heart attack.' She repeated the story in her head. 'Clean up the bath will you. It stinks.'

Emily went into the dining room, shutting the door behind her. Where's the brandy? She used her finger to wipe out the dust from a glass on the tray next to the bottle. Her entire body began shaking, shook so much that she had to grip the bottle with both hands to pour. Two hands around the glass, she sat on the edge of a chair and took a large gulp, welcoming the harsh liquid burn a passage down her throat. Tried to steady herself, sipping and breathing. What a mess. What should she do? Go to the hospital? Stay here with Ben? Those orange and red poppies in the flat looked pretty attractive right now. One more mouthful from the bottle, readying herself. Ben hadn't moved.

'Come on I'll make us some hot tea.' Sugar for shock, she recalled from somewhere. 'Just turn the taps on in the bath.'

She rang the Epworth at the hour.

'Ok Ben. They're saying it was a large heart attack. He needs surgery to get the blood flowing. He's going into theatre shortly. They're checking his head. Heart attacks are quite common. Most people recover well from them, these days. Are you listening?'

He was sitting on the chair where he had been eating dinner only an hour ago, elbows on the table, shoulders collapsed, head hanging, tea untouched.

'I'll call them again tomorrow, ok?' she looked at him. 'Why don't you head to bed, try and sleep, take the tea with you. I'll stay here tonight, my room's there. We can talk in the morning.'

Ben nodded and left the room. She stood for a moment, listening to slow steps, as though he was pulling himself up the stairs, and then his door closing.

Hide the alcohol. She found an empty box in the laundry and began filling it. Beer from the fridge, brandy, whisky and port from the dining room along with three remaining bottles of red from the wine rack. She carried the box out to the garage, her arms straining with the weight, returning to collect an unopened case of beer she had spotted at the bottom of the pantry. Took a final swig of brandy before pushing it all to the back of a shelf underneath the workbench. She dragged old sheets splattered with paint over them and moved a toolbox in front. Hoped she had found it all. Inside she picked up the boxes of pills from the floor and returned them to their hiding place, neat stacks behind jars of spreads, cans of soup, baked beans. She poured the contents of a bottle of carpet cleaner on the blood, scrubbing until she reduced the stains to a few pale spots in the midst of a wider wet patch.

She stood in the silence looking out to the dark, staring at the tree branches moving in the light wind. Was this her fault? She'd imagined she could have a reasonable conversation, calm it down. What if she'd said nothing? She thought back to the sequence of events. Did she make her father angrier? And Ben. Hadn't expected that. This idea of confronting her father with the truth, that went well. What did she expect? She closed her eyes as she recalled his fierce face directed straight at her, sending those missiles. She'd avoided being the target for most of her life. Her legs struggled to stay upright. She sat on the hard chair, trying to relax her shaking hands.

This all started with Ben. Why, why, why did he come here? Her father aggressive, nothing new there, repeats of the past. Both drinking. Ben fighting back this time. Why now? Their mother. That's when Ben couldn't stop himself. A surge of rage she hadn't seen in him before. She'd tried to keep him out of it but he seemed braver with her there, someone on his side, the two of them against their father. Could she have stopped it? What a feeble attempt, that burst of courage disappearing in the face of his anger. She saw herself immobilised, frightened, like she was twelve again. What a bloody fucking disaster!

Chapter Twenty-Five

Emily woke to hear Ben snoring. Six am, hours before he would emerge. A night of dozing and restless waking, her father's face appearing, scarlet to white, white to scarlet; falling. She lay, staring at the ceiling in the gloom of pre-sunrise light, wondering what to do. Realised she hadn't removed the bottles from Ben's room. Would he wake if she crept in now? Dismissed that idea, didn't want to risk starting the day with an altercation. Should she wait for Ben to wake up, go to the hospital, or return to the flat, give herself some space. Leave last night's events for a while. She threw on yesterday's clothes, carried her shoes downstairs to the front door and rang a taxi. Waited by the letterbox. Early enough to beat peak hour.

Inside the flat, relief flowed through her body. Almost home, even with the poppies. Socks drying on the windowsill, fruit in a bowl on the bench, bed made. As though nothing had happened in the twenty hours since she left. A shower. She scrubbed backwards and forwards, removing the smells, the blood, from her pores. The cheap towelling reddening her skin. She threw the face washer on the tiles and stayed under the hot water, letting it rain down on her head, warming her back, easing rigid muscles, clearing her brain. Smoothed moisturiser on her legs, her arms, in slow rhythmic strokes. Clean clothes. Almost normal again.

Strong coffee required. She left the flat somewhat amazed

to see daily routines continuing, joggers in the park, workers lining up for their morning fix in front of two black-shirted baristas exchanging jokes as they pumped out the orders. She glanced around the café as she took a seat, an older man poring over a newspaper spread on the table, three men in suits in close conversation, I wonder what their night was like; she thought. Smells of toast, coffee and baking aroused Emily's senses. Hungry, she ordered poached eggs with a large extra strong latte. Grateful for the coffee's quick arrival, she breathed in its aroma and drank, visualising the caffeine flowing through her network of veins, helping her to think.

What to do? She travelled thousands of miles to recover from her own disaster only to end up in the midst of much more. Ben homeless, lost his mother, probably Natasha, maybe Annie too. He clearly hadn't stopped drinking, and now this. Father in hospital, any number of potential scenarios there. Her ticket home was only a few days away. She munched through the white eggs on sourdough, stark against a side of bright green spinach. Frowned with the memory of her one attempt to have a straight conversation with her father. Determined to speak, not sure what she wanted to achieve, but had to speak for the first time. Her brave few words would be wiped from his mind, useless. He responded so harshly. Is that what he thought of her? Would he remember?

London was looking easy compared to this. She could book an earlier flight, leave tomorrow, maybe even tonight? She didn't allow herself to dwell on that temptation, she would not run away again. It would take more than a few days to sort out this mess. Well, there was no job waiting for her, no boyfriend. One slight hope–last night might have shaken Ben up enough for him to agree to rehab, worth trying again, didn't matter what it cost, anything to help him back on his feet. Somehow making up for neglecting him. She nodded at the offer of a second coffee, staring into space. Her father was likely to recover, but what if he didn't? Whatever happened, she would not become her father's carer.

Caffeine buzzing in her blood stream, she followed the paths across the gardens, blinking against the unexpected wind, making calls. Surgery went well, expected to be out of ICU in a few hours, need to wait and see how he recovers. No point in visiting yet. Nothing she needed to do there. Ashleigh's voicemail. Oh yes, that's right, she's working today. She smiled at the lively warmth in her voice, even in a recording, "Sorry to miss you, I'm busy now, but please leave a message and I'll call you back, as soon as I can, talk soon." So much better than those trendy voicemails, "you know what to do."

'Hey Ash. Give me a ring when you have a moment', casually, as though nothing serious had happened.

Called a car rental. There was her father's, but it smelt of him. Forced herself to call the airline, decision made.

Mid-afternoon, Emily fiddled with radio channels as she drove up to the ground floor of the rental car park, following the green signs. She paused on a classical music station, recognising the piece. Braked halfway up the exit slope. Taken back to the church listening to Phillip sing. On that hard seat where she was overwhelmed by emotion, watching his focused face above the front rows, remembering their closeness after. Her eyes welled up, and she swallowed down a sob. She wished she could talk to him; wanted his warm support. Someone she once thought cared about her. She steadied herself; don't think about him. The boom gate rose, she turned towards Camberwell.

As she got closer, private school traffic filled the roads with four-wheel drives and BMWs stopping alongside the schools. She halted behind a tram, watching primary-aged girls in blazers and dresses cram themselves in. That was her, so many years ago. Her violin and bag tight in either hand, hat jammed down. She liked school, was clever in the classroom, had a small group of friends, enough to protect her from the prima donnas; all she needed to make it enjoyable. Very different from what Ben talked about. Parked cars preventing her from creeping past the tram, she followed it to the next stop where adolescent alpha males grouped on the pavement. Not ready to go home yet. Cool and tough, shouldering each other, laughing, taking up space, letting everyone know they were in charge. Two quiet-looking boys sat on a wall at a distance, heads down, knowing their place. That would be Ben. This is where it starts, practicing being top dog.

She parked behind her father's car, tensing as the shock of last night's events returned. Less than twenty-four hours ago she was standing right here, the red lights of the ambulance spinning, siren piercing their street as it drove off, their father strapped inside. No answer to her knock. Luckily, she'd thought to pick up a house key.

The sound of the television reached her as soon as she opened the front door. She stared down the hall where yesterday she was flattening against the wall, allowing the stretcher go past. Her hand stopped an inch away from the back-room door knob, hearing again last night's shouting, reliving Ben shaking her Dad, him falling, crumpled on the floor. She closed her eyes, back in the horror moment of silence that followed. The blaring television penetrated, she shook her head back into the present and went in. Ben was slumped in his father's chair, smoke haze around him, beer bottles on the coffee table. Had she missed another stash?

'Em … just having a little rest', slurring.

'Let's get some air in here.'

She opened the back door and moved a chair to sit in the open doorway.

'Have you eaten?' Stopped herself from interrogating him about the beer.

'Yeah.' He waved a hand towards a plate with toast crumbs on the coffee table beside him.

'What are you watching?'

'Dunno … it's funny.'

Some kind of American sitcom with canned laughter telling viewers when there was a joke.

'Dad's out of surgery.'

Ben nodded, keeping his eyes on the television.

'So we've got to talk about what to do.' He laughed with the invisible audience.

'Listen will you! Ben! Fuck.' She stood up. This was useless.

'You can stay here for a bit, until we know what's happening.' At least it was somewhere to live.

'I'm ok', looking up at her for a moment.

'For now, but we must think of something else.'

She looked at him, sitting in his father's chair, eyes returned to the television after a brief nod. A simple solution in one way but surrounded by so many awful memories. Back in his child's room, what would that do to him? And her dad would return at some stage. What then? This has to be short term. She'd try the rehab option another day.

Emily looked in the fridge. Three eggs, margarine, plastic wrapped sliced cheese, bread and a shelf of beer. Four trays of single pieces of meat in the freezer, together with a pack of frozen mixed vegetables. Enough food for a while. Was she a parent now? She checked behind her, her back blocked Ben's view. She fitted two beer bottles in her bag, stretched the zip closed over their tin caps.

'I'll drop in tomorrow.'

Ben nodded.

What a waste of a drive that was.

That idea of a holiday, Emily's recovery break seemed a long way in the past. She should have gone to the Bahamas, lain on a beach. Sorting out her family was never part of the plan, but here she was ringing the hospital every day to hear the same message, "stable but no improvement yet," and trekking out to Ben who was turning the back room into a replica of his Footscray house. Always in that armchair, his father's chair, television on, ashtray spilling over. His eyes fixed on the screen when Emily gave him hospital updates or suggested rehab places she had researched. Responding only by gripping his knees or the arms of the chair more tightly. Shoulders bowed, head protruding as he leaned towards the television, lined face, cigarette trembling in his hand.

She brought food when she saw Ben was only buying alcohol. Where was the cash coming from? Had he found his father's wallet? She cleared away debris, collected dishes, emptied the bin, washed his clothes. Sometimes made him a meal, hoping he'd eat it. He was a little boy again, waiting for her to look after him. No mention of Annie or Natasha. She didn't know what else to do. Good at solving problems, she could find ways through all those knotty people issues managers came to her with, but this was beyond her. She hung onto a thread of hope that Ben would emerge again, at least enough to talk about what's next.

One time, after yet another ground-hog day visit, her frustration reached boiling point as she drove back to the flat. She sat in the underground carpark and rang the airline, wanting to reinstate her return ticket. Before they answered she hung up, halted by the vision of Ben in that chair on his own. Emily, the sister who had never been there for him, was the only one left. Only a few months ago, she was keeping him at a distance, not her responsibility, his decisions, his consequences, she told herself. That last conversation with her mother, seemed a long time in the past, she remembered her annoyance at being asked to look after him. Now she wanted to do all she could. Stay at least until he had committed to a solution, until she was confident he was on the path to recovery. She thought about the people she helped at the community centre. Her brother must not be one of those. Not Ben.

Phillip returned to her more often. Beside her as she walked down to the gardens early in the morning. She would run fast, leaving him behind, her lungs working hard, pushing out her stress with each gasp. Sometimes at night when she was struggling to sleep. His warm body close, filling the bed, she could smell his skin. She would turn over, away from the longing pulling at her, curl up tight. He hovered, waiting.

She hadn't visited her father yet. Busy, she told herself, no point, he'd be asleep anyway. What kind of conversation could they have after that night? Emily had avoided hospitals ever since she had left the one of her birth. Institutions signalling prospects she didn't want to contemplate. Even the sight of them made her fearful that her strength, and good health could be at risk. No serious illnesses, no broken limbs, no babies. Had kept resilient against any form of her own disintegration. Today they wanted to see her.

She left the car at the flat and caught a tram along Bridge Road. A fast five-minute trip and she was walking through the double doors into a mass of gleaming white scrubbed walls contrasting corridors of thick blue carpet, as though a plush veneer could make you feel calm and luxurious in a place of illness and death. As soon as the lift reached the ward Emily's nostrils filled with disinfectant. No luxury trimmings could cover that unique smell. Not the reassurance of a fresh clean bathroom, but a sharp reminder of the multitude of germs present needing fierce eradication. Here, no matter how white the walls, how reassuring the carpet or the paintings, no matter how blindingly clean the sheets, how efficient the nurses were, the building seemed to seethe with bodies breaking down, leaking, disintegrating. Despite files of paperwork, extensive lists of strict processes and procedures, life was out of control.

The junior nurse at reception smiled at her,

'Emily, yes, Miriam, the Nurse Unit Manager is expecting you, I'll just let her know. You can pop along and see him first while you are waiting. He's in number nine, on your left.'

An automatic assumption she would want to see him, so she did. Unexpected nausea rose as she peered into number nine and saw her father lying with his eyes closed, as still and pale as her mother in the coffin. Her mind flickered for a moment, opening the door into that room at the back of the funeral parlour. She pushed the image away. His arms lay loose on top of the blue blanket, a dribble sliding out of his half open mouth, eyes shut. Moved closer, trying to ignore the nausea. This was the man they had spent their lives being frightened of. The one who controlled everything and everyone in his reach. The one with the loud voice, the angry eyes, the violent temper. Here, small in the bed, tubes attached, plastic nametag around his wrist. Reliant on others for food, water, treatment, probably the toilet. Did he remember what happened? She took a few steps backwards and bumped into a chair. Damn, caught it before it fell but he opened his eyes.

'Emily', a notch above a whisper. Barely the same man who had last spoken to her with such strength and vitriol.

'How are you Dad?' She wished she hadn't knocked that chair.

He shook his head slightly, then lifted it an inch off the pillow. 'I said, I said ...'

She had to move closer to hear him.

'Too much.' He lowered his head back down. His eyes closed. As though he'd been waiting for her, ready to speak. Was that some kind of regret?

Skirting the chair, she returned to reception and waited on one of the hard blue chairs lined up beside the desk, taking deep breaths to quell the nausea, confusion twisting through her mind.

Miriam, a younger woman not in uniform and Emily. Invited to sit in a secluded area, separated from hospital bustle with armchairs, coffee table, magazines and offers of tea. Calm and practical, perhaps in her mid 40s, Miriam exuded confident experience.

'I'll come straight to the point. We have asked to talk with you as we think he's progressing more slowly than expected. It's still early days but we want to have a preliminary conversation about options. Given his age and general poor health, we need to consider that he may not fully recover. Heart attacks are typically straightforward these days, but it seems other factors are slowing recovery. He doesn't seem to be responding to treatment as well as we hoped. It may be the fall has caused further problems, we are doing tests,' she frowned, 'there does come a point where the person has to want to get well.'

Emily appreciated her directness. Had been ready to resist layers of sympathy, assumptions about how she was feeling. Here there was just honest information. She realised she didn't even know how healthy he was. He drank more than he should, not a smoker, that was her mum. Did he eat well? Not from what she had seen. Did he have other health issues? Relieved, she was not asked to explain what happened. Another old man having a heart attack.

'I've asked Alex to join us. Alex is a social worker here at the hospital.'

Emily turned to the younger woman. Alex cleared her throat, pushing her curly hair behind her ears as she spoke,

'Hello Emily. Can I ask, are you the next of kin?'

'I guess I am. But I don't live here.'

'Are there any other family members?'

'My mother died a few months ago. My brother is here but has his own issues, he can't deal with this. My father has a brother interstate, but they are estranged.'

Emily chose her words, aware what a disaster they sounded. How does a successful doctor, middle-class family, living in the sought-after streets of Camberwell, private schools, well dressed, expensive cars; how does he end up with no one to look after him?

'We need to talk about care options. The medical staff will continue exploring diagnosis and treatment, but we could soon be at a stage of needing to consider an appropriate living situation. I understand he lives by himself?' Acknowledged

Emily's nod. 'Unless he makes a significant recovery he is unlikely to be able to return to that arrangement.'

'So, what happens from here?'

'We'll have the ACAT team assess his needs and recommend options. You may like to investigate alternate living arrangements. I don't know how you're placed?'

Panic rose in Emily's stomach. No! No! Trapped into looking after her father. Nursing homes, carers, difficult discussions with him. She struggled to keep control of herself, arranging her face into professional calm, clearing her throat to find her firm voice,

'That's going to be difficult. I have to return to London. Home. Soon. My boss keeps calling. I've been away too long.'

They didn't need to know. Who cares what they thought of her, she would never see them again, anyway.

'Of course, I want him to have the best care. Perhaps you can sort this out directly with him? He is a doctor. He'll understand.'

Alex flicked her eyes to Miriam, returned to Emily.

'Of course. We wanted to make you aware of the situation. Your involvement is entirely up to you.'

Emily stood up, she needed to leave. Now.

'Anything you and he agree to is fine with me. He has money. Just do whatever you need to do.'

She ran into the gap between the lift doors as they were closing. Willing it to go faster. Irritated as they stopped on the second floor. A woman with a scarlet face got in, leant against the side, signs of crying. Well, that was not her. She wished that none of this had happened, a sense of despair that they had come to this, but no tears.

The hospital behind her, she walked along Bridge Road to the next tram stop where she didn't have to wait and look at the building. They would manage her father. Her thoughts shifted to Ben. He was harder. Gentle waiting and support weren't working. She'd have to apply more pressure, use all her persuasive skills to get him into rehab, long term rehab, she would find a way. In between visits and phone calls she had researched options, prices, availability, she just needed him to agree. Then she could go home.

Chapter Twenty-Six

Emily frowned to see three missed calls on her phone. Unknown number. Sweaty from her run she turned on the tap to fill the kettle for breakfast tea. Who would call her here? A London head-hunter? No, the number was Australian. Maybe one of the rehab providers she had been talking with. A day in the Yarra Valley with Ashleigh yesterday had renewed her energy. An art exhibition, tasting wines and cheeses. Lunch at a winery in the sun, looking across to hills lined with rows of vines, watching long- legged birds swoop to the dams which filled the hollows at the bottom of the valley.

Message bank. All three from a Sergeant Dale at the Camberwell Police Station, asking her to call. She stood by the sink, phone tight in her hand, stomach lurching, not noticing water spilling out of the kettle spout. Ben. What has he done? Did they pick him up on a street somewhere, put him in the cells to dry out? She recoiled from a vision of her brother lying on a footpath, berating passers-by, swearing at an officer. They must want her to collect him. How embarrassing. Still, now that the police were involved, she could enlist them to encourage Ben into rehab. Not much progress there, despite her renewed attempts. She would use this. A rock bottom moment to make him accept help. Were the police able to direct him to rehab? She'd find out.

She grabbed the kettle as it tipped over in the rapidly

filling sink; turned the tap off and poured out the surplus water, setting it to boil. Rang the number, putting a tea bag in the cup as she waited for them to pick up.

'Sergeant Dale speaking.'

'Hello Sergeant, Emily Green here. You rang me earlier.'

'Miss Green, thank you for returning my call. You are related to Ben Green?' A serious but pleasant voice. She realised she hadn't dealt with the police before; any expectations were from television crime shows.

'Yes, I'm his sister. What's he done?'

'Would it be possible for you to come to the station?'

'I can do that. Is Ben there?'

'I'd prefer to speak to you in person Miss Green. I can come to you if you'd prefer.'

How would that work, would he bring Ben with him? She didn't want anyone to see police officers at her door, especially with a bedraggled Ben. What if the owner happened to be around. Better to go to the station.

'No, I'll come there. I can be there in an hour.' Emily hoped she sounded responsible, someone in control of herself. She wasn't the one with problems.

'Would you like to bring someone with you?'

Did he think she couldn't manage on her own?

'No, that's fine thank you, I'll see you in an hour.' She put the phone down before he could ask anything else. Odd. But then they must have their protocols.

Evasive, she thought, as she filled her bowl with muesli. Why didn't he explain more? I guess they need to eyeball me, discuss options. She bolted breakfast, hungry after her run, and sipped the last of her tea in the bathroom while she showered. Better drive if I have to pick him up. Luckily, she knew no-one here, no-one to recognise her getting a drunken brother out of the cells. This has to stop; today's the day. She would have a quiet word with the sergeant before seeing Ben.

She parked on busy Camberwell Road in a half hour zone, that would be long enough. Opposite the plain brown building with its gleaming blue and white sign. One of those ugly functional buildings for bureaucrats which proliferated in the '60s and '70s. The junior constable at the desk seemed to be expecting her. She led her down a narrow corridor past photos of men in uniform; jackets, hats, stripes and badges, indicating some kind of importance. She wondered where the cells were. Was Ben down the back somewhere lying on a hard bed?

The constable ushered her into a small room on the right, asking her to sit on a wooden chair at a square table, its varnish long gone. No space for other furniture, no pictures in here to relieve the bare fake wood-panelled walls, one window too high for anyone to see through it, so small that the fluorescent light would always need to be on. Is this where they interview criminals? She thought it looked like the rooms on British crime shows, where two officers would try and extract a confession.

'Sergeant Dale will be with you in a moment.'

Her badge said Constable Kelly, brunette hair tight in a ponytail, freckles. So young, Emily wondered what she looked like out of hours, partying with her hair down, makeup on.

'Would you like a cup of tea or coffee?'

'No thanks.'

Let's get this over with, rap on the knuckles, guess she'd have to pay a fine, discuss rehab options, pick up Ben and go. A man in uniform entered, a similar age to herself. She stood up to shake his large hand.

'Is Ben here? Can I see him? What's he done?' Her tone a notch higher, her heart beating faster.

'Please have a seat Miss Green. Has someone offered you a tea or coffee?' Checked her nod. 'Constable Kelly is joining us.'

The constable shut the door behind Emily and joined Sergeant Dale on the other side of the table, putting down a notebook and pen. Thickset, grey hair, a few more lines than her she thought, goes with the job. In charge. He took a breath and looked across at her.

'I am sorry to have to tell you this, Miss Green. There is no easy way to say this, but we found your brother Ben at what I believe is the family home at around seven o'clock this morning. I am afraid he was already deceased when we arrived.'

Emily stood bolt upright, her chair fell back, eyes wide in shock.

'What! No! No!' Frozen, poker straight, her insides contracting. 'No! I saw him the other day, he was fine, well not fine, but Ben fine. No! This is a mistake!'

She noticed a light hand on her arm. Constable Kelly beside her.

'Please Miss Green. Have a seat. This is a shock. I am very sorry for your loss.'

She sat back down, trying to concentrate on the sergeant's words.

'I appreciate this is difficult but if I could just ask you a couple of questions. When did you last see him?' His voice was gentle.

'Yes, yes, I visit most days, not yesterday though, the day before. I went out. I thought he'd be fine. But this can't be him. How can you be sure?'

The sergeant nodded, keeping his eyes on Emily. 'A neighbour, Chris Dunn was kind enough to identify him at the scene. Unfortunately, he confirmed it was Ben. Again, I am deeply sorry for your loss', he continued. 'You would be aware then, he didn't seem to be living well?'

'No, yes, I've been trying to help. He's an alcoholic. He's been through a hard time. I wanted him to go to a rehab facility. I live in London. I'm just visiting.' Her words poured out, 'What? How? I mean what happened?'

Sergeant Dale hesitated, he glanced sideways at the constable who was writing in her notebook.

'Please. Tell me. I need to know.'

'Miss Green, do you know the neighbour, Chris Dunn?'

'Umm, I left many years ago. Next door?'

She had vague recollections of a grey-haired man nodding at her as he was watering his front garden, one time she was visiting Ben.

'Yes, number twenty-four.'

Constable Kelly slid her notebook in front of him. He glanced down, checking as he talked.

'Mr Dunn rang us early this morning. He said something worried him. Last night he heard noises from the rear garden, he looked over the fence and saw your brother out in the rain shouting and dancing around in circles. He said he felt a little afraid as Ben looked crazed. Those were his words. So he didn't want to enter the property, but called out for him to go inside, which after a while he did. Mr Dunn said he was still concerned but things seemed to have quietened down. Then this morning Mr Dunn was up early and noticed all the lights of the house were on; when he opened his back door, he heard the television blaring. He said he thought it was unusual as most days he wouldn't hear anything until much later. This time he knocked at the front door, but there was no answer, so he called us and asked us to check up on him.'

Emily felt sick, churning sick, but willed herself to stay. She gripped the sides of the seat with sweaty hands, leaning forward.

'Where did you find him?'

The sergeant looked down for a moment before meeting her eyes again.

'We found him downstairs in the front bedroom.'

'In my father's bedroom? Really? Was he sleeping there?'

'I am so sorry you are hearing this Miss Green. Are you sure you want to hear the details?'

Emily nodded, she had to know.

'He was kneeling on the floor at the bottom of the bed, with his head face down on the bed. He didn't have any clothes on. There was a towel behind him, he may have been using it to cover himself.'

'So ... suicide?' Emily whispered, the horror of the image boring into her brain.

'We are not suspecting foul play at this stage, although we will wait for the Coroner's judgement. There were several empty spirit bottles and many empty pill boxes scattered across the back room where the television was. We can't be certain yet of the actual cause of death, whether it was intentional or an unfortunate consequence. We will need to have an autopsy done, but it is often difficult to tell with people who haven't looked after themselves for a long time, as I am guessing is the case with your brother?'

'Yes. Yes, ah, he has had ... problems for many years, but it's only in the last few months they got out of control. Well I think so anyway. I live in London. Maybe it's been worse than I thought.'

Sergeant Dale nodded. 'He had the look of someone who's been struggling for a long time. It can be hard to distinguish between deterioration and deliberate suicide. There was no note. The autopsy will identify the direct cause of death, but I will warn you it may not clarify whether it was deliberate.'

Emily pulled at her coat, heat waves of sweat rising, difficult to breathe. She ran to the door, pulling at the handle,

'Where's the Ladies?'

Constable Kelly was beside her, hand on her elbow guiding her down the corridor towards a door on the left. Emily ran the last few feet, pushing the stiff door hard, just making it to kneel in front of the toilet and vomit until she was dry retching. Her hands gripped the bowl, only releasing as the heaving slowed and her retching subsided. She tore off a strip of toilet paper to wipe her mouth, then flushed. Turning to the door, she put her hand on the wall to steady herself, blinking to regain focus. Then, repulsed by the sour gritty taste, she left the cubicle and bent under the tap, rinsing and rinsing.

Constable Kelly came in with a tall glass of water. 'This might help. Sip slowly.'

'Thank you.' The glass felt cold against her hand. 'I'm sorry. My brother. My lovely, lovely brother.'

Sobs rose in her throat until they took control. She turned away leaning against the tiled wall crying big choking moaning sobs. Her heart thumped against her chest.

'I'm sorry, I don't do this, it's just that ...'

'It's all right madam, you've had a shock. A terrible loss. You cry as much as you need to. Would you like me to stay with you?'

Emily shook her head. 'No, no I'll be all right. Just give me a minute.'

'I'll make you a cup of tea. Come out when you are ready. No rush.'

Her crying slowed to a stop, the gulping breaths that shook her ribs calmed. She straightened up, trying to think through the pain in her head. Several slow sips from the glass still in her hand then she lifted her eyes to the mirror.

'Oh God.'

A blotchy face and red dried out eyes, lipstick streaked beyond her lips. The lines in her face magnified, deepened, since she last checked, this morning seemed like days ago. She shut her eyes, then blinked them open again; they were waiting for her. She soaked a wad of paper towels in cold water, pressing them against her face, her eyes, used one to rub her lipstick off. A slight improvement. Abandoned an attempt to rub off the greyish marks that had transferred from the floor of the cubicle to the knees of her favourite jeans. She took a big breath and pulled the door. The constable waiting outside. How does she deal with what goes on in here?

'Thank you. Sorry. I'm ok. Thank you.' Few had seen her lose control like that. She looked up and down the corridor.

'No problems at all Madam. This way.'

She walked with Emily back to the room where Sergeant Dale was standing against the wall. The constable put a china cup in her hands, she drank tea, hot and sweet.

'So, what happens now?' pulling her dignity together.

'We will need a statement from you', said the sergeant. 'Would you be all right to do that now for us, then it's all done.'

'Yes, let's get it over with. What do you want me to say?'

'Could you recount the last time you saw your brother and his condition at that point? And your contact details. That should be enough. We'll look after things from there.

You will receive a report from the coroner with his final judgement about cause of death, based on the autopsy. I am afraid that may take a week or more, depending on their workload. The body will be released once the Coroner has made his judgement, so I'm sorry to say you will need to wait a little while before holding a funeral.'

The body. That was Ben now.

'How long were you planning to stay in Melbourne?'

'Well I guess as long as it takes. If there's anything that can be done to speed things up?' She looked at the sergeant. 'I can't stay here forever. I need to go back home.' Emily's voice wobbled, but she stayed firm.

'I understand. We will do what we can. Is there someone you would like us to ring, who could be with you?'

'Umm.'

Emily's mind was blank. Who was there? Ashleigh, thank God for Ashleigh. One person.

'It's all right I'll make a call.'

The sergeant nodded. 'You are welcome to stay here until someone comes if that would help?'

No. She'd drive herself home.

'Thank you. I'll go. Can I ask – how did you know to call me?'

'Mr Dunn gave us your name. We understand your father's in hospital. We found your number in an address book beside the landline.'

God, is the entire street aware of our disaster of a family?

'I have Ben's phone here for you. It might help you with who to call.' The Sergeant took it out of his pocket. Now it starts, she would have to ring people and tell them. Natasha. Emily stretched out her hand for the phone, ran her fingers over the scratched glass, something he had held, his long fingers wrapped around it, his mouth close. She took the pen and paper from the sergeant, keeping the phone in her left hand as she wrote her statement with her right.

Natasha first. A sharp intake of breath and then a whisper 'Ben.'

Emily was on the couch in the flat. Her coat still on. Ashleigh put a steaming cup near her, more tea.

'I knew he was bad, but this?'

'How ... when ... how long ago did you last see him?' Emily asked, hesitating, not wanting to appear to interrogate.

'Oh, err a few weeks now. He would say he was coming and then not show or he'd turn up drunk, without warning. I never let him near Annie when he'd been drinking. He wouldn't hurt her, but you just couldn't trust him in that state ... But that last time was ok. He was so happy to hold Annie ... sorry ... give me a minute ... it was lovely to see him with her. I wish ... God. How could this happen? I loved that man you know. I gave him so many chances but as I got closer to the birth, he was getting worse and I couldn't look after a baby in that situation. And me too, I needed support. Ben wasn't reliable anymore. I just had to decide. I always hoped things would change but I guess as time went on I realised that probably wouldn't happen, not quickly anyway. Now this ... if only I ... I don't know, maybe I could have done something ... been in touch more. It was so hard.'

'Natasha, it's ok. You had Annie to look after.'

Emily stared out of the window, past the tree branches, phone at her ear, the clouds rolling in, larger, closer.

'He rang all the time. I'd switch the phone off at night, when he was bad. He'd keep ringing. Out of it. Sometimes abusive, sometimes crying or just incoherent. It was awful. Oh God I hope he wasn't trying to call me when ….'

Emily stopped her. 'No, no I have his phone, he didn't call anyone.' So, he was calling both of them.

They sat with silence for a moment. Ashleigh pointed to the cup in front of her.

'I loved him for years. More than anyone else. He was such a lovely man. What happened to him? His mum. That hit him hard. I guess his demons caught up with him.' She stopped. 'I can't talk anymore. I'm going to cry. Call me in a couple of days? The funeral. Please, I want to help.'

Emily drank from the cooling cup, Ashleigh beside her on the couch.

'Poor Natasha. And me. And what was it like for Ben, those last few hours. All on his own. God, I can't imagine. And I wasn't there for him. I'd taken one day off from visiting, just one day …'

'Hey, none of that', Ashleigh interrupted with a firm voice. 'This was absolutely not your fault. This is the end of a lengthy period of decline, not one day.'

'The one person in my family I thought I could help, I seriously wanted to. Too late, way too late. Fucking useless.' She bent over holding her stomach tight with both arms, rocking back and forwards, crying again with a deep guttural sound.

Ashleigh curled both arms around her. 'You tried. You really did. Remember all those visits, all that cleaning up, shopping, cooking for him. Remember the list of rehab places you researched; you even knew which ones had a place available. Think of the money you were offering to support him, and you, unemployed. You did a lot. What else could you have done? You gave Ben opportunities, options.

For some reason he wasn't able to take them. Do not even think about blaming yourself.'

'I couldn't save him', she choked out.

'No-one could. I'm sure he knew you cared about him.'

Emily sat up, blew her nose several times, took deep breaths, her body ached as though she was bruised.

'I'll have to tell my father.'

'Yes, but not today, unless you're certain you want to. It won't make any difference. I'm going to make you a sandwich. How about you wash your face, eat, then we can go for a walk, breathe some fresh air? Yes?'

Emily nodded.

Chapter Twenty-Seven

Emily stopped at the bank of small metal letter-boxes each time she passed, often several times a day, impatient for the autopsy report. When the brown manila A4 envelope arrived, bent in half to fit in the box, she ran back upstairs, tearing it open. Just inside, elbowing the door closed, she pulled the document out, scanning through the pages of formalities and information, looking for something that would somehow help to make sense of that night. As the sergeant had warned, there was no clarity whether death was deliberate or accidental. Pills, alcohol, malnutrition all contributed. Not suspicious in the Coroner's eyes. Confirmed that he had been on a downward slope for a long time. Years. Accelerating after her mother's death.

She sat on the couch, the pages of the report spread out on the coffee table. Re-reading for a clue. Anything. She remembered all those times on the phone when she was too busy to talk to him, annoyed with him. What if she'd been more supportive, what if she'd listened more? Could she have helped him back then? Stop it getting to this stage? When she last left Melbourne he still had Natasha, he was excited about becoming a father; she thought life was looking up.

That day. What if she hadn't gone to the Yarra Valley? Visited him instead, she would have stopped him, at least got help. Did he feel abandoned because she didn't visit? Oh God, no. If only she'd thrown away those pills, been stronger about getting rid of all the alcohol. She shook her head. He would have found a way. She should have forced him to go to rehab, she was far too gentle. She leaned back on the couch. Why did she let him stay in the house? It must have been awful. Is that why he moved downstairs? Too many memories in his own room? But his father's bed? Maybe the stairs were too much if he was drunk. Deep down she knew living there was contributing to his decline, but thought with her father absent ... she didn't know what else to do. By the time she realised he needed serious help, he was already falling into a pit. Slipping and sliding so fast he couldn't hold on to the sides, couldn't reach for her hand.

The day before the funeral. They had been ready for a week waiting for Ben. Emily, Natasha and Ashleigh, calling friends, gathering photos, choosing paintings, arranging music. Emily turned over to check the clock again. Six o'clock. Late enough to get up. She untangled the sheets from another night of twisting and turning. Awake or asleep, that last image of Ben stayed in her mind, naked and vulnerable at the end of his father's bed. She couldn't imagine being in such a state of utter despair. Is this what happens if you can't see a way out, if you don't believe in yourself anymore? Her own period of falling apart was nothing compared to his. She always knew she would manage. She stared upwards at the patterns on the ceiling created by a glimmer of dawn through the blinds.

It was time to tell her father. Had given herself the deadline of the funeral. Had to wait for the report, she told herself. He would never know the difference. She was strong enough to protect herself now, determined not to look weak in front of him, ready to guard against dissolving into tears, speech prepared. Clear her head with a run in the park first.

Showered and dressed, then Ashleigh at the door, balancing coffee and muffins. 'Breakfast,' she smiled, 'or perhaps second breakfast?' noticing the bowl in the sink.

'Only fruit. Coffee smells wonderful. Thanks for coming.'

'So, what's happening today?' Ashleigh pressed her finger on the last crumbs of the blueberry muffin and licked them off. 'More funeral prep?'

'I think we are pretty much ok for that. Just have to prepare the room tomorrow, put the paintings up.'

'I'll be there early.'

'You've been so great Ash. This has taken over your life.'

'No problems at all. You'd do the same for me. Now, today?'

'Time to tell my father. But I have to go to the house first.'

Ashleigh raised her eyebrows. 'Is that a good idea?'

'The hospital rang, they want clean pyjamas.'

'Do you have to?'

'They called days ago, I've been avoiding it. I think I'd better see him by myself, but could you come to the house with me?'

She had tried twice before. One day planned to go but somehow didn't. Another morning drove as far as the end of the street, saw the edge of the driveway and turned around.

Emily sat in the passenger seat, feeling the caffeine, accelerating her heartbeat as they drew closer. Ashleigh parked under a tree whose long branches and broad leaves took over the nature strip blocking the northerly sun from the house.

'Wow, it's decades since I've been here. And then it was hardly at all. Dropping you off, mostly. You usually came to mine.'

'Yeah, I don't think I ever invited friends over. We didn't

have many visitors, occasional afternoon tea with relatives. Even that sent Mum into a spin.'

Emily readying herself. Now she was here, it was hard to move.

'Why don't you stay here. You just tell me where to find them.'

'It's ok, I'll be fine. Let's do it.'

She pushed herself out onto the nature strip and continued momentum into the driveway, then stopped behind her father's car. It was strange to see the house, looking the same as always. As though it should have streaks of blood leaking out of the door and windows, as though the walls should crumble after such events. But it sat in its place in the street, a quiet closed face in a line of many. Calf length grass and weeds taking over from flowers, the only sign that something was amiss. She hoped no-one was watching her. The neighbours had already seen much more than she would want them to. Glanced over the fence to number twenty-four. Driveway empty, relieved there was no sign of the helpful Mr Dunn, didn't want to have that conversation. She hesitated on the porch.

'Let me go in first.' Ashleigh took the key from Emily's hand. 'Stay here.'

Emily obeyed, watching her march down the hall and disappear into the back room. Imagined what Ashleigh might be seeing. She closed her eyes, jabs of pain shooting through her head. Her eyes flicked open again with the sound of a door closing, fast footsteps, Ashleigh filling the doorway like a security guard.

'Not the back room. Don't go near the back room', breathing heavily.

Emily nodded, then hesitated in the doorway of her

father's bedroom. It was cold, dark and still. Very still. Smells of alcohol, cigarettes, urine. A dim shaft of light from the hall reached the end of the bed, outlining a towel lying on the floor. Emily could see nothing else, her gaze riveted. The pain jabs in her head became hammers. No thought, no emotion. Only pain and silence. Ashleigh's voice penetrated.

'Let me, you don't need this, I'll find them. How about you wait outside.' Ashleigh gently guided Emily into the hall and then returned, shutting the door.

Emily wandered down the hall, towards the back room as had been her habit in recent weeks, then stopped at the closed door, remembering Ashleigh's words. She saw the door of her father's study open and entered. His briefcase against the wall, notebooks and pens on his desk, as though nothing had changed. And the model cars, dustier than when she had last seen them. She picked up a green and silver Rolls Royce, turning it over in her hand. That time when she and Ben were small, playing with the cars, all those times when her father exploded, when his anger ricocheted around the house, crushing her brother, bullying her mother, terrifying them all. That last time when he raged at them both.

'My fucking father!' She threw the car against the wall, watching it fall in pieces and picked up a second. 'This is for you.' She stamped on its red roof, grinding it into the carpet. One by one she threw, dropped, stamped until the shelves were empty. Shouting with a new-found ferocity. She stood surrounded by broken doors, twisted bumper bars, rolling wheels, smashed bonnets, bent windscreens. Her heart thumped hard in her chest, her breath coming short and fast. She turned to see Ashleigh standing in the doorway staring at her, eyes round. Emily pushed past her, running out of the house, yanking at the car door handle, gasping, and crashed into the seat heaving with sobs.

She became conscious of her surroundings, Ashleigh beside her, a water bottle being pressed into her hand.

'Here, drink this.'

She sipped, recovering her breath.

'Sorry Ash, I'm ok.'

'How about we go back to your place for a while?'

'No, it's ok, over now. I've run out of time, funeral tomorrow. I'm fine, just need to fix myself up in the hospital bathroom.' She gave a slight grin. 'Can't have him see me like this.'

Driving to Richmond. Ashleigh broke the silence.

'We can employ someone to clean the house. I'll organise it. I'll keep the key for now if that's ok. You don't have to come back.'

Emily nodded. She found painkillers in her bag and swallowed four in one gulp.

'Look, I know things have been tricky with Phillip, but do you want to, maybe call him? Times like this, perhaps the past doesn't matter so much.'

Emily looked out of the side window. A flash of his face, the warmth of his body. Too hard. She shook her head, not looking at Ashleigh.

The hospital loomed on the right.

'I'll jump out Ash.'

'There's a car park, I can wait in the café.'

'Thanks, I'll be fine. Let's be in touch about tomorrow. Thanks.'

A quick hug, then she was watching the back of Ashleigh's head as the car rejoined the stream of traffic towards the city.

When she couldn't distinguish the car any longer, she turned to face the hospital.

She gripped tight inside as she walked through the glass doors, her nostrils again assailed with the smell of the place, looking for a bathroom before going upstairs. She splashed cold water on her face, relieved she'd remembered her make-up bag. Drops in her eyes, layers of foundation and powder covering blotchy skin. Ready. She breathed in strong Emily, resilient Emily as she stood in the lift, holding the plastic bag of pyjamas, standing tall behind a family with balloons and flowers, lifting her chest, readying herself, practising her words in her head, visualising, slowing her breathing.

A male nurse at the ward desk, busy on the computer. No sign of Miriam. Good, she didn't want to have further conversations. He lifted his eyes,

'Yes, go on through, room 9, he's just had tea.'

She tapped on the open door, not waiting for a reply. Half sitting up this time, propped by pillows, watching television, an empty cup on his table. He nodded in recognition and gestured to the visitor's chair beside the bed.

'Hello Dad', louder than she had intended, clearing her throat to remove the slight crack in her voice. 'I brought pyjamas. You're looking better.'

He shrugged. 'Maybe. They say I can't go home.'

'I know. For the best. They'll find you somewhere. Dad, I have to tell you something.'

'What's that?'

'It's Ben. He died, last week.' She'd said these words so many times in the last week, but still had to search for them, deep within.

'Ben?' his eyes widened under a heavy frown. 'How?' A struggle to form the word.

'There was an autopsy. Alcoholism, malnutrition, pills. Suicide in a way.'

His face paled further from his hospital grey. Eyes, staring at her, large in his shrunken body.

'No. No... Vivienne, now Ben. It can't be.'

'Only months between them. Ben was hit pretty hard when Mum died. She was an enormous support to him. Dad, if only you'd recognised the lovely talented man he was. He needed you.'

Her father lowered his gaze. 'I tried. I did. Tried to teach him what I know. I wanted him to be strong, do something with his life. He never listened. And now this.'

'Ben would never be what you wanted, surely you could see that. He achieved a lot in his life. You mightn't think it was worthwhile, but it was important to him. You were too hard Dad, way too harsh.' She was able to speak quietly, a voice of deep sadness, her explosive anger spent in the study.

He nodded. 'Perhaps, sometimes. I loved you all you know. I ... I don't always show it, but ...' He struggled to sit up against his pillows. 'But I did. I loved your mother, Ben, you'. He thumped his fist on the blanket with a burst of energy. Emily froze, a habit of many years. 'I tried to protect you all, do the right thing for you all.' He sank back against the pillows, his breathing laboured.

Protect us! We needed protection against him. How could he possibly think that was love? In some warped way, in his own mind, he believed he did.

'We were all so scared of you.' In the following pause she felt a release in her body, draining decades with one sentence.

It shocked her to see his eyes fill with tears. She struggled to stay in control, not going to cry in front of him. For a few seconds they held eye contact, Emily looking into his weak watery eyes. She broke the gaze, standing up to look out the window, across roofs to city towers, until she trusted her voice again. Not here.

'Funny, I'm the strong one, much more like you, not that you noticed.' She ignored a murmur from the bed and picked up her bag. 'And now it's us two left. Well, I'm going home soon, after the funeral. I don't expect to be back. Our struggling, broken mess of a family is over. I've talked to the staff here; they'll work with you to find a comfortable living situation. You'll be ok, no need for me to be involved. I'm going to find my life again, put all this behind me.'

She paused at the foot of his bed. On the rare occasions when she thought of him in years following, she recalled this picture, him alone in the hospital bed, head drooped.

'Bye Dad.'

Then down the hall not looking anywhere except right in front of her, straight down the stairs, out the doors, away from hospital smells into the noise of Bridge Road cars and trams. Not wanting to stop, she passed the line of people waiting for the tram, past shops and cafes, dodging shoppers, faster, just short of a run. Her leather shoes were rubbing the skin off her heels. Across the park, pushing her legs forward, ignoring the growing blisters, head down, avoiding any possibility of contact, however small. The end of her street in sight, she increased her pace to a jog, ran up the steps scrabbling in her bag for the key, found it, dropped it, struggled to fit it in the lock. Inside, door closed, she shook uncontrollably as though ice was entering her veins. She curled herself tight under the quilt until her muscles slowly eased. No more fear, no more conversations. After tomorrow it'll be over.

Chapter Twenty-Eight

Two deaths. Two funerals. Emily sat with Ashleigh and Natasha, looking at Ben's coffin in the centre of the room, the weight of the year pressing down. Twenty years of distance from her family and then this year. For a moment she was back in that apricot painted funeral parlour, staring at her mother's coffin on the stage, sitting with Ben and her dad, as other families do, cringing at Peter Ash, at her uncle, loaded with confusion.

This farewell would be different. Surprised by the numbers pouring in to join the circle. As Ben would have been. She imagined his pleasure at being surrounded by so many people. There for him. Some crouched around the coffin, pasting on their gifts of paintings or tiny sculptures, looking for remaining patches of bare wood between the art works already there. She thought again of the figure at the end of his father's bed. He would not be alone on this last journey.

Together with Natasha she had plunged into funeral preparations. Something they could do. Trying to assuage a shared guilt of "if only I …". Emily worked her way through people to call. She dreaded the first few, but as she continued down the list, she found some solace in others' grief, loss, guilt. After the shocked silence or tears, there was often awkwardness.

'Didn't know it had got so bad.'

'We kinda lost touch … I wish I'd called him … I should have made more effort.'

'I just thought he was busy doing his own thing. Ben was like that, you wouldn't see him for months and then he'd be on your doorstop.'

'If only I'd known he was in such a dreadful space, I should have …'

More pieces of the story.

Andy with the bungalow. 'I really wanted to let him stay, but he was in too much of a mess. I've got kids.'

Derek from the studio. 'Yeah, there was a bit of a fight. Not with me, some others. He was off his tree. They told him to go. Had enough. Lucky I was there when he came to pick up his stuff. I drove him back. Don't know how he thought he would get it all home. I should have followed up.'

They had transformed the serene cream walls of the funeral parlour into a crowded art gallery. Natasha had gathered paintings from friends, galleries and from the Footscray house.

'The landlord didn't realise I still had a key', she had grinned. 'He'd put most of it on the porch, anyway. Thank God I got there before they threw it in a skip.'

Ben screamed at them from the walls; magnificent uncomfortable works, chaos and fear reaching out of the canvas, reminding them of his battles that sat underneath a thin surface most of his life, taking control at the end. Except for one. An unfinished piece, perhaps his last.

'Wow', Emily had gasped as they unrolled it, cross-legged on the floor of Natasha's small lounge-room, Annie sucking her fists on a blanket beside them. A pregnant Natasha, sitting naked, a depth in her eyes as she looked back at the artist, emanating strength and beauty. She sat suspended in space in rich colours, the chair pencilled in, faint outlines of alternative backgrounds receding with the power of the figure.

'Ah, I wondered where that one had got to.' Natasha picked up Annie and held her close.

'This is such a contrast to his other works. So much love and happiness here,' she smiled across at Natasha whose eyes were filling up, 'for you'.

The piece dominated the room from its central place on the wall opposite her. Not because of size, there were others larger. All Ben's works were powerful, but this one drew you in close, captured you, radiating warmth, adoration, love, a unique peace. People were nudging each other, twisting around to look at it, turning back to smile at Natasha. A moment of light for Ben.

This time Emily wanted to speak. She stood close to the coffin and addressed herself to Ben. Reminded him of his best times, his talent, his achievements, his loves.

'Ben, I'm sorry I didn't hear your cries for help sooner.' Hearing others murmur. 'I'm so sad you have gone, my lovely brother', speaking through a choke in her throat. 'I want you to know I love you, that we love you. I hope you can feel the warmth here.'

She returned to her seat, crying now, tissues coming out around the room. The funeral celebrant offered an invitation, and many contributed; stories of better times, a few laughs, expressing sorrow ... Then Natasha stood, opposite her portrait, holding Annie in her front pack. A stillness surrounded them, eyes on her as she spoke, voice breaking.

When she had finished, she knelt and placed Annie's hand on the coffin, leant down with a kiss beside her tiny hand.

'Bye Ben.'

The slow, raw notes of Andy's saxophone led the procession out of the building. They gathered outside, a tight mass close around the coffin. Emily grasped Ashleigh's arm, as Jodie stepped forward and sang, an older version of the wild guitarist at warehouse parties. She lifted her pale throat away from her long black hair, studded bands circling her wrists.

> *May the road rise up to meet you*
> *May the wind be always at your back*
> *May the sun shine warm on your face*
> *And rains fall soft on your fields*
> *And until we meet again, my friend*
> *May God hold you*
> *In the palm of his hand.*

'I reckon Ben would have heard that. He's on his way now.' Ashleigh put her arm around Emily as they walked up the path to the hall they had hired for the wake.

'At least we said goodbye well. So many people, more than I'd expected. Just all too fucking late.' She kicked a stone into the grass alongside the paving.

'I don't know that anyone could save him. You offered help, but he had to accept it.'

They stopped at the side of the door into the hall, hearing the band getting started.

'He kept ringing me in London, I couldn't deal with it, was barely surviving at work, I got annoyed with him, wanted him to sort himself out, leave me alone. But he needed me. I told Dad Ben needed him. What a hypocrite.'

'This is years and years of history, not a short-term fix. You were seeing the end of long-term damage. At least you were in touch this year,' Ashleigh nudged her in the ribs, 'after trying to deny that you even had a family'.

'Yeah, well I paid for it this year.' Emily rolled her eyes.

'Stop that, no amount of self-flagellation will do anything. Everyone here wishes they'd done more. We're sending him off with love and a party, just what he would have wanted. Come on, let's have a drink.'

'Look!'

Emily pointed Ashleigh to the life-size photos of Ben on every wall. Ben in happier times wherever you looked. A band was playing at one end, a few people dancing, a trestle table of drinks, another loaded with Turkish breads, dips, pizzas. Ben's kind of party.

Ashleigh laughed. 'Bit different from cups of tea and sandwiches. I'm going to find the Ladies.'

Emily picked up a glass of wine and wandered over to a table spread with smaller photos. She ran her fingers over a younger Ben, long and lean, flowing hair, smooth skinned, clear-eyed, happier than Emily remembered.

'Warehouse days.' Natasha joined her, Annie sleeping. 'You were at some of these parties, weren't you? It's where I met him. Everyone knew that was the place to go, the best parties, lots of artists and musos. I liked him from the beginning.'

She picked up a photo of them both, Natasha laughing at the camera, Ben's mouth pressed against the side of her head looking like he wanted to be swallowed up in her.

'It was always us, really. I mean there were others, but I always came back to Ben. He was the one. I hung in there as long as I could. He was excited about Annie coming. I thought, hoped, he would pull himself together when she was born. Maybe it was all too much.'

'Where was this?'

Emily pointed to another one of them both. Natasha and Ben laughing, a few years older, dressed up, holding glasses of champagne to the camera. Ben leaning back, relaxed, his body, his face, warm wide-open eyes, all saying this was a brilliant time in his life. Not the bowed, hunched man of this year, his face lined and strained, eyes shrunken into his skull.

'Yeah, that's one of my favourites. It was at an exhibition opening and he had sold a sizeable piece. He was on top of the world. How does someone go from that to this? How does that happen?'

She kissed the black hair peeping out of the pack as Annie wriggled.

'I was remembering going to his first-year exhibition, before I left the country. You came.'

'Yeah, that was when I met your mum, I was trying hard to make a positive impression. I knew she mattered to Ben.'

'She was nervous too. Mum was so proud of Ben. She would want you to like her.'

Emily had a clear memory of her mum entering the long room at the back of the art school, in her new blue heels and matching handbag, her face alight with pride and excitement, looking for Ben, rushing towards him as he came to meet them, all spruced up in a dark jacket and an ironed white shirt.

'I remember him walking us slowly around the exhibition, talking about the artists. Then when we got to his pieces he disappeared. I turned to look for him and he was standing way back, watching as we looked at his works. He was so nervous we wouldn't like them. Didn't he win a prize? I thought, at last he's in the right place; success, friends, so different from before.'

Natasha smiled. 'That was a great night. I remember, it was in the common room, full of unwashed coffee cups the rest of the year but it looked like a gallery for the occasion; glasses of wine, floors polished, all the crappy couches hidden away somewhere.'

'It hit me that night how good he was. You know, before then, he was just the little brother who enjoyed drawing. But when I saw those huge powerful paintings, they blew me away. My brother, the artist.'

Natasha nodded. 'I started a year after him but I sometimes heard teachers talk about him. He was seriously good.'

Emily laughed. 'He could have been rich and famous. But you know Ben – never part of the mainstream. He would have been horrified to make actual money.'

'Yeah, not what mattered to him. He always did things his own way.'

'Make sure Annie knows how special her dad was.'

'She'll know all right. She'll be sick of me telling her. He really wanted to be a dad. But never made it.' Natasha buried her face for a moment in Annie's hair.

'Um, yes, I've been thinking.' Emily stroked the little arms hanging loosely from the front pack. 'I guess I'm Annie's aunt. I haven't been especially good at family, but this little one is kind of part of Ben, the only piece left. Do you think I could be her aunt? You know, act like a real aunt. I'll be in London, but stay in contact?'

'Definitely! She doesn't have much family either. I'll send her over. You might regret it', Natasha laughed, then put her hand on Emily's arm. 'Thank you. That's lovely. And you will be important to Annie. So, you're going back?'

'Yes. Time to go. It's been such a terrible year for many reasons, for both Ben and me. I never expected to come back, ever. But here I am, twice in one year, two deaths. London's my home though, I'm ready to sort things out there. Find myself a job', she gave a quick laugh. 'That was always the most important thing to me and I've hardly thought about it while I've been here.'

'A very tough year, for both of us,' Natasha smiled. 'Sounds like this is goodbye.'

'Yes. Odd to say this but I'm glad I was here. I missed a lot of Ben's life but at least I spent time with him this year. I hope it helped him, even a little. I don't know how I'd come through this if I hadn't seen him. And it's been good to be with you, even in these circumstances, and to meet Annie. You always have somewhere to stay in London.'

Natasha hugged her, Annie's warm round back between them.

She caught a taxi home, wanting to be by herself. How could so many terrible things happen in one year, less than a year? So much to deal with, forcing her to face her demons after years of avoiding them. Despite her determined efforts, she couldn't cut those ties, finding that they mattered after all. She'd always thought she could divorce herself from her family and her history, just a matter of deciding, helped by geographical distance. In those mythological stories, people went through fires or deep torment to emerge purified. Well, in time, she might become a slightly better person. In the midst of all this there was something liberating about letting that self-protective wall collapse. It had taken a lot of energy to maintain it, thinking it would keep her safe, make her free.

Chapter Twenty-Nine

One last visit. Emily paused at the edge of the driveway, steeling herself. Ashleigh had assured her the cleaners had finished, it should be easy to enter. She had refused Ashleigh's repeated offers to come with her; she needed to do this by herself, not entirely sure why she was returning but here she was. Her father's car loomed in front of her, its usual pristine paint streaked with dirt, leaves stuck to the roof. She could do this. Strode to the house, ignoring the envelopes and papers spilling out of the letter-box, skirting the car. An automatic jolt of tension as she faced the door, squeezing her tight, no longer necessary, she told herself. She turned the key in the lock and entered a fresh, clean smell. Anyone's house.

Averted her eyes as she passed the closed bedroom door and continued upstairs. Ben's first. She sat on the bed, looking for a sense of his presence but nothing of her brother left in this neat bare room. A refuge no longer needed. She noticed a small photo pinned near the bottom of the otherwise empty noticeboard, on a careless angle. Perhaps the cleaners had found it. She smiled at her and Ben together, very young, laughing, the camera capturing them rolling around in the grass. Reminding her there were good times. Where was that taken? She peered closer. It looked bigger than their backyard, maybe a park. Perhaps their mum took them out more than she had remembered. She took the pin out and tucked the photo in her bag. Add it to her collection.

Into her room, she pulled up the blind, letting the light flood in. She stood looking out across the treetops, watching their uppermost leaves move in the breeze, the same trees she had come home to as a child, a teenager and then this year. 'You've seen a lot', she murmured. She released the blind again and left. Down the stairs, she hesitated at the back-room door; those daily visits in Ben's last weeks, knowing that each time she opened this door she would find him slumped in their dad's armchair, his eyes lifting slightly, barely acknowledging her arrival, everything about him screaming loss and despair. Flashes of what had happened here, long ago; and that night, her father shouting, falling, crashing. A deep breath before pushing the door to enter a clean open space, shining windows bringing sunlight in. Surprised to discover she could be here without memories suffocating her.

Her mother's studio. She sat in the swivel chair and looked out at the garden, a view her mother would have seen every day for decades. As a child she remembered sometimes sitting on the floor reading in here while her mother drew, music playing. A moment of peace. The cleaners had gathered the sketchpads into a neat pile at the rear of the table; she flicked through pages of pencil sketches, experiments, some ink drawings. She put one in her bag and left.

On her way through the house she paused at the doorway of her father's study, surveying the empty shelves, the floor cleared of shattered cars. A few days ago she was here, throwing, shouting, destroying, remembering as though she was viewing a film of someone else, so unlike her. She spied a small wire wheel poking up from the carpet fibres, missed by the cleaners. Picking it up, she rolled it around in her hand and slipped it in her pocket. She expected to be sad for a long time, but her anger stayed here.

'I can leave now', she whispered. Then firmer, louder, her voice ringing through the empty house. 'I can leave now.'

She put her key on the hall table and walked out, hearing the front door click shut. She stepped off the porch and turned for one last look. It seemed possible to let it all go.

Case by the door, ready, long before Ashleigh was due; Emily waited on the couch. Glanced around at this room of red and orange poppies, smiling at the irony of living through weeks of despair and loss surrounded by such intense brightness. She felt the room's warmth from the day's sun, the blossoms outside the window were just past their peak, an entire growth cycle had taken place while she was here. She had come to recover. That idea seemed a long way in the past, disconnected to what happened.

She would be all right, confident she could rebuild her life in London, clearer about what was important. She felt something hard in her pocket and pulled out the small wire wheel. Perhaps it didn't need to come with her. She put it on the coffee table for someone else to find. She sat in the peace, drinking in the warmth, then picked up her phone, scrolled through her contacts to Phillip's number.

Postscript

Their favourite café or a new one? Or no café at all? His house? Her house? Walk? Somewhere confidential or public? A casual invite or something more to convey its importance?

Emily stared at the tube tunnel – bricked walls through the dusty window opposite on the way to Hyde Park. Had she made the right decision? A walk in one of London's busiest parks. Too neutral? Too public? What message would it send?

She had called yesterday, three days after returning to London. Wanted to make it sound casual, lay awake the night before trying out alternatives. "Hey why don't we catch up, haven't seen you for a while." How would that work? The last time she'd seen Phillip was in their regular Wednesday restaurant, finishing their relationship with ugly anger, running out the door. Unwarranted, she could see that now. Unfair, unreasonable. A moment when her stress burst out of her, aiming at someone who loved her.

That was before Australia, before her father's heart attack, before Ben. Couldn't go there, not for this meeting. After that scene, probably never again. Nor their Sunday breakfast café, which returned memories of Phillip asking about moving in together and her resisting. No, somewhere that would not take them back into their previous relationship. A walk in a park they hadn't frequented, easier than his eyes opposite across a cafe table – she could falter with that level of intensity.

Phillip said after his concert – a relationship milestone she reflected – that music let a little more of your emotion out. She'd found that death did that too. Through the nightmare of those weeks she shut her mind against his frequent visits, when he awakened her senses, seeing him as clearly as if he was there, feeling the comforting warmth of his body. It's over, it's over. But he reappeared. She knew it was Phillip she wanted to be with. She, Emily, who prided herself on not needing anyone, admitting to a longing that strengthened rather than faded. And now she would admit it out loud.

She got off the tube a stop early, wanting a longer walk to ready herself before their meeting point at Speakers Corner. Appropriate, she thought, her stomach knotting as she strode along the perimeter of the park. She had something to say, a speech if you like. But only to Phillip. Breathe Emily, breathe. Confident after yesterday's phone call that he hadn't rejected her, heard his relief when she suggested meeting, the eager warmth of his reply, saying yes before she'd finished the question. She reminded herself now, despite her shaky stomach, this would be all right.

Determined to use those words, 'commitment' and 'love', repeating them to herself as she neared the Corner. The last few weeks had torn away her protective fortress, exposing her in ways she would not previously have allowed. For the first time she would lead an emotional conversation, risk herself. She caught sight of Phillip ahead and halted, watched him pace in circles between the tourists, smiled to see him wearing the jacket she'd bought. She closed her eyes, autumn sun sinking into her skin. Come on Emily, it's time. She flicked open her eyes to see Phillip standing still. He'd seen her.

Acknowledgements

I would like to acknowledge and express my deep appreciation to the many who supported me in the development of The Long Fingers.

Enormous thanks to my writing group - Sarah Louise Ricketts, Lyndal Meehan and Zac who stayed the distance with me, providing valuable feedback on the shape of my story and writing style over years of development. To Toni Jordan who set me on the path of learning the craft of novel writing through her course 'Refine Your Novel,' opening my eyes to the complexities involved.

To my editors Julia Stiles and Christine Edwards who believed in the book and helped me to improve the plot, characters and clarity of my writing.

Thank you to others who read the manuscript, in part or full, in varied stages of its development, offering useful insights, in particular - Sue Sherman, Rhonda Dunmill, Barry Scott and Jenny Mitchell.

As I approached the unknown in publishing, Claire Saxby offered wisdom and warnings from her extensive experience. My publisher Sylvie Blair at Book Pod was terrific to work with, patient and transparent, demonstrating a commitment to achieving a quality final publication.

Thanks to my talented illustrator, Anthony Stevens, who

sought to understand and express the intentions of my work visually.

The support and continued interest from many friends and family members was vital in sustaining my belief in myself as a writer and that I was doing something worthwhile. Without their confidence in me, I might never have brought The Long Fingers to publication. To a few among many, I would like to especially thank Anne Gaylor, Annie Coleman, Tracey Banks, Davida Graham, Olivia Graham, James Bester, Bea Jones, Clive Bourne and Annee Miron.

About the Author

Gwyneth lives in Melbourne's inner west. She came to Australia as an English migrant arriving on one of the last welcomed and paid-for boats. From a young age, writing has been a way for Gwyneth to explore ideas and make sense of experiences. She began her writing career after finishing many years of juggling busy corporate jobs and bringing up her two daughters. Her first published writing was a series of travel experience blogs called 'Detours.' Gwyneth's recent writing delves into the understated and hidden, often exploring themes of identity, control and courage. *The Long Fingers* is her first novel.